MW00643393

BLESSINGS

BLESSINGS

A NOVEL

CHUKWUEBUKA IBEH

DOUBLEDAY • NEW YORK

This is a work of fiction. Names, characters, places, and incidents either are the product of the author's imagination or are used fictitiously. Any resemblance to actual persons, living or dead, events, or locales is entirely coincidental.

Copyright © 2024 by Chukwuebuka Ibeh

All rights reserved. Published in the United States by Doubleday, a division of Penguin Random House LLC, New York. Originally published in hardcover in Great Britain by Viking Books, an imprint of Penguin General, a division of Penguin Random House Limited, London, in 2024.

www.doubleday.com

DOUBLEDAY and the portrayal of an anchor with a dolphin are registered trademarks of Penguin Random House LLC.

Book design by Anna B. Knighton
Jacket painting: Summer Vibe in Takwa Bay I, *2021 © Tosin Olusegun Kalejaye*
Jacket design John Fontana

Library of Congress Cataloging-in-Publication Data
Names: Ibeh, Chukwuebuka, author.
Title: Blessings : a novel / Chukwuebuka Ibeh.
Description: New York : Doubleday, 2024. |
Identifiers: LCCN 2023034777 (print) | LCCN 2023034778 (ebook) |
ISBN 9780385550642 (hardcover) | ISBN 9780593687543 (paperback) |
ISBN 9780385550659 (ebook)
Subjects: LCSH: Gay men—Nigeria—Fiction. | Gay men—Family relationships—Nigeria—Fiction. | LCGFT: Gay fiction. | Novels.
Classification: LCC PR9387.9.I13 B57 2024 (print) | LCC PR9387.9.I13 (ebook) |
DDC 823.92—dc23/eng/20230801
LC record available at https://lccn.loc.gov/2023034777
LC ebook record available at https://lccn.loc.gov/2023034778

MANUFACTURED IN THE UNITED STATES OF AMERICA

1 3 5 7 9 10 8 6 4 2

First United States Edition

To my dearest aunt

ULOMA AMADI

(1976–2015)

PART

ONE

ONE

PORT HARCOURT, 2006

In October, he came. His arrival was without forewarning, without ceremony. A slight rap on the door that mild evening, just as the sun was making a final appearance before retiring, and there he was, in his bathroom slippers, hefting a GHANA MUST GO sack on his shoulders, next to Obiefuna's father, Anozie, both looking weary from the long travel. When Anozie had talked about getting an extra hand to assist in the shop, Obiefuna had not known what to expect, but, somehow, it was not the tall figure who now stood hugging his bag to his chest, a slight downturn to his lips as he stared at his dusty feet. He towered a foot above Obiefuna's notably tall father, but it was the even darkness of the boy's skin that made Obiefuna's eyes linger on him a while longer when he opened the door to let them in. The boy seemed undecided whether to follow Anozie inside or turn and head back the way he had come. He stepped in after a moment's hesitation, tactfully shrugging off Obiefuna's attempt to help him with his load.

"Welcome, Daddy," Obiefuna said, still not taking his eyes off the boy.

Anozie grunted a response. "Where's your mother?" he asked, settling on the sofa with an exaggerated heave. The journey from their hometown of Igbo Ukwu lasted no less than six hours on average and had the ability to leave a person feeling thoroughly incapacitated.

As if on cue, Obiefuna's mother, Uzoamaka, emerged from the kitchen. She halted at the dining room and looked straight at the new boy, sitting with his head slightly bowed on a stool opposite Anozie. She took note of his bags and the situation in one appraising glance. "Welcome," she said to Anozie, and nodded in response to the boy's prompted greetings.

"Get me a cup of water," Anozie told Obiefuna. He avoided Uzoamaka's eye. Exactly a week ago he had travelled to Igbo Ukwu to attend the town's union development meeting in his capacity as the assistant secretary, and was not expected home until tomorrow, and certainly not with an extra. He waited until Obiefuna returned with a glass of water and he had drunk from it, setting the glass on the table, before turning to face Uzoamaka.

"This is Aboy. Remember him? The late Okezie's third son. He's just finished secondary school and wants to learn a trade. His uncle followed me home after the meeting and begged me to take him in. Everyone thinks he will learn fast."

Uzoamaka looked across the room to assess Aboy again. He sat with his legs slightly spread apart, crossed at the ankles in front of him, encircling his bags protectively. He pulled them towards him as Uzoamaka studied him. The crinkling of the sack filled the quiet of the living room.

"Obiefuna, show Aboy where to keep his things," Uzoamaka said, finally, in English.

Aboy looked startled to hear his name, but he rose from the stool and walked down the short length of the living room, following Obiefuna through the corridor and into the small bedroom he shared with his brother, Ekene. There Aboy finally let go of the sack, watching as Obiefuna put it away in the wardrobe. Obiefuna turned to Aboy because he had said something.

"What?"

"Where's the latrine?" he repeated, in Igbo.

"Latrine?"

He nodded and, taking note of Obiefuna's confusion, made a slight squatting posture. It took Obiefuna a moment to understand. "Oh, you mean the toilet?" he asked.

Aboy hesitated, and then nodded again.

"Come with me," Obiefuna said. He led Aboy out of the room, back into the corridor, and pointed to the door of the toilet at the far end. Aboy walked with uncertain movements to the door and prised it open with a cautious push. Obiefuna wondered how long he had been waiting to go. Had he endured the long journey from the village with full bowels? Aboy inspected the bathroom with a perplexed expression that prompted Obiefuna to step into the toilet and tap at the water system, proceeding in halting Igbo, "This is where you'll sit and do it. And then flush with a bucket of water. Understood?"

Aboy seemed to give it a moment's thought, and then he nodded. He turned to Obiefuna with what Obiefuna would regard in retrospect as his first full smile since his arrival.

❖

THAT NIGHT, Obiefuna stood outside his parents' bedroom, ear pressed to the door, sifting through their bedtime conversation.

"Anam asi, I should have at least been informed you were coming with him today. How can you bring someone from nowhere into our house and expect me to be happy with it?" Uzoamaka protested.

"But I had no idea myself I would be returning with him," this from Anozie. "I told you how Shedrach followed me home after the meeting. Matter of fact, he even made the request right there in front of the whole umunna. What was I supposed to do? Turn him down?"

Uzoamaka hissed, "Why am I not surprised? Those conniving snakes know exactly how to get what they want."

Anozie chuckled. "It hasn't been easy for the family since Okezie died, Uzoamaka."

"It hasn't been any better for this family," she snapped back.

Anozie exaggerated a tired yawn. "He won't be here for very long." His voice had slowed to a sleepy drawl. "You'll be surprised at how quickly the years will fly past. And I intend to make him useful to me in the meantime."

EKENE WAS AMUSED by him.

"What sort of name is Aboy?" he wondered. They were on their way to Ojukwu Field for after-school football practice. It was a hot day; the heat of the coal tar penetrated Obiefuna's thin soles and scalded his feet. But it had no effect on Ekene in his thick-soled football boots, his eager air.

"There's nothing wrong with his name," Obiefuna said. He felt disappointed. It was hard to read Ekene nowadays: he could not tell if, in addition to amusement, Ekene felt any warmth for Aboy. He wanted Ekene to like Aboy. Although Ekene was thirteen months younger than Obiefuna, he had long resigned himself to needing Ekene's approval, revelling in the simple pleasures Ekene's validation brought.

Ekene shrugged and continued bouncing the ball. He possessed, at only fourteen, the grandeur of an adult, and the world-weariness that came with it. People said he was the spitting image of their father, with his narrow, unsmiling face and calculating eyes. He had also inherited Anozie's temper, except his was more spontaneous, the outcomes more shocking. At ten, he had buried the tip of a ballpoint pen in the lower back of a classmate after the boy pulled his chair out from under him as he was sitting down, causing him to land on the floor; had called his Form Four class teacher a prostitute for publicly berating him after he failed a test, receiving their father's strokes afterwards with impossible endurance. Just last year, he had nearly overturned a panful of hot oil onto Obiefuna for beating him in a playful brawl. Over the years, Obiefuna had learned to relate to him with an unstated wariness. Their relationship was hinged on the mutual understanding that Obiefuna's authority had its boundaries.

There were just a few boys around when they arrived at the field, roaming about, and jogging with footballs of different sizes; some of them were in faded jerseys and worn-out boots but most were shirtless and barefoot. Tobe spotted them from afar and hurried over.

"Men them!" He shook their hands, Ekene's a little longer. He snatched the ball from Ekene, bounced it. "What's up?"

"No problem." Ekene looked around the field. "Where's everybody?"

"They're late again o," Tobe said. "And Coach is not even here yet."

Ekene glanced at his bare wrist. "It's almost five na."

Tobe shrugged. "Does he care? We're not the big teams after all."

Ekene shook his head, a disappointed smile on his face.

"But we can still practise on our own, can't we?" Tobe said suddenly. "Nobody has to watch us to select for their 'academy.'" He rolled the last word around in self-mockery.

Ekene laughed. "Sure."

Tobe shouted, "Who's ready to play? I one!" In the distance, someone shouted "I two!," as the boys around scrambled to where Tobe stood with the ball.

"I choose Ekene," Tobe said, crossing a hand over Ekene's shoulder.

"I choose Paul," a lanky boy with sickly-looking brown hair, who had earlier shouted, said. Paul moved over to stand beside him.

"I wanted to choose Paul!" Tobe groaned. "We're always on the same team."

"Not my business." The lanky boy shrugged. "Besides, you already have Ekene. That's a full squad alone."

Tobe turned to Paul. "Who would you rather be with, Paul?" he challenged.

Paul shrugged and strolled the distance across to Tobe, and the other boy called out, stunned, "Paul! Where are you going? I chose you already! Abeg, come back here!"

Paul stood in the middle of the semicircle and raised both hands, as if exasperated, even though his delight was clear. It was satisfying when one team wanted you, but it was dizzyingly exhilarating when two teams were about to go toe-to-toe over you.

"But why are we even dragging Paul when we have so many

talented people here?" Chikezie chipped in on cue. "Look at Obiefuna, for example."

The laughter was expected; the shaking of heads and stamping of feet and quiet chanting of "No-no-no" had by now become a routine. Still, the hurt was as fresh as it had always been. From within the crowd, somebody said, "I'd rather be a one-man team than choose a basket," prompting more laughter. Even Ekene smiled.

And so Obiefuna sat on the grass and held T-shirts and slippers and water bottles. Even Chikezie had made several teasing attempts to leave his effects with Obiefuna, only quitting when Abdul, the biggest boy in the group, who also served as the referee, intervened, and warned him to leave Obiefuna alone. The match ended with a 3–2, Paul's side winning, but Ekene had scored the two goals for his team, and everyone agreed he was the man of the match. His opponents shook his hand and retrospectively commended the same skills they had decried during the match, concluding that his team could have done much better with two of him on their side.

On the way home, Obiefuna asked Ekene whom he thought Paul had truly wanted to go with, and Ekene laughed, looking light and happy as he was wont to do after a good game of football, and said, "Please, don't start now."

TWO

Of all the things there are to worry about during pregnancy, a name for the child was what troubled Uzoamaka the most. She thought the suggestions from her friends—Chidera, Tochukwu, Ngozi—too regular, too simplistic, Anozie's suggestions too practical, or, like everything about him, having a curious, archaic ring—who named their child Nnanna? She wanted a name to capture her gratitude for his decision to stay past the second month, for allowing her to witness his first kick by the fifth, a simple, wondrous proof of her body's capacity to sustain life, after many miscarriages had led her to believe otherwise. And, although she quite liked the suggestion from Anozie's mother, Obiajulu—"The mind is now at rest"—she thought it was the kind of name a grandmother would give to her grandchild, a fond name, heavy with sentimentality. Not one to appear on a birth certificate, to be used stripped of context, by the general, uncaring public.

In the end, she had settled for a bit of both: the final decision, which she scribbled with certainty on his birth certificate, was straightforward and practical while also retaining its touch of sentimentality. Most of all, it felt apt. "May my heart not be lost." For his arrival had solidified, in some odd way, Uzoamaka's sense of place, restoring to her a lost ability to believe in the concept of miracles.

His birth, on a still Friday midnight in August of 1991, had taken her by surprise. He had arrived two weeks early, so that she mistook her early contractions for an out-of-character disturbance from him. She was up on her feet in the kitchen, putting away the plates from the evening's dinner, which she had had alone because Anozie was away, and she thought at first she might sit down a bit to rest her back; and then, after a full hour of trying unsuccessfully to find a comfortable position and get him to relax, she rose from the chair and walked down the stairs to the neighbours' door and requested a ride to the clinic to have her baby. Ironically, it was the man, Mr. Adebayo, who flew into a panic, scurrying about his living room for proper clothes and emerging still underdressed. In the car, he darted worried looks at her so often she feared the car would swerve off the road and slam into a ditch. She shrugged off his attempt to help her out of the car when they arrived at the clinic, walking the distance to the labour ward herself; and, in a few hours, she held the shrieking baby in her arms, watching with tears in her eyes as he furiously announced his presence in the world, and an end to her longing.

The midwives were enamoured by him. They commented with approval on his healthy birthweight, his lack of jaundice, which was endemic at the time, the ease of the labour. Uzoamaka herself had been a thing of wonder in the ward, and she revelled in the attention from the other patients seeking to catch a glimpse of the baby, light-headed with contentment and already tired out by the time Anozie arrived, his joy at the brink of bursting. He told her the car was outside, ready to take them home, and together they looked down at the baby in the crook of her arm, nursing at her breast. A child, after all these years.

Uzoamaka liked to recount, at the slightest prompting, the circumstances surrounding Obiefuna's birth. His arrival had not just been an answer to the nights of endless prayers and tears that had lasted for years but also a reversal of their life's course and fortune. Three months into the pregnancy, Anozie secured a massive supply contract by chance, being in the right place at the right time, with enough income finally to move them out of their public yard and into a better one uptown, where they had a kitchen and bathroom to themselves. Her hair-braiding business suddenly bloomed, with too many customers insisting on having her attend to them even though she was visibly pregnant and there were other free stalls around. A few weeks into the eighth month, Anozie, following the lead of his friend Udoka, had bought tickets for a raffle with a sizable percentage of his earnings. She nearly lost her mind when she found out, going for days without speaking to him, and when he informed her a week later that he had been notified that he was to receive his grand prize in Benin, being one of two lucky winners out of over two hundred people, she dismissed it as a lie, a mischievous attempt to get her to start talking to him again. And, when he arrived from work the following day, laughing and crying in her arms as he told her that the prize was a car, the new model Mercedes-Benz, she screamed and jumped around the house until she felt a protesting kick, a warning to be still, and yet a small and abiding reminder of the greater miracle that was now her life.

"You know, he brought us all these blessings," Anozie used to say in the early days following Obiefuna's birth. It was just like him to state the obvious with the self-satisfaction of one wielding esoteric knowledge. Of course she knew. She regarded the baby with certain gratitude. He was faultless, free of the anxiety-inducing behaviours characteristic of newborns. He was popular at the market for his ready, dimpled smile and his full hair, which was soft to the touch and made people assume, initially, that he was a girl. Other mothers told her she was lucky—how the baby accommodated, and even slept in, the arms of strangers, allowing her the space and time in which to work, how he ate everything he was fed, saving them the energy and cost of scouting for special meals, doubling in weight with healthy, radiant skin, rarely falling sick. He was lovable and playful with everyone, effortlessly gaining their affection. Her customers took to dropping tips specifically for the baby, and when he began to babble the "thank you" she taught him to say, they laughed and stared at him in speechless wonder. He was not even a year old when he began to totter about on unsteady legs and pronounce babyish variations of the names of the regular faces he saw. The general teasing was that he was an old man in a child's skin; the general belief was that he was a special child.

But when Uzoamaka woke up with that familiar morning sickness again and confirmed her next pregnancy, she was, for reasons she could not name, mildly worried. She found it difficult to share in Anozie's joy, however infectious, and when his mother breezed in from the village with a trailer-load of foodstuff and a bigger trailer-load of goodwill, she wanted to ask the woman to leave right away. The mere thought of putting on a cheer she hardly felt, of performing happiness for its own sake, exhausted her, and she vomited her way into the sixth month, losing weight and appetite at every turn and needing to take an early leave from work, on the doctor's recommendation, to rest. And, even when the baby came (born through Caesarean because he would not stay in the right position), small and overwhelmingly shrill, she tried and failed to feel something concrete. For him, Obinna or Chidera or even Ozoemena would do. But Anozie called him Ekenedilichukwu, "Thanks be to God," and, in her dark, fleetingly misanthropic moments, she would wonder what there was to be grateful for when the child had nearly taken her life.

The considerable differences between the two children would become apparent as they were growing up. It was surprising and sometimes heartbreaking to watch her Obiefuna lose all his babyish charm, turning into a reserved, self-effacing child, and unconsciously relegating authority to the brash, forthright Ekene. Obiefuna transitioned before her very eyes into the exact opposite of his baby self, and Uzoamaka looked on with growing despair as he tried and failed to be accepted by his peers and became susceptible to bullies; and, more distressingly, he was now a source of irritated concern to Anozie.

"That boy," he remarked often, with none of the grateful wonder that had characterized early musings on Obiefuna, "he's abnormal."

The first time, she had demanded an explanation for his statement, raising her voice to match his when he told her off, knowing deep down—and further angered by the knowledge she was unprepared to admit—that there was indeed something unusual about the boy. He spoke little, kept few friends, was likely to come home with bruises from a fight he had lost or in tears because of something mean one of the neighbourhood kids had said; and, while Ekene reminded Uzoamaka of the boys of her childhood, some of whom had been the objects of her childhood crushes, Obiefuna brought to mind the fun, loyal girlfriends she had grown up with. Sometimes, she was distressed by the nagging feeling that a terrible mistake had been made. But sometimes, such as when Obiefuna took to the dance floor, she was convinced that there was nothing remotely closer to perfection. He astonished her with his moves, his ability to manipulate his limbs into impossible angles. He was known in the neighbourhood for his gift, and she looked on with elation at parties as he outdanced the other children, ignoring the irritated snorts from their parents. It was among the many areas of his upbringing on which she and Anozie disagreed. Once, they had attended the baby dedication of one of Anozie's old friends, and Obiefuna, in his usual fashion, had scooped all the dance prizes there were. Anozie, nursing a cold bottle of beer, had taken in the sight with a mere uninterested glance. He was in a jocular mood, exchanging pleasantries with friends and presenting gifts to the parents of the child, and on the drive back home he hummed merrily to the Oriental Brothers. But when they arrived, she was still unbuckling her sandals at the front door when Anozie turned round to slap Obiefuna across the face. Uzoamaka stood upright to see her son slammed against the wall from the force of the smack, corresponding welts appearing almost immediately on his face.

"What is wrong with you? Anumanu!" Anozie swore, his voice getting stuck behind his throat as it did when he was working himself into a fit of rage. "Are you a woman in a man's skin? Asim, i bu nwoke ko i bu nwanyi?" he demanded, undoing the hook of his belt for a proper assault. It was then that Uzoamaka wedged herself between them and dared him to lay a finger on her son one more time, telling him to wait and see if she would not feed him his own penis. They stood staring at each other for a long time, he surprised by her audacity, she seething in her newly found, compounding rage, the silence fraught with expectation, until Anozie put the belt down and stormed into the bedroom.

The boy cried until dinner was ready, all the way through dinner and late into the night. She sat by his bed, rocking him gently and whispering, "Ozugo nu, sorry," and a whole lot of promises. She held his head to her breast—his temperature was rising—and felt her blood rise to her head from rage. How ridiculous, how callous and absurd to expect perfection from a child. He was only eight years old, unaware of what "proper" behaviour entailed. But, as she put out the light in the room, having managed to subdue his tears and put him to sleep, she wished he would be a little more conventional.

THREE

It was difficult for Obiefuna to imagine what his life, what their lives, had been prior to Aboy's arrival. It seemed as if, with Aboy, Obiefuna's life had finally begun, a life he had been waiting to live. Aboy appeared to fit effortlessly into the fringes of their existence, as if a space had already been cut out for him, waiting for him. He fit into his new role at the house without the sense of bewilderment Obiefuna had expected, taking on his assigned chores with charming grace. In the mornings, Obiefuna woke up to the sound of Aboy's heavy footsteps on the stairs as he hauled water from the public tap downstairs to fill the drums in the kitchen. As Obiefuna swept the floors and Ekene washed the plates from the previous night, Aboy had his bath in preparation for heading out to the market and opening the shop ahead of Anozie. Sometimes, whenever they managed to get ready at the same time, Aboy offered to walk Obiefuna and Ekene to school, suffering the consequence of having to take the longer route to the market. It was only on Saturdays that he stayed home until noon, doing Anozie's laundry for the week in the yard downstairs. Obiefuna liked to watch him from the railings. He was in perpetual good cheer, steadily whistling a happy tune under his breath. Sometimes, sensing Obiefuna's presence, he looked up and gave a small wink that made Obiefuna smile, delirious with happiness. Aboy was at ease with his new life, eager to assimilate. His English had improved in the ten months he had been with them, and he no longer had to repeat Uzoamaka's instructions over and over when he was sent on errands or take a moment to ponder a response when Obiefuna or Ekene spoke to him. And he was a wonder at the shop. Obiefuna sometimes listened as his father extolled Aboy's agility to his mother, commending his initiative, which sometimes brought extra profits; Aboy had, by observing a similar practice in other shops, suggested Anozie undertook the task of home delivery for bags of cement in order to add the cost to the purchase and get more gain after having split the profit with the delivery man. Anozie was impressed by how well Aboy ingratiated himself with the customers, so that even long-time customers now wanted to be attended to only by him. Anozie bragged about Aboy's certain future success. He would easily make a name for himself while still serving, which would be invaluable when he was free to start up his own business. "The boy has not a single dishonest bone in his body," he declared and went on to tell the story of how, as part of the customary test for a new apprentice, Anozie had colluded with a fellow trader who posed as a customer and overpaid Aboy after making a purchase. The man had been stunned to speechlessness when the boy, on discovering the error, ran a whole mile to refund the extra money. Anozie, too, had deliberately placed money in the pockets of clothes to be laundered, only to have it duly returned to him, not a single note missing. "That boy? A wonder, I tell you," he concluded approvingly to Uzoamaka. She made vague, sleepy sounds of attention, not sharing her own stories, if she had any. Obiefuna could not tell what his mother felt for Aboy. She was courteous to him without being friendly, ultimately regarding his presence as a passing inconvenience. Only once did she raise her voice at him, threatening to slap him, when he spent too long on an errand and came back with the wrong item. She sometimes complained, too, when he skipped night baths: he spent all day in a sweaty stupor, hauling bags of cement onto lorries, and came home coated in a film of white dust and exuding the metallic smell of limestone. Even his eating pattern was curious: he cleared away the grains of white rice on his plate before licking the stew, and his moulds of fufu were as large as a child's fist—Obiefuna and Ekene had giggling fits watching him swallow them in one gulp. He sometimes put on a show to entertain them, flattered by their keen interest. He laughed often, a sound that came without warning, like the soft, almost reluctant rumbling of thunder after a light rain, making something flutter within Obiefuna. Other times, he moved around the house in a brooding silence and spent minutes at a time looking into the distance. Obiefuna yearned to know what he was thinking in those moments, but he never asked. They didn't last long. Soon enough, Aboy would emerge from them with a puzzling animation, recounting his adventures in the village, stories that Obiefuna did not know whether to believe, such as how he climbed trees with one arm tied to his back and how he walked miles from the river with two gallons of water hoisted on his shoulders and a third on his head, without losing a single drop.

He frequently talked about his future plans.

"When Oga settles me, I will open one big shop in this Port Harcourt, and it will be the biggest shop in the whole world." Although he laughed when he said this, there was a force of conviction in his voice that told Obiefuna he believed this himself—or believed in his ability to try. Obiefuna wondered if he had a girlfriend in the village, if he thought of her often. Although a corner of the room had been designated for Aboy's use, with an old mattress retrieved from their parents' room, Obiefuna sometimes woke up early in the morning to find Aboy in bed with him and Ekene, the feel of Aboy's erection straining against Obiefuna's thigh from underneath the shorts he wore to bed, his eyes closed, the soft snore from his lips an indication he was truly asleep, completely oblivious to the state of his body. Once, Obiefuna woke up to the sight of Aboy's forehead next to his, his breathing warm on Obiefuna's face. Up close, Obiefuna could see the wide flare of his nostrils, his burgeoning moustache. He reached out to touch Aboy's cheek, running his fingers lightly over the width of his face. His fingers lingered on the lips, tracing their hard texture, trying and failing to shut out the voices in his head. He inched closer, unable to resist the force that pulled him. Aboy's lips were hard and firm. Aboy stirred, his eyes still closed, but in the ever-so-slight curve of his lips Obiefuna detected a smile.

In the morning, Aboy did not talk about it. He showed no inclination to recall what had happened the previous night. Obiefuna watched him go about his chores, avoiding Obiefuna's gaze, leaving the room the moment Obiefuna walked in. In Aboy's eyes, something had dimmed, something between them had cracked, and when he looked up the following Saturday to see Obiefuna watching him, he simply looked away.

Did Aboy now hate him? Had he imagined the smile?

Aboy seemed wary of coming close to him, but there was also something in his demeanour that told Obiefuna Aboy was not exactly repulsed by him. There appeared, in his carriage, a half-heartedness, as if Aboy felt the spark Obiefuna felt, and his fear came from the thought of the consequences. Obiefuna imagined Aboy's future. He would be the owner of a big shop in the market and would have amassed enough wealth to come back for Obiefuna, and they would run away to a hidden place to be together forever. He turned away from washing plates one Saturday morning to see Aboy watching him.

"You've been holding that plate for an hour," Aboy said.

"Do you have a girlfriend?" Obiefuna blurted out.

Aboy raised a brow, but he did not seem surprised or puzzled by the question. He eased away from the wall and came to stand beside Obiefuna. "Are you jealous?" he asked. He was smiling.

"Me? No. I just—"

"Shh." Aboy placed a finger on his lips. He steered Obiefuna sideways, so that Obiefuna was facing him squarely, a plate and a soapy sponge in his hands suspended in the air. He looked into Aboy's eyes, at the dark, tiny pupils in the midst of the vast whiteness of his eyeballs. At first, he saw nothing, only a mesmerizing contrast of black on white, and then he saw his reflection in Aboy's eyes, witnessed his own smile. There was a stall in time, an instant when Obiefuna was convinced it was himself and Aboy alone in the world. It was a moment he wanted to live in forever. They were interrupted just then by a shuffle, and when Obiefuna turned he felt his heart stop at the sight of his father standing by the door with his hands behind him. There was no doubt he had been there awhile, had seen enough. The moment lengthened, the silence brittle.

"Have you finished washing the clothes?" Anozie said, referring to Aboy, but his eyes rested on Obiefuna and they never left him, even as Aboy walked the length of the kitchen with his head lowered, brushing past Anozie at the door, even as Anozie reached behind him to shut the door with a firm click, even as he reached for the nearest thing he could find: a cord lying helplessly on the kitchen worktop.

PART

TWO

FOUR

OWERRI, 2007

The walls surrounding the building were tall and unpainted, with sharp broken bottles jutting out unevenly atop them. On a sign next to the red gate were the words REHOBOTH SEMINARY in unmissable red print.

"We're here," Anozie said, turning to Obiefuna and speaking for the first time since they had left Port Harcourt. Obiefuna remained quiet, staring through the window at the defaced walls of the school as Anozie filed into the line of cars making their way through the open gates and parked under a slender coconut tree in the compound. Anozie got out of the car first and turned round to get Obiefuna's box from the boot. Obiefuna let himself out after him but remained standing by the door. A man walked up to them and shook his father's hand with both of his, slightly bowing. Obiefuna vaguely remembered him as the man who had spoken at length with his father a month ago when they were here for the entrance exams. Now, as they talked, Obiefuna looked at the procession of curiously young boys clutching school bags and rolling boxes up to where they would be searched. On the outer gate, in front of what looked like a chapel, solemn-faced men stood behind long tables, leafing through the boxes mounted on them.

"Obiefuna," Anozie called.

Obiefuna turned to face him.

"This is Mr. Josiah. He works here. He will be your guardian."

Obiefuna stared at Mr. Josiah. If he stood on his toes, he would match Mr. Josiah's height. The man's smile was too wide, too watery, and Obiefuna worried spittle would drool from the corners of his mouth.

"I've given Mr. Josiah some money for your upkeep," Anozie continued. "Meet him if you need anything or if you need to call me." His tone made it clear he did not expect Obiefuna to follow through on the latter.

Obiefuna nodded. His father turned to Mr. Josiah, who seemed in a daze.

"Oh, come with me," Mr. Josiah said, snapping back into consciousness. He led the way to the search area and helped Obiefuna to hoist his box on the table in front of a stern-looking man. He mumbled an inaudible reply to Obiefuna's greetings and yanked at the zip of the box.

"Bring out your prospectus," he said.

Obiefuna dug into his pocket and retrieved the slim booklet listing his required possessions. At intervals, the man read from the prospectus and rummaged in the box for the item. There was an almost deliberate disorderly vigour to the way he overturned the neat folds of clothes Obiefuna's mother had taken care to put together the night before. The man pushed the provisions aside as if they offended him somehow, nearly overturning the ceramic cup in the box. He held it up and flashed Obiefuna a look. "We don't use this here. Your cup must be plastic or aluminium. Your father will go home with it."

He rummaged further and stopped. "Where's your white bed sheet?"

"Sir?"

"Are you deaf?" The man yanked at his own ears. "Your white bed sheet for Sundays."

"I don't have, sir," Obiefuna said. His father had been meticulous in going through the prospectus, even ticking off the purchases he made each day. It surprised Obiefuna to realize he had missed this.

"What did the prospectus say?" the man asked.

Obiefuna kept his eyes on the table, embarrassed at the high pitch of the man's voice, which was already drawing attention to them.

"Well, I can't let you pass if—" The man stopped. "Is that a brown belt you have on your waist?"

Obiefuna glanced down at his own waist as if seeing it for the first time. This one, he had to admit, was an intentional transgression. His mother had mentioned it at home, but they had been in too much of a hurry, and his father had shrugged it off as irrelevant.

"Take it off," the man said. "Only black is allowed."

Obiefuna was fumbling with the belt when he felt hands on his shoulders. Mr. Josiah said, the watery smile not leaving his face, "Sir Offor, abeg easy on my boy."

Sir Offor did not return the smile. "His things are not complete."

"The father has given me some money to buy a white bed sheet and black belt. They did not know."

"It was in the prospectus," Sir Offor countered with a half-snort, waving Obiefuna away. Obiefuna zipped the bag and hoisted it on to his head. He walked over to his father.

"You'll be all right here," Anozie said. "Read your books, go to church, and keep your head down." He paused. He seemed to hover, undecided on the next line of action. Finally, he reached out to place a hand on Obiefuna's shoulder. "One day when you're older, you'll understand why this was necessary." With that, he walked briskly to his car. Obiefuna watched him drive off, a cloud of red dust billowing after him.

"This way," Mr. Josiah said, steering him towards the second gate, which led to the main campus. The buildings stood about in a jumbled arrangement as if there had not been a plan and most had been erected as an afterthought. "You'll be placed in Ogbunike House," Mr. Josiah said as they walked. "It's the house for SS1 boys. You have the added advantage of being closest to the classroom complex. And it's kind of secluded, so you'll be out of sight of the more senior students." They walked further, Obiefuna uncomfortably aware of the eyes planted on him from the windows of the buildings they passed, until they came upon a faded brick building in the distance. It was partly hidden from view by tall grasses growing in front of it.

"Most of it will come down soon," Mr. Josiah said, as if reading his mind. From a low-hanging concrete slab, a group of boys playing table tennis stopped to stare at him. Mr. Josiah led the way up the stairs and down the corridor, stopping in front of the fourth door.

"This is your room," he announced, walking inside. "And this is your bunk." He indicated a vacant top bunk close to the window. The lower bunk had two boys sitting on it, their game of cards suspended, regarding him with open curiosity.

"Who owns this bunk?" Mr. Josiah asked, tapping the lower bunk.

One of the boys lifted his hand.

"Good. This is your new bunkmate. Help him get settled in," he said in a tone that was not a request. Obiefuna watched him leave.

"So, are you a rainmaker?" the boy asked once Mr. Josiah was out of the door.

"A what?"

"You know, do you, like, wet the bed at night?"

"Oh." Obiefuna took a breath. "No."

"Good"—the boy beamed, relieved—"because the last thing I want is your piss in my mouth in the middle of the night," he said. "They call me Wisdom," the boy added, extending a hand.

Obiefuna took it. "Obiefuna."

"You need help with that?" Wisdom asked, glancing at his box.

"No, it's okay," Obiefuna said, but Wisdom helped him unpack anyway, making a space in the makeshift wardrobe for him and clearing out the upper compartment of his own locker to temporarily accommodate Obiefuna's provisions. He disappeared from the room and returned a few minutes later with a bare mattress. In the middle was a stain the shape of a hastily drawn map and it had a faint odour of stale urine.

Obiefuna gaped at him. "I can't use this."

"Why not?" Wisdom patted the foam. "It's dry."

"I don't even know who the previous owner was."

Wisdom paused. He looked at Obiefuna with amusement in his eyes. "See this ajebo! You think you're still at home?" he said. "Look, it's a choice between this and sleeping on the floor. You should consider yourself lucky. Not everyone gets a bed to sleep in on their first day."

"When do I get mine?"

Wisdom shrugged. "Who knows? Could be tomorrow, could be next week. You might never get it until you graduate."

Obiefuna sighed. Included in the prospectus had been the instruction to deposit money for a mattress, cupboard and bucket. He still had the receipt his father had given to him nestled in his breast pocket, to present to the bursar whenever the products were available. He watched as Wisdom installed the mattress on the bunk above, wrapped in Wisdom's spare bedcover. He climbed down after he was done and gave the bed one satisfied tap. "This should do."

Obiefuna nodded, touched. "Thank you."

"No worries."

That night, Obiefuna dreamed of walking all the way home, to the sight of his mother and Aboy on the staircase, waiting for him.

WISDOM WOKE HIM the following morning by tapping his back repeatedly. Obiefuna sat up in bed and peered down at Wisdom, squinting in the harsh glare of the lamp on his face, unable to place, for an instant, where he was. In the distance, he could make out the fading echo of a bell and feet shuffling out of the room, down the corridor.

"That's the rising bell," Wisdom explained, putting out the lamp. "Let's go for prayers. Quickly, before the seniors come."

Obiefuna descended from the bunk and felt his way around with his feet, in the dark.

"What are you looking for?" Wisdom asked.

"My slippers."

"Did you leave them on the floor last night before going to bed?"

"Yes, right here." Obiefuna tapped his feet on the ground next to Wisdom's cupboard.

"Ah, no. You don't do that," Wisdom said. "The owners have collected them."

"What owners? They're mine. My father got them for me at home before we came here."

Wisdom gave a short laugh. "What I mean is . . . You know what, never mind." He reached into his locker and produced a pair of oversized sandals. "Manage with these for now. Let's go."

As they walked out of the door, Obiefuna asked Wisdom if he would ever see his slippers again.

"No," Wisdom said, simply.

PRAYERS WERE SHORT, led by the chapel prefect, an equally short SS3 student who stomped his feet at intervals, holding on to the waistline of his trousers, as if worried they would slip off otherwise. Afterwards, Obiefuna stood in a queue at the tap with the plastic bucket Wisdom had provided for him. The bathroom was swarming with students, so he opted to join some boys who had their baths on the small field in front of their house, Wisdom laughing at how he had become an outlaw on his very first day. By the end of the day, he was well settled into his class, already briefed by Wisdom on the routines. At prep, he flipped through his mathematics textbook, trying to focus on the exercises and understand the formulae, but his mind couldn't hold them long enough to extract any meaning. He was further distracted by the low but insistent drumming of the boy behind him. He fought a growing urge to turn round and tell him off.

"It's not making sense, eh?" said the boy next to him. Obiefuna looked at him. Earlier he had observed him with an indistinct interest, noting the way the boy studied him up close from time to time, trying to get Obiefuna's attention.

Obiefuna shook his head, giving in, finally. "Nothing."

"Don't stress it. We have all term." He said, "Let's talk."

Obiefuna turned to give the boy his full attention. He had a curiously shaped head, an odd contrast with his smooth, handsome face. His smile was awkward, undecided, as if he had yet to make up his mind about Obiefuna. "About?"

"Anything," the boy said. "Where did you move from?"

"Port Harcourt," Obiefuna said.

"What was your old school like?"

"Very good," Obiefuna said. He wondered if he sounded shallow. He had loved that school, had thrived there even amid a fair competition. He remembered the kind, soft-spoken teachers, the friends he had slowly accrued. The result of his Junior WAEC exams had been released a month ago and the headmistress had phoned his parents personally to give her congratulations.

"So why did you transfer here?" the boy asked.

Obiefuna looked back at the book spread open in front of him. He panicked for an instant, wondering if the boy had seen the look in his eyes, if this strange student had been able to see past the façade and read him somehow. The scars on his back were yet to fully heal, occasionally becoming tender when he had a bath. How could he describe the sting of the cord that Saturday morning as it struck skin? And yet, even in that moment, he had been primarily conscious not of the pain from the thrashing but of the fear in his father's eyes. He still remembered his mother's alarm when she returned from the salon to see the marks, how she had spent the whole evening screaming at his father, her voice bouncing off the walls of the house late into the night as Obiefuna tried to sleep, his back taut with pain. Afterwards, she asked him what had happened, and he lied that he had broken a plate, grateful that Ekene had already disposed of the day's rubbish. She looked at him with doubt in her eyes, but she did not probe. He remembered, too, the look on her face when his father broke the news that he would be sitting the entrance exams at the seminary in a few days' time. His mother protested, pointing out his outstanding performance at his current school; but Obiefuna looked across the table to find his father's eyes on him, and the coldness of his gaze prompting him to say, "I want to go, Mummy," and she had turned to him in surprise, aware that something beyond her grasp had just passed between father and son, something that categorically excluded her. Again, that look of doubt had returned to her eyes. Again, she said nothing.

A sudden silence descended on the class. A senior student had walked in and he stood now by the door, regarding the class with one sweep of the head, his face set in a frown. As he made to leave, someone hissed.

The senior student turned back to the class. "Who did that?"

This time the silence lasted even longer. Obiefuna waited for someone to speak, for the boy to confess. But nothing happened.

"Everybody kneel down," the senior student said. Obiefuna wondered, as the whole class dropped to their knees, where the whip the senior now held in his hands had come from. He glanced sideways at the boy next to him, who had made the sound. The boy looked straight ahead with such a perfectly blank expression on his face that Obiefuna wondered if he had been mistaken. The senior student walked up and down the row, issuing measured threats if the culprit was not named. Obiefuna's knees hurt from the tight position in which he was wedged behind his desk.

"You, stand up," the senior student said suddenly, pointing to Obiefuna.

Obiefuna hesitated before he rose. His chest hurt from the furious beating of his heart.

"Tell me who made the sound," the senior said.

Obiefuna cleared his throat and swallowed. Next to him, he could feel the boy tense. He could feel, also, all eyes in the room fixed squarely on him, waiting. He began to perspire.

"Since you're not going to talk, come out. You'll serve as an example to the others."

Obiefuna let himself out from behind his desk and walked all the way to the front.

"Hold that wall," the senior said, tapping the cane on the desk.

Obiefuna turned to the wall. Steadying himself for the whip, he was startled when someone shouted, "Senior, he's a new student!"

The senior student paused, looked at him curiously. "Are you a new student?"

Obiefuna nodded.

The senior gave him a gentle tap with the cane, as if in regret at the fun he had just missed. "And you're already allowing them to spoil you." He sized him up with a smile. "Go back to your seat."

Obiefuna felt light on the way back to his seat, as if he might float should he lift his feet any higher. A soft murmur followed the senior's exit. The boy next to him nudged him, staring at him in open wonder.

"You're a real one," he said.

Obiefuna nodded. He was quite stupid, all right. He wondered if the boy had really been ready to see someone else suffer punishment for his own offence. Obiefuna wondered, too, if the boy was the one who had shouted the information that rescued him.

"My name is Jekwu," he said.

IT WAS JEKWU who showed him the ropes, providing him with the hacks necessary for survival. Best to wake up and have your bath before the rising bell went off and the bathroom became too crowded; best to store water in the mornings after breakfast, when the tap was free, so you had some in reserve for afternoon or evening baths. Whatever you did, never miss chapel, or forget to dress your bed with white sheets on Sundays. Obiefuna learned to soak little quantities of raw garri in water before night prep, so that he arrived after prep to meet a bloated, bland-tasting but wholly satisfying ration. He learned to cut his soap into smaller pieces to make it last longer and to dissuade people from asking to share with him in the bathroom. He learned to fold dry clothes underneath his pillows before bedtime, so that they had straight lines on them by morning. He learned to stay out of the way of seniors: never look them in the eye, cross to the other path when they were sighted, never even smile. He learned to make the most of his time there.

Still, boarding school tired him. He hated the sharp sound of the rising bell, swift and resounding, which made the insides of his ears throb, jolting him even when he was awake. He hated the eternal sense of urgency that pervaded the air. He hated having to hurry to devotions held at the school court, to class, to the refectory, to bed. He hated the excruciatingly long prayer sessions at rising and at the end of prep. He hated the veiled suspicion with which everyone regarded each other, seeking to outwit and at the same time avoid being outwitted. He hated having to take his bath in the bathroom, an open yard next to the perpetually messy toilet, where faeces lined up on the ground and flies gathered in the hot afternoons so that his first instinct, always, was to throw up. Jekwu laughed the first time he complained and reassured him that he would get used to it, and even the thought of getting used to it dampened him.

He hated the senior students—towering, malevolent figures who seemed to get off on sadistic behaviour. Corporal punishments for even the most minute offence came in vicious, sickly creative forms. The stories terrified Obiefuna: the group whipping by seniors; the peculiar ex-prefect, mercifully expelled, who took pleasure in burning the fingertips of those who defied him with a lighter; gluttonous senior students who seized the meals of juniors and made them watch as they ate. A classmate showed Obiefuna a triangular-shaped scar on his arm: a senior student had flung an iron at him, newly emptied of burning coal. It was unthinkable to report any of this. Snitches were despised, surprisingly even among the victims. Obiefuna understood before long. The boys endured what they endured because theirs was a system that promised reciprocity. The time would come when they, too, would be seniors, at the helm of affairs, free to let off the frustrations accumulated over their years as juniors. The promise of this future gratification made the present suffering bearable, even desirable, for suffering would toughen them and make them more brutal, more skilled in knowing how to break a body. The analogy sickened Obiefuna to his stomach. He observed the junior students below him, innocent and unassuming, blithely unaware that they had, simply by being young, signed themselves up for unimaginable horror. He felt worse at the thought that they would be broken into a state of compliance and inherit the idea of reciprocity themselves, and that they would pass it down to the ones who came after them. And he hated the small but firm certitude in his gut that it was only a matter of time before he lost his calm reason and became the very thing he despised.

He hated the food. The tea at breakfast was a whitish, insipid liquid that the boys supplemented with their own beverages. Lunch was the predictable garri and a variety of soups similar in their watery tastelessness: the eguisi soup with unground seeds sticking out, the ogbono with excess palm oil floating on top. Only Sundays were different. Obiefuna came to appreciate the egg sauce served with bread and a better-tasting tea at breakfast. But it was the lunch he most looked forward to all week: white rice and stew, made occasionally with meat. He was irritated, however, by the long queues at mealtime, the boys pushing and shoving at each other until they threatened to overturn the cooler holding the food on the table. Most of his classmates repulsed him: brash, semi-young men, too old to still be in secondary school, sporting a crude and vulgar sense of humour. He was astounded at how gravely offensive things became trivial to them (he would never have fathomed that an insult like "bastard" was something one could take in one's stride, as though it were as benign as "stupid"), their tendency to break into sudden, unchecked fights. He hated the heavy smell of unwashed bodies and body odours that could not be hidden under harsh-smelling colognes, the strong smell of urine that hung in the air every morning from the corners of bed-wetting students. He hated the tendency of things to go missing—swiftly and without trace. And he hated, most of all, the ridicule you were bound to get if you complained about any of this. Because he had quickly observed the haughty airs the boys put on with new students, he felt grateful for Wisdom and Jekwu, their nearly unquestioning loyalty, the closest to kin he had. For there, in the vast seminary, he felt cut off from the world, overwhelmed by a pure and intimate sense of his ordinariness. If he screamed with all his might, no one outside the walls would hear him.

He thought about Aboy often. In his passing daydreams, he saw himself in the kitchen, standing in front of Aboy, reaching out to kiss him; but, just when he was close enough, Aboy's face transformed and gave way to his father's, to those eyes bedevilled by a heart-stopping deadness. In the brief calls made through Mr. Josiah to his father, messages transmitted back and forth in clipped monosyllables to save cost, he could make out only an obscure picture of the situation at home. Once, he happened to call when his mother was within reach and she informed him, at the end of the call, that Aboy and Ekene had sent their regards, and, as he handed the phone back to Mr. Josiah and made his way out of the room, he was filled with a bubbly warmth in his chest that stayed with him for days.

Obiefuna was permanently assigned Saturday labour on the school farm. It was a rare stroke of luck. The SS1 boys, regarded as the school's workforce, were usually saddled with the most gruelling tasks: washing the toilets, handling the school waste, levelling the tall grasses around the school when necessary. Farm labour, basically reserved for the SS2 students, felt like a miracle. At the farm, there were too many labourers for the few tasks that needed to be done, and, although Obiefuna did not mind joining in the harvests, even found it enjoyable, he and the other SS1 boys apportioned farm labour were mostly restricted to weeding with a hoe. The agricultural prefect, Senior Chijioke, was popular for his friendliness to subordinates, blurring the lines between supervisor and supervisee. At the end of each session, he let a junior student climb the orange and guava trees and rain down fruit, letting each labourer have a piece with the instruction to eat it right there and not take it back to their dormitories. Obiefuna found the weeding soothing: his movements were rhythmic, the plants giving way beneath his hoe, conversations thriving around him. One Saturday, as he worked, he noticed a group of seniors sitting on a felled tree, munching on the sugar canes they had cut down earlier. Obiefuna could make out snatches of their conversation from where he was. The senior speaking had a force to his tone—as if the conversation were an argument, even though the others simply looked on with an awed expression on their faces—as he spoke about a place called Green Gate, where, Obiefuna gathered, he had gone the previous night. Obiefuna knew who he was. Senior Papilo—so named after the Nigerian football star Nwankwo Kanu, whose skill he was said to perfectly embody—was the captain of the school football team. He was equally one of the most feared seniors on campus, notable for his spontaneous temper and his creative punishments. A non-prefect, he inspired greater reverence than even the most senior prefect. His description of Green Gate was lucid, the occasional pauses building anticipation. Obiefuna worked on the weeds around the group, unable to stop himself from inching closer, intrigued by the forbidden nature of the information being shared. So utterly absorbed was he in the story and in his imaginings of this place Senior Papilo described that he did not immediately notice the silence that had settled in, the palpable tension that now pervaded the air. He looked up with slow, cautious movements and, to his absolute horror, saw that Senior Papilo was staring directly at him.

"Come," he said.

Obiefuna averted his eyes and pulled at the weeds with extra vigour.

"I swear to God, if I repeat myself . . ."

Obiefuna straightened up from the weeding and touched his chest to confirm that he was the one being asked, hoping the blankness on his face was projecting his feigned innocence. Senior Papilo held his eyes without confirming. Something about the way he tapped at the sugar cane in his hand told Obiefuna that the senior would make a lunge for him if he wasted any more time. He approached the group with his head bowed, contrite, cursing his curiosity.

"You're going to repeat everything you just heard, word for word," Senior Papilo said.

Obiefuna looked up at him.

"I see you enjoy Big Boys' gist. Figured we should invite you to formally join us, no?" he asked the other seniors. They responded with brief cackling.

The moment was tense. A light breeze from around the trees rustled the cassava leaves and settled in Obiefuna's ears. His heart thumped fiercely as if about to pop out of his chest. He could feel the sweat trickling down his back as all the seniors stared at him. His legs had begun to itch.

Finally, one of the seniors, obviously keen on getting back to the conversation that had been interrupted, tapped Senior Papilo and made a pleading gesture with his palms, and Senior Papilo waved Obiefuna away.

Obiefuna went back to uprooting the weeds, making sure to move as far away from them as possible.

JEKWU LAUGHED when Obiefuna told him.

"I thought you wanted to listen to gist? Why did you run away?"

Obiefuna laughed along. He was still unable to shrug off the sense of trepidation he felt. He was unable, too, to blink away the sinister look in Senior Papilo's eyes, which had made him certain for a split second that he would drop dead without being touched.

"Senior Papilo is like that, sha," Jekwu said, "very wicked human being." He touched Obiefuna's shoulder, leaning close to whisper in his ear, "If you ask me, I'd advise you to avoid him. Don't let him notice you, for good or bad. You'll regret it either way, trust me."

Obiefuna had not planned to get himself noticed by Senior Papilo, or by anyone else for that matter. And so it was terrifying for him when, a few days later, he casually glanced away from the blackboard, through the window of the classroom, to see Senior Papilo strolling past with some of his friends. Before Obiefuna had the chance to look away, Senior Papilo looked to his right and their eyes met; and for the rest of the day and for days afterwards, Obiefuna thought about the look in Senior Papilo's eyes, that slight, suggestive smile that tugged his lips to a corner. It disturbed him somehow.

FIVE

Uzoamaka's mornings now brought a sour taste. It stayed on her tongue long after she had brushed her teeth, ruining every meal she took. She attributed the feeling, at first, to being unwell. The heavy downpours lately, unusual for early October, had brought with them mosquitoes, and Anozie had a terrible habit of leaving the windows open. She had the street pharmacist prescribe malaria drugs for her, and religiously swallowed tablet after tablet. By the second week, she knew enough to decide her sickness was not physical, merely a reaction to Obiefuna's absence. It was like having a precious possession yanked from her hands. She had watched him the morning he left, as he let himself into the car next to Anozie, and she had felt in that moment a searing pain in her chest, as if she had been stabbed, which metamorphosed, as the days progressed, into a dull ache that lingered.

She had underestimated the impact of his presence, the sound of his laughter ringing out, and she was randomly invaded now with flashes of the ordinary things that he used to do. She had also underestimated his quiet popularity, and she was often surprised by the frequency with which people enquired about him.

A WEEK INTO the resumption of school in September, Ekene had returned with a written note from the headmistress requesting Uzoamaka's and Anozie's presence. Anozie, conveniently, had to attend to a work call, so Uzoamaka went alone.

"I understand that you have only the best interests of your child at heart," the headmistress began, once the perfunctory pleasantries were out of the way. "But it would help us if we at least knew what we were doing wrong."

"You did nothing wrong, ma," Uzoamaka said.

"Then why pull the boy from here? Is this about the Senior WAEC? We're known for good grades. Besides, Obiefuna was going to be fine anyway. He was doing so well."

Uzoamaka stared at the table. She was slightly disconcerted by the headmistress's small, pinched face, by what looked like a compulsive neatness in the arrangement of materials in the large room. Next door, the voices of children repeating a definition rang in her ears.

The woman shook her head, resigned. "Well, I'm sure you know best. It just puzzles me. Especially with your other son still here with us. It makes no sense at all."

Uzoamaka offered a tight smile in response. There was no way she could explain to this woman that she herself was, in fact, just as mystified by the change. She had imagined herself used to Anozie's spontaneity by now, but this decision left her ill at ease. She spoke little for the rest of the day as she went about her work in the salon, untangling braids, washing, setting, relaxing and perming, but, back home, she updated Anozie about her school visit using the same words as the headmistress. It made no sense to move the boy from a relatively cheap, quality school to one in an entirely different state, just because he was worried about the boy's performance in the WAEC.

"Who said I was worried about his performance?"

"Then what is this, Anozie?" she said. She hated the tremble in her voice. She wished there was something within reach that she could slam against the wall. "Why isn't he here?"

"Because as long as he's my son I get to make some decisions regarding him, and they don't have to make sense to you or to that silly woman," Anozie said. "He will remain in that school, Uzoamaka. That's final. I don't want to talk about this issue again."

Uzoamaka called her sister, Obiageli, to complain. They had not always had the best relationship, strained further since their parents' passing five years ago. Obiageli brought an unreasonable sense of competitiveness to everything. Uzoamaka's problems would be one more way for her to feel good about herself. Obiageli listened, making small sympathetic sounds as Uzoamaka spoke, and at the end she decided that the situation really wasn't fair, but perhaps Anozie knew best. Uzoamaka hung up.

THE EVENING NEWS held mostly horrors. A pipeline explosion in Lagos had killed a hundred people; the riots in Jos steadily left a pile of bodies. Close by, just two streets away, armed cultists had raided the neighbourhood and carried out a gang rape. Amid her new state of permanent anxiety, Uzoamaka was conscious of a more intimate, muddled feeling of unease, an awareness that something had gone wrong in her house. She had been too angry to make sense of the tension in the air, but she had always been somewhat in sync with Anozie, and she could tell when something was depriving him of sleep. She was startled sometimes to emerge from sleep and find him wide awake, sitting up in bed with his arms folded across his chest, looking into the distance. Uzoamaka did not press him for information. They had, over time, become accustomed to a pattern of playing hide-and-seek with each other, holding out for as long as possible to see who would give in. Anozie was often the first to surrender. In another few days, he would tell her what the problem was and put her mind at rest. But the expected timeline passed, and he told her nothing. She returned from work late one evening to find Aboy at home. He stood by the kitchen worktop, his back to the door. He made funny sounds with his throat, and she thought, at first, he was singing. But he turned, on sensing her presence, and she saw that he was crying.

"Madam, please help me, beg Oga," he said. "I have nowhere else to go."

ANOZIE WAS UNYIELDING. He had always been an exacting man. He did not typically go back on his word. She had over the years gained the ability to temper most of his extreme decisions and get him to reconsider. But she also had learned her boundaries, aware by now that there were instances when there was no turning back for Anozie. Dishonesty was his greatest pet-peeve, and the reality of a thief serving under him was enough to set him on edge. He had given Aboy two weeks to leave, and, as the days drew nearer, Uzoamaka felt the air in the house become even thinner, as if they all shared a limited supply. Aboy left his meals untouched. "You will not tell your people I refused to feed you in my house!" Anozie told Aboy. "You will not steal from me and soil my name, too."

The thought of his leaving filled Uzoamaka with a vague terror. Even now, with his departure imminent, he carried out his chores with maximum efficiency: hauling water from the public tap to fill the drums, washing Anozie's pile of dirty clothes in the tub downstairs. That weekend, she had felt too unwell to go to the market and sent him instead—smiling inwardly, as she handed him the shopping list and some cash from her purse, at the thought of Anozie finding out she was entrusting him with money, something Anozie himself had, until recently, done without a qualm.

"I'll be back soon, ma," he had told her, and she felt her heart sink at his instinctive need now to reassure her. She wanted to say that she'd never imagined otherwise, but instead she said, "Don't be long."

He nodded and proceeded to the door. Uzoamaka headed towards the kitchen.

"He's going to be okay," Aboy said from the door.

Uzoamaka turned round. "What?"

"Obiefuna," Aboy said. "I know you're worried about him. But he's a good boy. He knows to stay out of trouble."

Uzoamaka stared at him awhile before she nodded. Strangely, it sounded a little more reassuring coming from Aboy; there was something steadying about the practical and yet particular sincerity of his tone, as if he were merely pointing out the obvious, while at the same time speaking from a place of intimate knowledge.

"Aboy," she said, "why did you take your oga's money?"

He closed his eyes and exhaled. When he opened them, what she saw was a defencelessness, bereft of guilt, and something she would later interpret as disappointment. "Madam, I swear on the grave of my dead father, I did not steal Oga's money."

Uzoamaka watched him in silence. She was reminded of Anozie's satisfied gloating late into the night as she drifted off to sleep. The boy had been for Anozie a prayer answered, inspiring in him an absolute confidence Uzoamaka knew was rare for Anozie's exacting character. She was familiar with an unfortunate phenomenon that sometimes occurred with apprentices. Some masters had been known to use their boys to their very limits, only to turn on them in the end and accuse them of misdemeanours, all in a bid to evade the responsibility of "settling" them at the end of service, as the agreement stipulated. But Aboy was just a year into his five years of required service. Anozie stood little to gain from his ousting. Besides, he was not that kind of man.

"Why else would your oga want you gone?"

"He's . . . angry with me," Aboy said with a slight stutter.

"But why?" Uzoamaka pressed. She did not understand it. Aboy had seemed only perfection to Anozie, to the household. "What did you do to him?"

There was an instant, as she stood watching him from across the room, when she saw his lips part, when it seemed like he was going to speak. But he shrugged and shuffled the shopping list in his hand, and, with lips suddenly set firm, she knew she would never get a response, that the conversation, as far as he was concerned, was over.

Aboy left the house on a Saturday, a day before the deadline Anozie had given him. Anozie was away at work, Ekene yet to arrive from the field. She was making lunch in the kitchen, and he appeared by the door to tell her he was set to leave. She followed him back into the living room. "Where will you go?" she asked.

He shrugged. "Maybe to the village."

Uzoamaka sighed. He might as well never have come. What

kind of man had she married? "Aboy, have you begged your oga? Whatever it is you did, he could give you a second chance if you apologize."

"He won't, madam," Aboy said. He had his eyes to the ground as he spoke to her, as if scared of looking at her. "He would never forgive me."

Something about the sudden force of his tone made Uzoamaka take an unconscious step backwards. He hesitated a moment longer, as if in silent apology, before letting himself out through the door. She remained standing, staring after his retreating figure, until she could no longer see him, and then she returned to the kitchen. The dull ache was again in her chest, bringing back to her an odd sense of deprivation. She picked up the knife to slice the utazi leaves for the soup, but for several moments she could not get her fingers to work. She was momentarily blinded by a flash of light across her mind's eye, and after she blinked it away, she was buoyed by clarity. Uzoamaka turned to the door and let herself out, running down the short flight of stairs that led outside. Aboy was standing in front of the yard, bag clinging to his shoulder, ready to board a bus.

"Aboy!" she shouted. He turned in her direction, alarmed, and, as she approached him, she sensed something else—fear. He was prepared for something she was going to say, something she had just realized. But Uzoamaka only untied the end of her wrapper and retrieved a slim wad of folded naira notes that she squeezed into his palm. "Give this to your people when you get home," she said. "And be careful on the road." In her sparse clothing, her bare feet coated with dust, she felt a little dramatic, a little foolish.

Aboy looked at the money in his hands. She saw his eyes fill with tears.

"God bless you, madam," he said.

Uzoamaka nodded. She could tell that his gratitude extended beyond the money: he knew she believed him. "Go well, my son," she said. "Ije oma."

He nodded. He looked as if he were going to hug her but decided against it. She remained standing by his side, without speaking, until a bus pulled up and he got in. Then she turned round and went back into the house.

SIX

The boys had a special anthem for Visiting Day. It was sung generally in the morning, before the gates were opened to visitors. Obiefuna spent the entire previous week learning the words by heart. He was caught up in the excitement of seeing his mother, seeing Ekene, after so long. From the accounts of other students, he made out that the day was an elaborate affair, with some parents travelling many miles across several states to attend, often turning the whole thing into a showy family reunion, complete with cooler upon cooler of food as if it were a party. On Visiting Day, the kitchen provided only one cooler of food for the whole school and yet there were almost always leftovers. Obiefuna's mother was one to make a show. He fantasized about the prospect of having much more than he could finish, impressing his roommates with his mother's unmatched cooking. But on the

Friday preceding Visiting Day, when he called to find out their intended time of arrival, he was informed by his father that they would not be visiting.

"What?" Obiefuna blurted out before he could stop himself.

"We're busy right now, Obiefuna," Anozie said.

Obiefuna gripped the phone closer to his ear with a force that made Mr. Josiah look up at him from his desk, which was piled high with the papers he was grading. Obiefuna shut his eyes tight and pinned his toes to his footwear to stop himself from reeling. On the other end of the phone, he could hear his father's patient breathing, the huffing sounds a quiet challenge.

"Why?" Obiefuna asked.

"Hmm?"

Obiefuna hung up. He passed the phone across to Mr. Josiah.

"No show?" Mr. Josiah asked.

Obiefuna shook his head.

"Brutal," Mr. Josiah murmured. "Don't look too gloomy. You're a big boy. Do you really need Mummy?"

Obiefuna forced a smile and turned round to go. As he walked back to the house, he hummed a song under his breath, and kicked about a stray container, all in an attempt to distract himself. Immersed in the game, his head down, he did not make out the feet approaching early enough to avoid bumping into them. He looked up to apologize and felt the hair on his arms instantly stand on end at the sight of Senior Papilo. Obiefuna reached down to wipe the slippers that didn't need wiping, stuttering his regrets. He dreaded what he thought would be the collected, contemplative look on Senior Papilo's face.

"Sorry, senior," he tried again.

Senior Papilo shrugged. "You can make it up to me tomorrow." There was the hint of mischief in his voice.

"My parents are not visiting," Obiefuna said.

"Why not?"

"I don't know."

Senior Papilo looked down at him awhile. Finally, he said, "Come to my room tomorrow. Ask anyone to show you. Let me give you something." He headed off.

Obiefuna stared after him. He had not always known what counted as a miracle, but he was certain this was one. It was common knowledge that Senior Papilo was one of those people who had subordinates lined up on Visiting Day, eager to offer tributes. Obiefuna proceeded with a gallop to his house, pausing by the tennis court to do a brief twirl before he mounted the stairs. He looked from the veranda at the classroom building, thought how grand the school structures appeared in the waning light of evening. Tomorrow seemed so long in coming.

By morning, the whole school was up in one energetic burst. Functions were hurried over, as some parents tended to arrive early, hovering at the main gate, biding their time until the formal bell went off at 9 a.m. and the inner gates were opened for them to come in. The boys were already dressed and lining the pavements of their dormitories as they waited to be summoned. The more desperate ones hurried to the gate and spent the whole time on the lookout for their parents. It struck Obiefuna that it was similar to the prison-visiting in the sitcoms he liked to watch with Ekene back home. He idled about the tennis court with Jekwu, absently watching a game, until someone came to tell Jekwu that his father had arrived. Jekwu returned shortly, bearing two bags, one containing food and the other provisions. Obiefuna followed him upstairs and helped him to unpack. Jekwu transferred the food to large plates and rose to exit, needing to return the flask to his father, who was waiting by the gate.

Obiefuna was given the task of looking after the food until he returned. When he was gone, the boys in the room gathered round the corner with spoons in hand. Some of them toured the rooms with the hope of getting themselves fed off other people's goodies, since they had none themselves. Obiefuna brushed aside their conspiratorial eagerness, insisting everyone wait until Jekwu arrived. One of them tapped him and pointed towards the door. He looked to see a junior student standing there.

"Are you Senior Obiefuna?" the boy asked timidly.

"Yes?"

"There's someone looking for you at the gate."

Obiefuna frowned. He was aware that it was a tradition among the boys to prank each other on Visiting Day. Bored, they went round giving false summons to people whom they knew were expecting visitors. Those who fell victim to the prank often had to undergo the long journey to the gate, only to discover there was no such summons. He sighed and looked away.

The boy walked up to him and tapped him. "Senior, I'm serious."

"I'm sure you are," he said drily. He looked up from the food to behold Jekwu's roommates' questioning stare. "I'm not expecting any visitors," he explained.

"Well, you're the only Obiefuna in our class," one of them said. "And the boy looks very sure."

Obiefuna turned to him again. The boy met his eyes squarely. It was unusual to be pranked by a junior student, but that might be the idea. Someone could have sent a junior student to make it more believable. For a moment, Obiefuna silently dared him to laugh and confess it was a prank, but the boy stared right back, unflinching. Finally, he gave up. "You'll take me to him."

The boy looked displeased. "Senior, he's standing—"

"Keep quiet and sit here." Obiefuna tapped on the side of the bed. "We'll go once the owner of this food comes back." The boy would be made to pay if this turned out to be a joke.

Jekwu barged into the room a few minutes later. He registered the crowd gathered round with displeasure. As he settled down, Obiefuna rose, briefly explained that he would be back soon and headed out with the boy. They walked to the gate together, and as they neared, Obiefuna began to believe it was real. Who could possibly have come? Had his father been pulling his leg? He knew, though, that his father was hardly one for jokes. Perhaps his mother had asked one of her relatives who lived nearby to check on him. The junior student halted and pointed forward. In the distance, Obiefuna regarded the tall figure in faded T-shirt and trousers in silence. Dust swirled around him. Aboy was the last person he had expected to see. He made for an odd picture standing there, arms folded across his chest. He turned after a moment to face Obiefuna, and something about that smile told Obiefuna Aboy had seen him all along. He walked quickly, consciously checking himself from breaking into a run, and hugged Aboy, holding on to him for a long, long moment.

"Obi," Aboy said quietly when they disengaged, searching his face. "How far?"

"I'm fine," Obiefuna said. He felt an intoxicating happiness, as if he had been drinking all day.

"What have they been feeding you? You've become so thin." He tugged at Obiefuna's biceps playfully. Aboy had on him the acrid scent of cheap cologne. He carried a small bag in his right hand while his left was intertwined with Obiefuna's. He was looking around him, seeming to search for something. "Where do we sit?"

Obiefuna led the way into the chapel. The benches had been

removed and replaced with white plastic chairs specifically for the purposes of Visiting Day. At different sections, families sat around; the air was stuffed with the aroma of assorted meals.

"I brought you this," Aboy said, when they were seated. He passed Obiefuna the bag.

"Thank you." Obiefuna peered into the bag. He could make out a takeaway pack from an eatery. He had imagined Aboy would come with a home-cooked meal.

"Did Daddy ask you to come?" Obiefuna asked.

There was a pause. Aboy tilted his head to the side to watch Obiefuna's face and Obiefuna saw something like realization slowly dawn on him.

"You don't know," Aboy said.

"Know what?"

"Your father kicked me out. He said I stole money from him."

Obiefuna tried not to drop the bag. Aboy was shaking his head from side to side, the thin stretch of smile betraying his emotional state. Even as the question formed on Obiefuna's lips, he was instantly repulsed by it. Of course Aboy was innocent. Obiefuna knew his father to be many things, but how could he have orchestrated a set-up this callous, this basic and yet so garish? How had he been able to convince anyone?

"Your mother did not really believe him," Aboy said, as if reading his mind. "But there was nothing she could do."

"Oh," Obiefuna said. There was nothing else he could say.

Aboy said, "I'm currently staying with Ikem and Dibueze—the apprentices from the next shop—in their one room in Mile 3. I'm doing small jobs by the day to provide food and add to the rent."

"I'm so sorry, Aboy."

"Don't talk rubbish," Aboy chuckled and reached behind

Obiefuna's head to give him a gentle tap; and then his hand lingered. Obiefuna felt a jolt as Aboy caressed his ears. "I just wanted to see how you were doing, Obi," he said in a low murmur.

Despite himself, Obiefuna could not help but smile as a warm feeling spread all over him, numbing his toes. He reached out to take Aboy's hand. Aboy hesitated, his eyes seeming to dart about, as if to make sure they weren't being watched, and then he gripped Obiefuna's fingers briefly and let go.

"Your father doesn't know I'm here. So please don't tell him, or even your mother or Ekene."

Obiefuna nodded. "Of course."

Aboy stood up to go. "Stay well, Obi."

Obiefuna watched him head to the gate, his broad shoulders, his slightly bowed legs, his ungainly walk. He watched until Aboy disappeared from sight.

Sunday took on a slow start. Still reeling from the thrill of the previous day, the boys shuffled to class for Sunday School as if in mourning. Even the sermon at the main service was more subdued than usual, unbearably long, and Obiefuna fought to stay awake. He was relieved when the final grace was shared, and everyone rose to exit the chapel in order of seniority. He was on his way back to the house with Jekwu amid a cluster of his classmates when he heard hissing coming from the senior house. Everyone picked up pace, looking straight ahead, none daring to look up, as this would mean sacrificing oneself for whatever errand there was. Obiefuna was almost successfully past the senior house when one of the boys tapped him and pointed in the direction of the hiss. "It's you, Obiefuna."

Obiefuna looked up. It took him a few seconds to register Senior Papilo, and he felt the coldness of realization numb his spine. How could he have forgotten the promise to visit him yesterday? He handed his Bible and hymn book to Jekwu and turned round to Senior Papilo's house, dreading every footfall that led upstairs. Senior Papilo was waiting for him at the final landing, and he silently led the way down the corridor and into a large room, stopping at a spacious corner at the far end. Within the already impressive outlook of the room, the space set itself apart somehow, exuding a quiet authority. In place of a bunk, he had a bed that was balanced on stacks of old cupboards. On the wall above, boldly scribbled in capital letters, was the word PAPILO.

"Kneel down," Senior Papilo said in a low voice, his back turned to Obiefuna.

Obiefuna began to speak. "Senior, I'm so sorry, I forgot—"

Senior Papilo tilted his head backwards to look at him, without fully turning, and Obiefuna found himself descending to his knees, the rest of his apologetic explanation cut short. He wondered why it mattered so much to Senior Papilo that there had been one less mouth to share the treasures he must have received yesterday. But then Senior Papilo's quirkiness was what defined him. He might have interpreted Obiefuna's failure to turn up as a defiance of sorts, a slap to his authority.

Obiefuna remained kneeling as Senior Papilo changed and left for lunch. Senior Papilo returned just when Obiefuna's knees had begun to hurt. He carried a plate of food in his hands. The smile on his face faded as he approached. He locked the food in his cupboard and sat on his bed. He was fiddling with an egg, tapping the shell lightly as if checking to see if it would crack. For a while he seemed engrossed in the act, oblivious to Obiefuna's presence. When he finally looked at Obiefuna, his expression was one of distracted puzzlement, as though he did not recognize him. "Is that a handkerchief you have under your knees?" he asked suddenly.

Obiefuna glanced down at the handkerchief he had placed

on the floor to prevent his white trousers from getting stained. He made to remove it, but Senior Papilo raised a hand to halt him. He reached under the bed for the bucket underneath and scooped out a bowl of water. He sprinkled it on the ground and shuffled his slippers on the wet floor until it was messy enough. "Lie down on this."

Obiefuna looked at him. He wondered just how far he could hold his own against Senior Papilo. He wondered, too, if he would be the first to disobey him. What was the worst that could happen? But he lifted himself from his kneeling position and lay down on the muddy mess, feeling the cold floor hard against his chest, the wetness seeping into his skin.

"Look up," Senior Papilo ordered.

Obiefuna looked up at him.

"What's your name?"

"Obiefuna."

"Where are you from?"

"Igbo Ukwu."

Senior Papilo looked at him closely. "I'm from Isuofia. You know there?"

Obiefuna shook his head.

"It's the closest town to Igbo Ukwu. We're like brothers."

Obiefuna nodded. So a kinship had been established. He wondered if Senior Papilo would let him go now.

"Why did you lie to me, Obi?"

"I'm not lying, senior, I honestly forgot."

"You told me no one was coming to see you yesterday," he said. "I believed you. I even offered to take care of you because you were looking so dejected that day." He sounded deeply hurt. "But you turn round and make a fool of me."

Obiefuna kept his head bowed.

"Go on," Senior Papilo said. His voice had returned to quiet malevolence. "Tell me you were not the one I saw yesterday at the chapel with one man." Obiefuna was silent. "Boy, look at me when I'm talking to you." Obiefuna looked up. "Were you or were you not the person?"

"I was."

"So why did you lie?"

Obiefuna took a breath. "I did not know he was coming."

Senior Papilo stared him down. The smile on his face was not kind. "Have you heard about me, Obiefuna?" he asked.

"Yes, senior."

"Did they tell you that the one thing I hate more than lies are lies that are stupid?"

"I swear to God, senior," Obiefuna said. "It's just . . . complicated."

"Hmm." Senior Papilo paused. There was an instant when he seemed to be considering the situation. Obiefuna's heart welled with hope.

"Take off your shirt and lie down," Senior Papilo said finally. He stood up and walked to his wardrobe.

"Senior, please . . ."

The egg swished past Obiefuna's ear and smashed to pieces on the wall behind him. Senior Papilo was dutifully extracting his leather belt from the trousers he had pulled off a hanger. He wrapped one end of the belt around his palm and waited for Obiefuna to take off his shirt. The first swing landed on Obiefuna's bare shoulders, tingling pain burning up his skin. The second landed on his back and the third on the side of his face. They came quickly, twirling in the air seconds before they struck flesh. At first Obiefuna was too dazed to cry, but he decided seconds later that he would rather die than give Senior

Papilo the satisfaction. He counted up to sixteen before the beating stopped. Senior Papilo put the belt down and gave him a final sizing-up before he told him to get out of his sight.

Obiefuna walked back to his house. Jekwu was still dressed, waiting for him in his room. Without asking any questions, Jekwu helped him out of his clothes and soaked them with bleach. Obiefuna crawled into Wisdom's bed, refusing the food Jekwu offered. He dithered between sleep and wakefulness, finally drifting off to the sound of idle chatter. He did not know how long he slept, but soon enough he felt hands tapping him. He shrugged it off, wishing Jekwu would leave him alone. But the voice that said "Obiefuna" was too deep to be Jekwu's. He opened his eyes to behold Senior Papilo's face. For a fleeting instant, he wondered if he was dead and this was hell, but Jekwu's face appeared next to Senior Papilo's as Obiefuna sat up straight in bed. Senior Papilo extended a plate of food to him.

"You missed lunch," he said casually, his face expressionless.

Obiefuna stared at the food, rice flecked with sardines, the food which Senior Papilo had brought back from the dining room and saved in his cupboard earlier. Obiefuna shook his head. "I'm not hungry."

Senior Papilo rose from the bed. With the same lack of expression, in his usual levelled tone, he said, "I want to see this plate empty by the time I come back. And when I say empty . . ." He paused and looked at Obiefuna. His eyes transmitted the rest of his message. Obiefuna would not dare to throw the food away.

As soon as he was out of the door, Obiefuna handed the plate to Jekwu. Jekwu glared at him, shook his head. "I don't want any trouble," he said. "Besides, you really need to eat."

Obiefuna took a spoonful of rice, unsurprisingly tasty. It was rumoured that the graduating class had their meals cooked separately, and with enough spices. He ate quickly, relishing the taste of the sardines, and soon he was scraping the plate. It was after he was done that the oddity of the situation occurred to him. He could sense where this was leading, and he did not like it. Not someone like Senior Papilo, whom he had concluded was a psycho. He took the painkillers Jekwu offered and lay back in bed. Later, after prep, Wisdom retrieved the plate, now washed, from the locker, and told him to return it.

"He said he would come for it," Obiefuna said.

"You expect Senior Papilo to come to this house just to pick up the plate you used to eat?" Wisdom enunciated each word slowly, to make Obiefuna see his own ridiculousness.

Obiefuna took the plate to Senior Papilo's house. Senior Papilo sat perched on a bench in his corner of the room, lifting dumbbells, rippling muscles glistening in the light from the bulb above. He looked up at Obiefuna and set the dumbbells down. "Looks like someone did not forget this time around," he said with veiled amusement. He reached for a small towel hanging by the window to wipe away the sweat on his face and round his neck, gesturing off-handedly to his cupboard. Obiefuna could sense Senior Papilo watching him while he put the plate back. As he made to leave, Senior Papilo held his wrist. "Look at me," he said.

Obiefuna turned to face him. Senior Papilo's eyeballs in the yellow light took on the almost translucent sheen of fine honey. Senior Papilo pulled him downwards until he was in a squatting position, sandwiched between Senior Papilo's open thighs. He kept his eyes on the sweat that trickled down Senior Papilo's neck to his chest, disappearing through the tufts of hair around his navel, as Senior Papilo studied his face in the light, running his finger gently over the welt on one side of his face. "Jesus, I can be a beast sometimes," Senior Papilo said, smiling through his regret. He cupped Obiefuna's chin in one palm, tilting it upwards so that Obiefuna's eyes met his again. "This is what happens when I get provoked, Obi. And I was just trying to be your friend." He sighed.

"I'm sorry," Obiefuna said. He did not know why he apologized. Only that there was something in Senior Papilo's eyes, almost pure and sad, that made him want to set the course of the previous day back in motion, so he could erase Aboy's visit and be with Senior Papilo.

Senior Papilo held on longer, his face inching so close that his nose almost grazed Obiefuna's, and then he pulled away. Obiefuna could still smell the mustiness of his sweat, could still feel his heartbeat. "I forgive you, Obi," he said after a while. "God knows I forgive you."

THAT WAS ALL it took to become Senior Papilo's boy. There had not been a direct statement of intent on either side, but Senior Papilo took on the role of a School Father in the following days and Obiefuna grew into the role of a "boy"—and he supposed that was how it went. Jekwu joked, his tone not hiding its underlying disapproval, that it was the oldest story in the book: senior student marking out a junior student to bully, with the sole intention of manipulating him into submission. Obiefuna did not know about being manipulated. He was only aware of the mesmerizing effect Senior Papilo had on him. It was like a spell, this something about Senior Papilo that drew him in and held him. On sports days, he was on the lookout for Senior Papilo, clapping the longest when Senior Papilo displayed one of his many skills on the pitch, taking a quiet, personal pride in the uproar that followed every well-placed goal. He came to fancy Senior Papilo's oddities, which seemed to have, in Obiefuna's mind, a unique quality. Fundamentally, Senior Papilo lived a simple life: he detested clutter, he abhorred dishonesty or sloppiness, he hated having to repeat himself. Obiefuna learned to be alert, to carry out chores with demonstrative efficiency. He learned to pre-empt Senior Papilo's needs, creating a routine for the chores, intensely gratified whenever he managed to extract from Senior Papilo a rare, approving smile. In the afternoons after class, he retrieved Senior Papilo's uniform and had it washed alongside his and hung out to dry before the time came for his extra-mural classes. Shortly before night prep, he ironed the uniforms with coal and delivered Senior Papilo's to him immediately after prep (once, he walked in on Senior Papilo punishing one of his other boys, and Senior Papilo had pointed at the shirts Obiefuna delivered and said that was how a shirt that had been ironed should look).

Obiefuna liked the benefits that came with being Senior Papilo's boy. He could easily skip Saturday functions now, spending the mornings in Senior Papilo's corner, on his wide, soft bed, reading a book, or sleeping, or eating with Senior Papilo. Senior Papilo's generosity stunned him. Obiefuna's understanding of the school's father–son relationship was one where the son was essentially the provider and the father the protector. But with Senior Papilo, nothing was ever requested, or even expected, of him. Senior Papilo never failed to save up food for him whenever he missed the refectory while engaged in a chore (so that he took to deliberately missing the refectory, as Senior Papilo's supplements were tastier and filling). Senior Papilo's soakings lived up to their name, consisting of an entire row of cabin biscuits and spoonful upon spoonful of milk; Obiefuna worried that he would get a stomach upset afterwards. But it was the takeaways he most looked forward to, which Senior Papilo got on the Thursday nights he scaled the walls to go into town. It was the only time he had all four of his boys, each from a different class, together, watching with smug pride as they wolfed down the plates of fried rice and chicken and salad so elaborately packaged in foil.

On other days, Obiefuna suffered the crushing weight of his decision. Senior Papilo could summon the most spontaneous, the most terrifying, temper. He was particularly inventive with his punishments. Although Obiefuna had envisaged, from watching the other boys endure dreadful punishments, that his own day would come, he was ill-prepared when it did. Sometimes he was punished for things that were manifestly beyond his control. On the days it rained and the uniforms could not dry and therefore could not be ironed (Senior Papilo forbade any of them from pressing a hot iron on his wet clothes), Senior Papilo made him lie on the floor beneath his bed until midnight, when inspection would begin. When his attention slipped and he missed a word of Senior Papilo's instructions, he was whipped with a leather belt across his bare shoulders. Afterwards, Senior Papilo would survey the injury with an almost sad expression, going on and on about being forced to hurt him, prompting Obiefuna to apologize. Still, it was, fundamentally, a fair trade, and it had its benefits. It made the other seniors leave him alone, some of them, out of loyalty to Senior Papilo, going as far as to exclude Obiefuna from mass punishments. And when, in July, it came the time for Senior Papilo's graduation, Obiefuna nursed a stubborn lump in his throat. "Will you miss me?" Senior Papilo asked him once, throwing Obiefuna off-balance as they ate together from a plate of soaking that Senior Papilo had made. The food got stuck in Obiefuna's throat, and he took his time swallowing as he nodded. Senior Papilo traced his eyes for a long moment. For once, for a split second, Obiefuna thought he could interpret what that dewy-eyed glassiness in Senior Papilo's eyes meant. And then Senior Papilo looked away and looked at him again, and, just like that, it was gone.

SEVEN

After he emerged from the bliss of babyhood, Obiefuna picked up several undesirable traits, among which was his susceptibility to illness. A sickness would seem to sprout out of the blue, torturing his tiny body and raising Uzoamaka's blood pressure, until something appeared to snap and it disappeared almost as swiftly as it had come. A few days past his fifth birthday, he developed a fever. It was beyond comprehension. She had woken up the night before to the sound of someone heavily mounting the stairs, a steady thud that lasted well past half an hour, neither approaching nor receding. When Anozie took out a lamp to investigate, he assured her that there was no one and that the security gate at the base of the stairs was still firmly locked. He shot her one of his accusing stares that said it had all been in her head, and because the boys were asleep in their room and the sound of the thud stopped after she returned to bed, she did not argue with him.

But the next day, Obiefuna had not risen well. He lay stretched out on the bed, burning with a fever that threatened to scald the back of Uzoamaka's palm, his body so still that the slow rise and fall of his stomach gave the only indication he was still alive. His breathing was laboured and heavy, the occasional sound from his slightly opened lips sounding to her like the groans of a dying man. He was placed on a drip by the doctor for a few days, and she kept vigil by his side for the duration, dousing him in capfuls of olive oil, forcing mashed meals and tablets she had procured at the pharmacy down his throat, terrified of taking her eyes off him and knowing with a stubborn certitude that they would have to take her before they harmed a hair on his head. On the fifth day, he began to kick in his sleep, mumbling something she did not understand. She crouched beside him, afraid to touch him and afraid to move away, begging him in between sobs not to lose the fight. His kicking slowed after a while, and he returned his hands to his sides, fists rigidly clenched. She held a light to his face, and although his lids were open, eyeballs squarely meeting hers, there was a deadness to them that told her he was far gone. She knelt beside him and held his hand in both of hers, her head pressed to them, and it was in that position that he found her the next morning, staring with wide-eyed puzzlement as she ran her hands all over him, unbelieving, the boy who had nearly died before her own eyes.

Uzoamaka had always felt that she alone understood him. She had first begun to regard him with renewed interest when, at a crusade she attended with Obiefuna while pregnant with Ekene, the prophetess, a towering giant of a woman with a deep, masculine voice, had paused by Uzoamaka's seat as she walked down the pew in the course of her preaching. She lifted Obiefuna, barely a year old then, fast asleep, from Uzoamaka's thigh and cradled him in her arms as she walked the short length of the row, all the while speaking in tongues, returning him to her afterwards without a word. Anozie had dismissed the incident as irrelevant. "So a female pastor sees you, an obviously pregnant woman, carrying a child and decides to relieve you of the burden for a few minutes. Big deal?"

But a second incident had humbled him. A few years down the line, Anozie ran into debt from gambling, and the fiery-eyed, bad-tempered Udoka, from whom he had borrowed, swore to make their lives miserable if Anozie did not hand over the money he owed. Udoka, turned up without warning at the shop and at their house, once even at Uzoamaka's salon, threatening to involve the police, his village oracle, cultists. One evening, as they were having dinner, they heard a banging on the front door, the weight of the fist causing the table to vibrate, and Udoka's voice boomed from outside, demanding to see Anozie, threatening to break down the door if he was delayed. Uzoamaka hurried Anozie to the bedroom and hid him in her box of wrappers, intending to tell the man he was not in, but before she could get her story in order, Obiefuna, then four years old, had trotted to the door and opened it for the man. Uzoamaka's first thought, after recovering from the shock of the sound of the door opening, was that the man would take Obiefuna or Ekene as collateral until his money was returned, but when she hurried into the living room she was left stunned by the sight before her. There was Obiefuna, small with spindly legs, holding on to the door frame and looking up at the large, thick-set man before him with a defiance even Anozie lacked. The man stared down at Obiefuna, dumbstruck, his fist suspended in mid-air. And then, still silent, Udoka turned and left. Obiefuna closed the door after him and walked past Uzoamaka to the dining table, hoisted himself onto the chair and quietly continued with his interrupted dinner. When she told Anozie later, he turned and looked at Obiefuna, who had fallen asleep on a chair in the living room in the middle of watching a cartoon with Ekene, and she saw, in Anozie's eyes, not quite belief but something close to wonder.

It had always been easy, when he was a child, to get Obiefuna to talk to her. His soft-voiced innocence had often been just what she needed to get through a hard day. She loved the evenings, when she walked home with her sons after finishing work, a boy flanking her on each side. Obiefuna would go on and on about the things that had happened at school, reliving the events with frenzied gesticulation, as if eager to transport her into the actual moments, his gusto bringing a smile to her lips even on the worst days. During the years when they were growing up—as she became more and more despondent because of Ekene's rascality, Anozie's flagrant show of preference and her own inability to keep a third pregnancy—the little, fleeting moments like these were what somehow kept her going. Once, after a particularly gruelling day at work, she had been exhausted and dispirited, the cackling of the plates at dinner and Anozie's aloofness compounding her crankiness. And then, without warning, Obiefuna said in his childish voice, "Mummy, sorry," much to everyone's surprise, and that was all it took to make her lean forward at the table and burst into tears.

She thought back now, increasingly, to his childhood. She remembered arriving home with him from hospital, Anozie mounting the stairs ahead of them to hold the door open for her. Visitors had poured in, and in such large numbers that there wasn't space to seat them all. For the first month she was hardly alone with him, and when she searched across the room she was likely to find him in the arms of someone else. There were times when it felt exhausting, when she wished her situation otherwise, but she was convinced even then that their mere presence solidified what she believed: that her boy was not like any other. As she watched him grow, putting away the baby clothes that so quickly became obsolete, marching with him to kindergarten on that first day, she had laid out in her mind, without even being consciously aware of it, a life course that he would follow: the excellent grades he would receive in school, the top-rated universities he would attend, the high-paying job he would have. She had pictured the beautiful girl he would settle with, the small children who looked like him running around her home and getting on her nerves while she complained fondly to friends, all of them aware she would not have it another way.

Uzoamaka watched Anozie eat. He ate with a deliberate slowness, moulding his garri with an almost showy precision before dipping it into his soup. He had a habit of chewing with his mouth open. It was the one reason why he never ate outside, lest he rile everyone with the sight and the grating sound of his chewing. She had become accustomed to quietly checking him when the sound became unbearable, but she held back today, steeling herself for what was to come. He washed his hands in the bowl of water before him at the end of the meal and rose from the dining table to head to the living room, getting set for the evening news.

"I'm going to see Obiefuna tomorrow," Uzoamaka announced.

Anozie turned round. "Uzoamaka—"

"I just want to be sure he's fine," she said.

"You talked to him on the phone the other day and he told you he's doing well," Anozie said.

"I need to see for myself."

"This unreasonable behaviour is exactly why the boy is where he is," Anozie said. "You can see him when he comes home for the holidays," he decided, waving one dismissive hand at her and turning away, to signal an end to the conversation.

"Anozie—" Uzoamaka began.

"Are you not listening to me?" he barked, turning back round. "I said you're not setting a foot outside this house to see anybody."

Uzoamaka bit back a scoff. She stacked the dinner plates atop each other and took them to the kitchen. When she returned to the living room, Anozie was reclining on a chair, watching the news. She stood by the room divider with her arms folded across her chest.

"Anozie, we've been married a long time. You know by now that I'm going to see him tomorrow, whether you like it or not."

He blinked, taken aback. "Really? It has got to this now?"

She eased away from the room divider, without responding, and walked to the bedroom. She could hear the water running down the hall—Ekene was having his night-time shower. She climbed into bed and pulled the sheets up to her chest.

"I just told you that the school will go on break in less than a month," Anozie called out suddenly from the living room. "What is so urgent that cannot wait until then?"

THE SCHOOL WAS BIGGER than she had imagined. Uzoamaka sat by the chapel, staring at the vast fields of the school compound, and marvelling at the contrast between the green expanses of the institution and its urban location. Harmattan had come early this year, and she wished, as she stared at the gleaming white walls of the chapel, coated now with a thin film of dust, that she had come with a shawl to protect her shoulders from the cold, dry wind. She recalled, with retrospective amusement, the earlier spectacle at the gate with the obstinate gateman who had refused to let her through, citing lack of purpose, as if her simple explanation of wanting to see her son was insufficient. She had banged repeatedly on the gate until the man was forced to summon his superior, and the older, wiser-looking man had only to give her a single look, taking note of the unwavering resolve in her eyes, before he held the gate wide open for her, with an appeal to at least wait until breaktime in half an hour. Obiefuna took so long to emerge that Uzoamaka experienced a moment of dizzying panic, convinced that he was not there, and that Anozie had done something terrible with her son. And then there he was before her, a confused smile on his face, a mass of hair on his head she would have levelled had he been at home. Did his uniform look oversized on him or had it always been that way? She hugged him twice, burying her nose in his hair. There was no lingering fragrance of the strawberry hair lotion he used at home. He did not hug her back as tightly as he usually did.

"Nwam." Uzoamaka ran her hands over his face. He usually knew better than not to be properly moisturized in harmattan season. She could spot newly formed acne on his forehead, dark sprouts of hair forming on his upper lip. When he called her "Mummy," she almost reflexively took a step backwards. It had been only three months. Her boy had transcended into manhood behind her back.

"You look nice," he said.

Uzoamaka smiled. It was an odd compliment from him, or perhaps it was the lack of enthusiasm with which it was given, stripping it of a genuine quality. She had taken the time to select her clothes for the day and applied a spicy perfume she reserved for special occasions. She wished he would not simply refer to her appearance as "nice."

"What's this on your face?" she asked when they were seated, pointing to the left side of his face, where a faint mark ran from his jaw up to the top of his ear.

"I fell down, Mummy," he said.

Uzoamaka drew back to look at him. It looked nothing like a wound from a fall, but what struck her the most was the memory of his using those same exact words to describe bruises he had received on playgrounds as a child, bruises she later came to know were inflicted by other children. Yet again, her son was being bullied. Anozie had pulled him out of a perfectly good school and brought him to a slaughterhouse.

"I'm fine, Mummy," he said, as if reading her mind. "I mean it."

Uzoamaka sighed, putting off the battle until later. "Have you made any friends?"

He nodded. "A few."

Uzoamaka did not know whether to believe him. She could not claim to know about the idiosyncrasies of sixteen-year-old boys, but surely bringing his friends along to meet his mother was not considered old-fashioned now?

"Your friends," she said. "Are they good to you?"

He glanced at her with eyebrows raised, not knowing what to make of her question. She did not like this new haughty air he put on. She might have pulled his ears in warning if they had been at home.

She tried again, leaning forward. "Obiajulu. Do you like it here?" she asked.

He shrugged. "The teachers are good."

It was not in his character to be deliberately evasive. She reached a hand under his chin and tilted his head upwards to have a good view of his face. He was unresisting, his neck darting in every direction she manoeuvred, as if held by a spring;

compliant in a sense but also defeated. Uzoamaka felt an almost physical pain from her heart sinking.

"You can always come home if you're unhappy here," Uzoamaka said. "You know that, don't you?"

He hesitated before he nodded. His attention was divided, his gaze fixed on something in the distance. Uzoamaka looked away. She wished she sounded more convincing, she wished she believed herself. The silence between them was suddenly filled by voices of children playing. In the distance, a faint bell chimed briefly.

"What is it?" Uzoamaka asked, hurt that, whatever it was, it seemed to have captured his attention in a way that she had been unable to all the while.

"The warning bell for end of breaktime, Mummy," he said. "And visiting."

Uzoamaka nodded. She felt a slow numbness spread through her, but she rose as he did, and passed the bag of provisions she had brought with her to him. They hugged, a moment too brief, and then they disengaged.

"Greet everyone," he said, half turning to go.

Uzoamaka nodded again, and then, just as the lie came to her tongue, because it had nestled stubbornly in her mind and refused to dissipate: "Aboy was asking of you."

Few things would stick more firmly in Uzoamaka's memory than the look on Obiefuna's face as he turned round to acknowledge her message: the joy so mesmerizingly captured in a lift of his brows, the instant sparkle in his eyes that she had been unable to elicit. She was reminded of stepping into his day-care centre when he was a baby, after they had spent several hours apart, his squeal of delighted anticipation on hearing her voice from outside the room, the pure, innocent joy on his face when his eyes processed her form, as if she were the most precious person in the world. It was one of the babyish appealing traits he had lost in teenage-hood, but there it finally was again after so long, although brief, although now self-conscious. Uzoamaka was only too familiar with this look, and, although it was directed at someone who was not her, she knew that her boy was in love.

EIGHT

The final day's sermon was on the theme of Christmas. The chapel had been given a makeover for the occasion, and now, as the chaplain went over the significance of Christ's birth and the value of newness, Obiefuna stared up at the ceiling fan above him, decorated with multicoloured balloons that swished as the blades moved. He was unaware of when the sermon came to an end, until Jekwu nudged him, prompting him to rise, as the others did, for the benediction.

"Merry Christmas in advance, my children," the chaplain said from the pulpit, and Obiefuna watched as the boys turned to repeat it to one another. Back in the house, he lay on his bed without packing, willing away the noise from his roommates, from the entire student body excited to leave.

"Do you not want to go home?" Wisdom asked.

Obiefuna sighed without responding. He felt a fatigue he did not understand. An odd premonition had wrapped around his shoulders from that morning and would not lift, so that when, finally, his father arrived and informed him, as they got into the car, that he would be spending that holiday and future holidays with his paternal aunt in Owerri, he wasn't surprised.

"Is Ekene there?" he asked.

"No," his father said and did not elaborate, and, as they eased out of the school gate, into the main road, Obiefuna understood then that his punishment was ongoing, and never to be questioned; to be accepted quietly instead, with as much grace as he could muster.

HIS AUNT'S HOME, on a quiet, tree-lined street off the Aladinma Housing Estate, charmed him. Obiefuna had only a vague recollection of the woman, from brief visits to the village when he was small, and he had been prepared to despise her. But he found himself enamoured with her and fascinated with the large house. He had a room to himself, previously occupied by one of his aunt's sons, who now lived abroad. He spent whole days alone in the room watching television, coming out only to greet his aunt before she left for work and after her return. His aunt disapproved of his weight and had the help serve him food at intermittent intervals, jokingly vowing to make up, in two weeks, what he had lost in months.

ON CHRISTMAS EVE, his mother called.

"Obiajulu," his mother said. It seemed such a long time since he had been called that. "Kedu?"

"I'm fine, Mummy," he said. He did not realize he had been holding his breath until he felt a little dizzy and put his hand to the wall to steady himself.

"I'm so sorry you couldn't come home to us," she said. "Daddy just thought it would be easier for you to go there since it's so close."

Obiefuna nodded, and then, realizing his mother couldn't see him, he said, "Yes, Ma."

"Is your aunty good to you," she asked.

"Yes."

"Ngwanu, greet her for me oh? And please be a good boy to her."

"Yes, Ma," Obiefuna said again. He handed the phone back to his aunt, and, as he walked back to his room, he remained light-headed. He had been so certain that she was calling to tell him that she knew, having easily put the pieces together, finally seeing what had been in front of her all along. Or perhaps his father had simply told her, realizing, suddenly, that he and Obiefuna had agreed no pact for secrecy, especially where his own mother was concerned. He wondered about Aboy. Last Christmas, Aboy's first and only with them, their father had come home with a chicken on Christmas Eve and saddled Aboy with the responsibility for killing it. Obiefuna watched with Ekene, excited, as Aboy dug a hole in the earth, holding down the squawking chicken with one hand and running the knife across the chicken's neck with the other, taking it out in one slice. For days afterwards, Ekene would re-enact the chicken's struggle, much to Obiefuna's amusement, but Aboy never laughed.

"It didn't even do it like that," he snapped one time at Ekene, startling everyone, and putting a permanent end to Ekene's show.

With the onset of the external exams in May, Obiefuna saw less of Senior Papilo. Since the SS3 students no longer had regular classes, only dressing up on the days when they had exams,

Obiefuna had less laundry to wash. And on the days when he did have papers, Senior Papilo was finished so early that he'd already had his clothes delivered by someone else before Obiefuna could reach the house. He sensed a new remoteness about Senior Papilo, attributable to his tension from the exams. Still, Obiefuna missed him. He would, in the middle of a lesson, or a random discussion with the boys in his house, peek out of the window to see Senior Papilo strolling in the distance with a group of his friends, and feel a crushed longing at those easy strides, that slight slouch that raised his right shoulder, how effortlessly he stood out. And so, when, on a Thursday afternoon after class, he received a summons from Senior Papilo, he was almost dizzy with an unfathomable gratitude. Senior Papilo was squatting next to his cupboard, pouring cornflakes into a bowl, when Obiefuna arrived. He reached into the cupboard for a spare spoon and handed it to Obiefuna.

"How did it go?" Obiefuna asked.

Senior Papilo shrugged. "Physics." His forlorn expression communicated the rest.

Obiefuna watched him scoop spoonfuls of milk into the bowl. He tossed a few cubes of sugar next, stirred evenly. His low-cut hair had wavy curls that ran diagonally across his head and shone from his meticulous application of hair oil.

"Are you going into town today?" Obiefuna blurted out.

Senior Papilo gave him a sideways glance from his squatting position. Slowly, his contemplative expression dissolved into a smile. "Why? You want to come with me?" he asked, returning the packet of cornflakes to his cupboard.

It would mean scaling the school walls. They could be suspended if found out, and if the reason for the scaling were to be uncovered—and he had a feeling it wasn't a good reason—they could be expelled. But Obiefuna thought of the few weeks left until the end of the session, after which he might never see Senior Papilo again, and so he said, "Yes."

Senior Papilo paused for a few seconds and then he proceeded to fix the lock on the cupboard. Finally, he turned fully to watch Obiefuna. Obiefuna could not read the expression on his face, and he wondered if Senior Papilo would burst into laughter or reach for a belt. Obiefuna felt time slip past him.

"Meet me at the school farm at eight o'clock," Senior Papilo said, finally. "Not a minute late."

At prep, Obiefuna flipped idly through his book, not attempting to grasp a word. He was about to do an incredibly stupid thing for which he could be expelled. He toyed with the prospect of not showing up, whipping up the excuse of a sudden stomachache, an assignment, preparation for a test, all of which he knew Senior Papilo would easily see through. At 7:45 he exited his class and made for the school farm. The gate was unlocked and squealed when he let himself in. He immediately made out Senior Papilo's silhouette among the slender coconut trees. Senior Papilo looked at his watch and gave an approving nod. He handed Obiefuna a shirt and a pair of jeans. "Chijioke will join us in a minute," he said.

Obiefuna tried not to flinch. Why was the agric prefect joining them? His first thought was a cult initiation, and he felt a queasy sensation in his stomach, his mother's parting warnings, the night before his departure for school, replaying too loudly in his head. He had heard stories of how new initiates were whipped continuously with machetes until those who were unable to withstand the training died. He searched Senior Papilo's face in the dark for a sign, but he could make out nothing from the senior's placid expression while he waited for Obiefuna to get dressed. Obiefuna was in the middle of buttoning up his shirt when they heard footsteps approaching. Senior Chijioke came into view. His confused glance moved from Obiefuna to Senior Papilo.

"He's coming with us," Senior Papilo explained.

"Are you crazy?" Senior Chijioke queried.

"Relax." Senior Papilo looked Obiefuna over and seemed satisfied with his brief assessment. "He can handle it."

"They'll never let him in," Senior Chijioke pressed.

"Of course they will. For the right price."

Senior Chijioke seemed unconvinced still, but he shrugged and led the way further into the farm. Obiefuna followed behind, feeling that queasiness again. Perhaps he should change his mind and turn back. Senior Papilo would be furious with him, but he could handle a few punishments. When they got to the wall, Obiefuna looked up at the sharp bottles jutting atop it. How did they intend to scale it? Without speaking, Senior Papilo and Senior Chijioke set to work clearing away a patch of grass at the base of the wall. Afterwards, Senior Chijioke extracted two blocks from the base, revealing a small hole large enough to crawl through. Senior Chijioke went first, fitting his legs through, and then the rest of his body. Senior Papilo nudged Obiefuna forward, opting to go last. As he fitted himself through the hole, Obiefuna imagined for a panicked second that he would get stuck, unable to move in or out. Outside, the path was deserted and stretched all the way to the main road, where they boarded a taxi.

They were quiet throughout the drive. Even Senior Chijioke was no longer his cantankerous self, and he stared out of the window in pensive silence. Senior Papilo was in front, next to the driver, tapping on his knees as he did when he was deep in thought, not turning once to meet Obiefuna's eyes. Finally, he mumbled something to the driver, who turned to him with a sceptical glance before he looked back at the road. Obiefuna could make out the slight lift of the driver's chin in a small smile. Obiefuna swallowed, feeling the swift rush of wind past his ears. The driver finally turned into a narrow path. Obiefuna peered out of the car at the fading lamps that lined the street, faintly illuminating the faces of the women who stood about on either side of the lane, inched forward as though waiting to hail a taxi. Obiefuna took in their low-cut dresses showing too much cleavage, their postures demanding attention, their faces shaded behind sunglasses. The driver stopped in front of a gate, still smiling his sickly smile. When they alighted, Senior Papilo led the way to a gate painted a green colour. A massive man in a shiny jacket blocked the entrance, and regarded Obiefuna with a vicious glare. Senior Papilo crossed a hand over Obiefuna's shoulder and extended a single naira note folded in his palm to the man. The man received it after a grudging pause and held the gate open, wagging a warning finger in Senior Papilo's face. Inside the vast yard, a row of paved bungalows lined both sides, and several women were strutting about. With a parting nod at Senior Papilo, Senior Chijioke left the group and walked towards a dimly lit corner of the compound. Senior Papilo guided Obiefuna towards one of the girls sitting on the pavement on the right row. She was holding a pocket-sized mirror to her face as she applied make-up by torchlight.

"Where Angel dey?" Senior Papilo asked.

The woman looked away from the mirror and fixed frosty eyes on them, her eyeliner suspended in mid-air. "I look like Angel keeper?"

"Sorry," Senior Papilo said, not looking sorry at all. "But you know where she dey?"

The woman snapped the mirror shut and put it in her handbag. "Angel dey busy with customer now. But I fit be your angel this night." Her expression had turned sly.

Senior Papilo snorted. He had the slightly agitated look he put on when his patience was being tested. "Which room?"

The woman stared at him wide-eyed. "You wan go meet them there?" she asked.

Senior Papilo glowered at the woman without offering a response. At first, she stared back in defiance, but she faltered eventually, as Obiefuna knew she would, and pointed to a door on the opposite row. As they walked away, Obiefuna turned to see her watching them. Senior Papilo knocked on the door the woman had indicated. Obiefuna shifted, slid his hands into the pocket of the oversized jeans to try to keep them from shaking. Did Senior Papilo really intend to interrupt them having sex simply because he wanted to see Angel? The door opened after a few minutes, and Obiefuna barely restrained a gasp as a large, thick-set woman appeared in the doorway. From her name, he had expected a younger, prettier woman.

"Angi baby," Senior Papilo called out.

The woman sighed almost wearily. "Papilo. How naw?"

"No shaking." He looked past her into the room. "I hear say you dey busy."

Angel frowned. "Busy? Who tell you dat one?"

Senior Papilo tilted his head back towards the other woman. Obiefuna turned just in time to see her avert her eyes.

Angel snorted. "Yeye girl." She looked at Senior Papilo. "I no dey work today o. Na off-day."

"Ah," Senior Papilo said, scratching his head, "why today na? I bring my boy come make him collect one round."

Obiefuna froze. Angel looked down at him, registering his presence for the first time. At first her face was blank, and then she burst into laughter. Obiefuna glanced from her to Senior Papilo.

"Na joke be dis?" Angel asked when she straightened up.

"Ah, Angi, no look am like small pikin oh. Na old man be dis. And dis thing no small." He reached down with a swift movement to cup Obiefuna's bulge in his palm, causing Obiefuna to suck in a quick breath.

Angel watched the spectacle with amusement. "Anyway, as I talk before, I no dey work today."

Senior Papilo reached for his wallet. "I go pay double."

Angel sighed in feigned exasperation. She looked at Obiefuna again, laughter lurking in her eyes, but he knew then she would give in.

"Okay," she said finally. "Just because say na fine boy sha." She winked at Obiefuna and eased inside away from the door. Obiefuna looked at Senior Papilo. He stared back at Obiefuna with eyebrows raised and motioned for him to go in. Obiefuna took a deep breath and stepped inside. The room was small and square with a lingering smell of damp. It was bare, save for a mattress made up as a bed next to the wall, a tiny plastic table and a built-in wardrobe that held only empty hangers. The walls were almost completely covered with posters of American superstars. There were no chairs where he could sit, and so he stood in the middle of the room and tried not to listen to Angel's conversation with Senior Papilo. He saw her retrieve the money from his hands and shut the door behind her. Quiescently, she reached behind her back to undo the zipper of her dress, slid it off and piled it in a disorderly heap on the table. She took off her underwear, not glancing at him once, not showing surprise at the fact that he was yet to undress. When she was completely naked, she slid into the bed and propped a pillow under her head. Obiefuna stood where he was, staring at her.

"What is it?" she asked, finally looking at him.

Obiefuna sucked his tongue to unfreeze it. He wondered if Senior Papilo had left him and gone back to school. He wanted to turn towards the door and let himself out of the room, but his legs had turned to jelly. Angel got on her knees and crawled to the edge of the mattress. She reached out a hand to him and pulled him to her, until he towered over her, glancing down at her.

"Na your first time?" she asked in a low voice.

Obiefuna nodded.

Angel studied his face closely. "How old are you again?"

Obiefuna swallowed. Something in her eyes told him it would be useless lying to her. "Sixteen," he said. "Almost seventeen," he added, unnecessarily.

He felt her grip on his arm slacken. He wondered if she was going to push him away. That would mean returning the money Senior Papilo had given her. Perhaps she was aware that someone else would gladly take him for the normal rate. There was a moment when he felt her teetering, weighing up her personal ethics. Finally, sighing, she reached upwards to unbutton his shirt. She worked feverishly, her breathing coming in rasps. As she undid the hook of his belt, he kept his eyes focused on the picture of Rihanna on the wallpaper behind her, feeling a small discomfort at the way the eyes stared right back at him. Angel pulled down his jeans and he stepped out of them, still looking at the poster. She took his penis in her hand.

"This one no be sixteen o," she said with a whistle, and he blushed. She fiddled with his penis for a short while, trying to decide what to do with it. When she took him in her mouth, Obiefuna let out a gasp. He could tell that this was not standard protocol, and he wondered whether to be flattered that she had chosen to make an exception for him. He felt himself grow in her mouth, hardening to stiffness. His toes had begun to curl on their own, and his knees felt as though they would buckle at any point. He wondered if part of the arrangement at the door was for Angel to rate his performance to Senior Papilo at the end of it, if Senior Papilo would begin to look at him differently if he passed. Angel pulled away from him and retreated further into the bed, spreading her legs. Obiefuna crawled in beside her, overwhelmed, at that point, by the urge to throw up. He sat up naked beside her and looked around the bed.

Angel said, "What is it?"

"I need a condom," he muttered.

She looked taken aback for a minute and then she laughed. "Small boy like you, which disease you wan carry?" She reached sideways for him and pulled him to her, guiding him between her legs. Inside her, he was enveloped with a warmth that threatened to knock him unconscious. He tried not to look at her face as he felt the tremor in his veins. She was adjusting to accommodate him when he felt a swift rush of ecstasy to the tip of himself. He gave way before he could stop himself and collapsed on top of her, panting, loathing his release. He heaved himself off her after a minute and reclined on the wall next to her. She sat up in bed, flustered, trying to comprehend what had just happened. And then she stood up and walked around the bed to retrieve her underwear from the table. Because she was quiet, he said, "Sorry."

She shrugged in the middle of getting into her underwear and said, without looking at him, "First time. Na so e dey be."

A FEW DAYS LATER, Obiefuna woke up with a fever. It escalated quickly, stiffening his joints, so that the nurse at the school clinic confined him to a bed, under her close observation. His throat felt sore and parched, his appetite had gone, and he was unable to eat the food Jekwu delivered from the refectory, managing only a few spoons when Senior Papilo arrived and fed him by hand. He drifted in and out of a fitful doze, only vaguely aware of Senior Papilo's presence next to him on a chair, the senior reaching out from time to time to feel his temperature with the back of his palm. There were times when he suffered mild hallucinations, when Angel's face, scrunched up with scorn, floated across his vision, at once taunting and terrifying. Obiefuna still remembered the moment after the incident when he had sat next to her on the bed, fully dressed, waiting; within him, something shrank even further in time to the clock's loud ticking, until Senior Papilo's knock on the door informed him that they were ready to leave. Senior Papilo had briefly searched his face without speaking, and, as they walked out, Obiefuna saw him wink at the woman who had lied to them about Angel earlier. They had arrived at the house just before lights out, and when Wisdom asked him where he had been, he muttered something about running errands for Senior Papilo.

"Jekwu said you left class before prep was over," Wisdom said. "We went to Senior Papilo's house to look for you and neither of you was there."

"Did I say I was running the errand in his house?" Obiefuna retorted, lacing his voice with an edge sharp enough to discourage further interrogation. He craved a bath, but he knew it was too late, and the senior students would be on the prowl soon to whip the students still up after lights out. When the bell went off a few minutes later, he climbed into his bed, uncomfortably aware of Angel's scent on his skin and the stickiness in his underwear. And he lay awake for a long time looking up at the whitewashed ceiling.

Now, he sat by the window in Senior Papilo's corner, watching as a group of junior boys trooped to the refectory for dinner. It was the third day into his illness—the worst phase of it had abated, but his tongue still had that lingering clammy taste, and a persistent ache raged in his head. Across from him, Senior

Papilo idly listened in to a conversation in his corner. More than once, he made out Senior Papilo's eyes on him. He could tell from the conversation that Senior Papilo would be scaling the wall again today to go into town. To see Angel? Would they discuss him? It occurred to him then, with a sigh, that he was still here, in Senior Papilo's corner, after everything. He caught his faint reflection in the mirror, smiling a small, wan smile. He had begun, lately, to look at Senior Papilo, at their friendship, in a different way. Was this something Senior Papilo did with all his boys? An initiation of sorts? Something told him it was not the case. He had been specifically singled out, and he could not make out why. So far, he had been deprived of a private moment with Senior Papilo, although he wasn't confident about what he would say if he had the chance. And, after today, he might never get that chance. Senior Papilo had finished his final exam the previous day. Obiefuna had watched from the railings, along with his classmates, as the senior boys spilled around the field, running through the dormitories in jubilation. Soon, they began a game of hoisting one another up and throwing each other into a small algae-infested pool close to the school farm. Senior Papilo was one of the last people to be grabbed—it took an army to subdue him—and hauled over, and he emerged from the pool wet and slimy, laughing. How did he do it? How was he able to radiate such light-heartedness when Obiefuna felt this undoing in him? As if the world were shifting from beneath him.

Afterwards, as he sorted through Senior Papilo's things for what he could keep, he tried not to drop to the ground. The other boys openly schemed for the valuables—the large, sturdy cupboard, the soft, wide bed, the sleek brown sandals and white canvas, the buckets. Obiefuna sat on the bed, holding on to the charcoal iron and uniforms he had naturally inherited, aware that Senior Papilo was watching him all the while. Later, with the boys long gone, Senior Papilo reached out to touch his knee and told him it would be all right, and he felt the urge right then to cry because it would not be all right at all.

Obiefuna felt Senior Papilo's hand on his shoulder and looked up.

"There's someone I want you to see," Senior Papilo said.

Obiefuna glanced through the rows of bunkbeds at the door. "Who?"

"Not here," Senior Papilo said. "We'll head for the school farm in a few minutes."

They followed the route that led to the brothel, but, midway, Senior Papilo asked the driver to pull over and they went into a supermarket. Obiefuna followed Senior Papilo, watching in astonishment as he took a few toiletries, including sanitary pads, over to the till. He followed as Senior Papilo crossed to the other side of the road and boarded another taxi, which drove in the direction from which they had come. Opposite the school, they alighted. Senior Papilo led the way down a short, narrow path. Obiefuna looked up to see the sign for the girls' campus. A lump formed in his throat. Was Senior Papilo trying to get them caught? He almost opened his mouth to call out, but Senior Papilo was already rapping on the door in front of them. The viewer slid open, and a pair of eyes peered at them. The man's expression became instantly guarded.

"Yes?" he demanded. It was apparent strange young men were unwelcome around here.

"Good evening, sir," Senior Papilo said. Obiefuna almost smiled at the acquired tone. "Please, I'm here to drop off some things to my sister."

The man frowned. "It's not Visiting Day."

"I know, sir, but she called us to say that her provisions had run out, and our parents asked me to stop by since I'm just around the corner."

"Who are you?" the man demanded.

"I'm a student at the university in town, sir."

"And who is this?" The man's eyes darted to Obiefuna.

"This is my cousin, sir. His name is Francis."

Now the man frowned at Obiefuna, as if daring him to deny the name. He opened the door slightly and extended his hand to take the bag.

Senior Papilo retreated. "Please, sir, I need to give her this myself. I also need to deliver a message to her from our parents."

The man glared at him. "Young man, do you know the kind of trouble I could get into for letting you in when it's not Visiting Day?"

Senior Papilo reached into his wallet for a naira note. "I'll be quiet and fast, sir," he said, extending an enclosed hand towards the man, "and you can have this one for beer."

The man sighed, hesitating only briefly before taking the note from Senior Papilo and stepping aside to let them in. Obiefuna was instantly taken by the beauty of the campus. It was far smaller than the boys' but with a graceful orderliness from what he could see: buildings designed with identical storeys and painted the same grey colour as the sky, flat-bed flowers hemming the driveway and classrooms, stuffing the air with a heady, sweet scent. The man motioned them into the gatehouse.

"What did you say her name was?" he asked once they were inside.

"Munachiso Amaeze. SS3C," Senior Papilo said.

"And what's yours?"

Senior Papilo exhaled. "Obiefuna Amaeze, sir."

Obiefuna shot a glance at him. Senior Papilo looked straight ahead, his face carefully blank, until the man was out of the door, and then he let out a short laugh. He reached sideways to adjust Obiefuna's collar, which didn't seem to need adjusting. "Get ready for when she comes," he said.

"Why?"

"She's coming with her School Daughter, whom I want you to meet."

So that was why Senior Papilo had him tag along. Obiefuna stared at some graffiti on the wall, no doubt the nickname of a girl who did not want anyone to forget she was once here. The man returned moments later with a fat, chocolate-skinned girl, followed by a smaller one.

"Papilo," she said, unsuccessfully masking her smile.

The man shot an icy glance at Senior Papilo.

"It's just something she calls me, sir," he explained quickly. "My real name is Obiefuna."

The man turned back to his logbook. As they talked about their make-believe parents, supplying codes at intervals, Obiefuna studied the small girl across from him. She was lithe, with an oval face that could pass for pretty, and a styled parting on one side of her head. She sat with her knees pressed close together, her gaze focused on her palms, which were intertwined on her lap, aware, Obiefuna could tell, that he was looking at her. He wondered how long it had taken Senior Papilo to orchestrate the meeting, what he hoped would come out of it. There was a knock on the outer door and the man gave Senior Papilo a warning glance before he exited the room. Senior Papilo hurriedly took Munachiso in his arms.

"I've missed you," he said into her neck, fondling her behind while she squirmed in his arms like an earthworm that had chanced on salt, suppressing giggles.

"I waited for you on my birthday and you didn't turn up," she said when they disengaged.

"Sorry, baby. You know how these things go." He picked up the bag from the seat. "But I didn't forget my gift."

She took the bag from him, her eyes shining. "Thank you." She kissed him on the cheek. They talked some more before Senior Papilo gestured to the girl behind her. "So this is the girl?"

"Yes," Munachiso said, turning. "This is Rachel."

Senior Papilo made appreciative sounds, nodding slowly. Obiefuna tried not to yelp as Senior Papilo turned to him with a jab on the shoulder, "And here's my boy. His name is Obiefuna."

Rachel looked up just then. Obiefuna was disconcerted by her gaze; it seemed to trace the width of his face without settling. He could see her teeth from where she bit down gently on her lip. In the silence, Obiefuna was suddenly aware that all eyes in the room were on him, waiting for him. He felt like an actor who had suddenly forgotten his lines.

"Obiefuna?" Senior Papilo prompted.

Obiefuna looked at him.

"Don't keep a girl waiting," Senior Papilo said with an awkward laugh. "This is the part where you ask her to be your girl."

NINE

Something about the face feels familiar to Uzoamaka. It is perhaps the state of the head—oblong shaped and closely shaved, now twisted to an unnatural angle so that it faces upwards, even though the body is essentially lying on its stomach, casually splayed on the pavement. His hands have been folded behind him as though in cuffs: a captive even in death. His open mouth emits a whitish tongue. All around him, flies are having a feast. But it is the eyes that Uzoamaka is unable to handle: open, staring up at the sky as if in supplication. None of the people who have formed a mini-circle around the corpse to snap their fingers and speculate on his identity and cause of death step forward to close those eyes. It is a bad omen in Uzoamaka's hometown, to die with one's eyes open like that. The spirit will never rest. And when you think of the boy, who cannot be more than sixteen, essentially a child who ought to be bringing succour to his mother or irritating her to no end, not splayed on the floor like a ragdoll beneath a blistering sun, with eyes open like that. Uzoamaka is deeply unsettled by those eyes.

And so Uzoamaka is not entirely surprised or alarmed when she sees the boy flashing before her vision throughout the day. It is those eyes that crystallize in her mind, seeming to tell her something she cannot comprehend. The next time she sees the body again, it is in a slightly adjusted position, the head now positioned naturally. But, most importantly, the eyes are closed. Because of the gentleness now on the face with the eyes closed, making it almost ethereal, Uzoamaka cannot help but stare. She is aware that she cuts a curious spectacle standing there alone in the hot sun to mope around the body and yet she is unable to look away. She is unable, too, to stop herself from inching close to the body, her steps deliberate and calculated, unable to stop the lurch in her heart. The face is slightly shaded from her view, and she has to turn the head all the way to an unnatural angle again to fully look at the face. The sun is at its highest point in the sky, and her skin is clinging to her blouse from the sweat. She is aware that all eyes are trained on her. Decisively, she flips the body over with considerable effort—how is he so heavy?—and lifts the shirt up, her eyes trailing over the body, willing it to become clearer and at the same time remain obscure. Her hand feels the warmth of the bloated stomach before she sees the birthmark, just as she remembers it: a splotchy dark mark just above the pelvis. It is perhaps the only thing that has not changed, a defining feature that somehow remains unaltered. He looks so peaceful, almost happy in death, she thinks, right before she clubs at him and screams. Through blurred vision, she sees people running towards her. They are tugging at her shoulders, trying to pull her away from him, but she is unable to tear her eyes away from that face, her hands from that body, unable to stop herself from saying his name, "Ekene! Ekene! Ekene!" like a war chant. In the throng of the voices, she finally registers one that is familiar, and she turns to look up at Anozie. He is suddenly the only one present in a room that is dimly lit and deathly quiet, and he is glaring at her in confusion.

"What is wrong with you?" he thunders in angry Igbo. "You almost rose the whole street."

Uzoamaka does not understand what he is talking about. She looks around her for Ekene, but she is surrounded by bed sheets and so she leaps from the bed and hurries to the boys' room. She rushes up to Ekene's bed and shakes him vigorously until he stirs and sits up in alarm. Behind her, Anozie's voice booms in her ears. There is so much going on that the only thing that feels sensible to do is to burst into tears, holding on to Ekene until dawn filters in through the window.

Now Uzoamaka sighed. Below her, the woman whose hair she was braiding shot her an offended glance.

"Sorry," Uzoamaka said with a thin smile, repositioning the head. Her apprentices, two young girls taking advantage of the university strike to acquire a skill, exchanged puzzled looks, no doubt confused as to why she, of all the people in the salon, seemed most affected by the news of the shooting.

"Splayed on the pavement just like that," the woman began again, snapping her fingers as if to reject the fate. It was she who had delivered the news of the shooting, having been—she claimed—at the location herself. She had about her none of the horror Uzoamaka expected, only the vaguely exulted bearing of one wielding most sought-after information.

"Na wa," another woman said. She had her hair stuck in the

hairdryer and spoke with her head unmoving, almost comical. "First we couldn't sleep for the cultists. Now we can't sleep for the military."

"But they said he was a suspect," one of the women said.

"Which suspect?" the newsreader fired back. "He was only trying to answer a call."

"But we don't know who exactly was calling . . ."

Uzoamaka stifled another sigh. As much as she found herself drawn to the conversation, she inwardly wished the women would stop talking. How easily her day had gone from wonderful to horrendous. It was the anniversary of Obiefuna's birth. He had turned seventeen that morning, and she had surprised him by calling to sing to him, just as she always did when he was home, carrying with her the delightful surprise in his voice all the way to the salon, only to be greeted by her apprentices with the news of the shooting. Now this loud-mouthed woman would not stop with the details. It had occurred at Ikeokwu Junction, just walking distance from her shop. The cult clashes had reached their peak, random bodies piling up by the roadside, unclaimed. There were rumours swirling round that the cult groups were the products of seeds sown by politicians, and even the governor's name was mentioned once or twice. It was believed that the governor's own party had backed a section of the cult group the year before to rig the elections in his favour. On emerging the winner, he reneged on his promise to properly establish them, and so they took to the streets, causing unspeakable havoc, with the same weapons the government had purchased for them. Uzoamaka thought the story too conspiratorial to be accurate, but the brazenness of the cult groups made her wonder. She joined a peace demonstration by women in the neighbourhood, marching through the market and all the way to government quarters, where they set up camp, singing and demanding action, until police vans arrived and released teargas to disperse the crowd.

The governor's response, after weeks of protest, was to declare a state of emergency, officially handing over the state's security to the military. The men swooped in without warning, wielding guns almost half their size, wearing menacingly starched camouflage and driving around town in shiny new vans with the warning inscription OPERATION HESITATE AND DIE. It was said that they walked around with their lips padlocked—Uzoamaka had yet to see that, but nothing was impossible with these people—and hands positioned at the trigger, ready to fire at a moment's notice. They announced new security protocols over the radio, declared nightly curfews, carried out random stop–search exercises and set up checkpoints at major junctions, where passers-by were required to walk with both hands raised, as if in surrender, not letting them down for any reason. Uzoamaka had heard stories of how an elderly man had wet himself because he was pressed and had been too scared to put his hands down. Week after week, the governor gave satisfied broadcasts over the radio extolling his own "ingenuity" in bringing about order, blithely unaware, or choosing to overlook, the eternal state of terror among his citizens. The most recent victim, Uzoamaka gathered from the conversation, was only a boy. His attention had slipped at the checkpoint when his phone rang, and he reached into his pocket for it. Perhaps it was a girlfriend calling, or his wife, or his mother. Perhaps it was the excitement that made him forget, in that instant, where he was, sensing too late, just when the bullets were pelting his skin, the ensuing chaos propelling him, exiting the world before he even touched the floor. Uzoamaka wondered if he had already taken the call before he was shot, what the person on the other end had made of the staccato shots, sounding like fireworks in July, the whirr of screams, the buzzing of the phone line, the permanent silence that settled in.

"But we can't really blame the army sha," the newsreader conceded. She would not stop. "Those Deebam boys were a real terror."

Everyone made variant sounds of agreement. Uzoamaka held the now finished hair together and reached for a candle to burn the tips. She would never understand how young boys woke up in the morning and decided, of all things, to become cultists, taking pleasure in hacking rival members to death in broad daylight, from the sight of young bodies bloating in the sun. Until now, they had been everywhere, not even bothering to hide their identity, moving past her shop with the same lopsided walk that was their trademark: dragging a foot as if it were only loosely attached to their hip, one shoulder comically raised while the other inched to the side, almost like a deformity. They were even adorned in the same colours—bright red or yellow or black handkerchiefs tied to their wrist or around their necks or peeping from their back pockets. Once at the market, the woman who sold second-hand clothes had dissuaded her from buying a pair of red shorts she fancied for Ekene, because red, according to the woman, was one of their colours, and Ekene might attract their attention if he were to "fly their colour." The woman told her about her neighbour's son, who had gone out wearing a pair of yellow shoes: for most of the night, his family had stones rained down on their roof, which only stopped when the boy went out to meet them. He returned two days later with machete-inflicted wounds on his back as proof of initiation, and now he stole money from street shops and openly fought his father. Uzoamaka wondered about Ekene. He was just sixteen, and she already found herself having to push back against early signs of rebellion, hating the note in her voice when she had to scream at him for keeping a late night, her absolute shock when she walked in on him one time smoking a cigarette in his room. It might have helped if Obiefuna was around—he had always exerted a quietening influence on Ekene, supervising Ekene's activities out of Uzoamaka's sight. But he all but belonged to Anozie's sister now, and Ekene had too much private time to himself, spent hours playing football in the field, kept company with people she knew next to nothing about. Once, she saw him from the balcony shaking a neighbour's son and ending with a sign she did not understand. He was only a child, and the implications of what he was doing eluded him; yet she waited until he had turned in for the night and then approached him with a cane. She flogged him repeatedly until they were both crying, she thinking all the while of that body splayed on the pavement, those vacant eyes boring into hers. Thinking, too, about how that death might have been averted if only the boy's mother had flogged him a little longer, a little harder.

TEN

The conventional wisdom was that there was no better time to be careful than in SS2. As Obiefuna wheeled his box through the second gates after the search, breathing in the warm air of the campus again after the session break, he felt a mix of elation and terror. It was Jekwu, later that night, who explained the code. The first months of SS2 were regarded as the most precarious for the students, only a term away from their being passed the mantle of school leadership, the prefectships. They would have to get through the final lap of torture from the SS3 students as well as from the outgoing prefects before they handed over. Even worse, the school had decided, for some odd reason, to have the two most senior houses right next to each other, so that Obiefuna could not successfully get through a day without a run-in with a bored SS3 student looking to punish him just for the fun of it. The strategy, Jekwu advised, was to avoid trouble if he could, endure it if he couldn't, and take consolation in the countdown of months until they became prefects themselves, when the school, and the world, really, would be at their feet.

It seemed to Obiefuna that with each new year harmattan announced itself earlier. And every time, it seemed to sneak up on him, the wind colder and more vicious. The school had gone to bed one night in November, as it had every other night, and by the next morning the campus was enveloped in a fog so thick Obiefuna could hardly make out figures within a few feet of him. At prayers, several boys turned up with their bed sheets wrapped around their shoulders, but the prefects were too cold themselves to bother punishing them. Obiefuna dreaded touching water to his lips as he brushed his teeth and dreaded even more having a bath. A crowd of boys swarmed the kitchen with buckets and tales of various allergies, only to be turned away by the kitchen staff. Wisdom suggested that they should jog around the field to stimulate inner heat, but Obiefuna gave up after the first lap, worse off than before, his ribs hurting. At the tap, he stood shivering as he watched his bucket fill with water, willing it in his mind to become warm. The bathroom complex near his house lacked its usual rowdiness. Many of the boys had gone back to bed after prayers, opting to skip morning baths. Some of them would ultimately go for "rub and shine." The thought of "rub and shine"—in which hand-and-leg washing, with cream and cologne application, was substituted for a proper bath—had always disgusted Obiefuna. But standing there at the tap with the cold snaking itself around his shoulders, Obiefuna seriously considered the prospect, if only for this one time.

"Very cold, abi?" someone said from behind.

Obiefuna turned to see Senior Kachi, the school's senior prefect. He had a towel wrapped around his waist and a sponge in his hand. Behind him, a boy from Obiefuna's class held Senior Kachi's bucket of water. Obiefuna ached at the steam rising from it.

"Do you need hot water?" Senior Kachi asked.

Obiefuna stared at him in shocked silence for a while before he nodded.

"Follow me," Senior Kachi said, turning towards the prefect quarters. Obiefuna followed behind, conscious of the envious glances the other boys shot him. Senior Kachi's room was a square, airy space, with three wooden-framed beds where the two deputy senior prefects and the chapel prefect slept. There was a smaller, built-in room in the corner, with a bed, which was Senior Kachi's. On the wall next to the bunk was a socket. A ring boiler was connected to the socket and half sunk into a small bucket of water. Senior Kachi switched the socket off and motioned for Obiefuna to take the water.

Obiefuna emptied the water into his bucket, relishing the heat that serenaded his face. "Thank you, senior," he said.

Senior Kachi did not respond. He had his back turned to Obiefuna, silently observing the fog through the window. But as Obiefuna made his way out, he turned at the main door to see Senior Kachi standing by the entrance to his room, looking at him.

Obiefuna came into wakefulness slowly. His eyes searched in the dark, until they made out the silhouette of the face which was peering down at him. The breath smelled faintly of cigarettes.

"Stand," Senior Kachi said, in a quiet command.

Obiefuna propped himself up on his elbows. Senior Kachi stepped aside to give him room, his hands sunk in the side pockets of his baggy shorts. Obiefuna retrieved his footwear from under his bed. When he made to grab a shirt, Senior Kachi stopped him. "Just come with me."

He filed in behind Senior Kachi as they made for the door. A cold blast of air hit his face as he stepped into the corridor. All through the short walk down the hallway, Senior Kachi did not glance at him even once. They were near the base of the staircase, the darkest corner, when Senior Kachi stopped and turned to him. "Obi," he said, simply.

Obiefuna looked at him. Even in the dark, he could tell that Senior Kachi's eyes were averted, his hand on his mouth. And because he would not act, Obiefuna did. He inched his face forward, flushed, Senior Kachi's breath too loud in his ears. He did not make sense of the hands placed on his chest in resistance until his lips tasted air. His heart stomped in his chest as he waited for the next step. Senior Kachi's hands travelled across his head and tucked behind his ears, as though to pull him close, but the senior prefect guided him downwards. Senior Kachi wore no briefs under his shorts. He smelled of lavender soap. Obiefuna took him in his mouth, with the firm grip on his head relaxing as he moved his tongue, occasionally coming up for air. He held on even as a rush of saltiness filled his mouth, a strange, nauseating taste. Senior Kachi pulled him up and tapped his head fondly, as one would a puppy, and told him to go back to bed.

He did not know how long he slept, but he woke up the next morning with a new lightness of being. Here was his first real thing. During functions, as he was assigned tasks, he was constantly on the lookout for Senior Kachi, but Senior Kachi, who was dividing the SS1 boys into groups, did not meet his eyes. It was later, as he worked with the other boys harvesting cassava at the school farm, that he realized he was being avoided. What had been magical for him, what had been of auspicious significance, was for Senior Kachi a minor, necessary release. Obiefuna had been merely an available tool. He thought of it that night as he lay in bed, struggling to sleep. Just before midnight he felt a presence next to him and turned to see Senior Kachi. Again, Obiefuna rose without a word, falling in line behind Senior Kachi, halting at the dark staircase and pliantly descending to his knees. This scenario was repeated day after day, and yet nothing changed in Senior Kachi's public demeanour with him. Obiefuna was instinctively wounded. He understood the need to hide, especially when you were Senior Kachi—senior prefect, pride of the school, a shining star, with a reputation to maintain—and yet he couldn't help the resentful hurt he felt. And day after day he thought about putting an end to it, his resolve dissipating as soon as Senior Kachi showed up at his bedside and led him away. As it turned out, the decision was made for him without his having to try.

One Sunday, Obiefuna was nestled in bed with Senior Kachi, both avoiding chapel. He heard the call for the benediction from where he lay, and watched from the window as the boys poured out in their white outfits.

Senior Kachi was watching, too. "Take a look at this," he said after a while.

Obiefuna leaned forward to get a good view. Boys were strolling in every direction, but somehow he knew who Senior Kachi was talking about. Something about that distinctive carefree sway of his hips, the flutter of his wrist, made Obiefuna chuckle. "Festus?" he said.

Senior Kachi sighed. "Is that his name?"

Obiefuna nodded.

"That boy disgusts me," he said.

Obiefuna hummed and said nothing.

"I see no reason why a boy would choose to behave like a girl."

Obiefuna remained quiet.

Senior Kachi turned to him. "You never tell me about your girlfriend, Obi."

Obiefuna shook his head. "I don't have one."

Senior Kachi looked surprised. "Why not? You need to get a girl, Obi."

"Why?" Obiefuna asked. He did not need to ask, but he did.

"Because you need one," Senior Kachi said. He leaned away from the window and stretched out on his bed. "Don't get this thing into your head. It's just a game. Every boy should have a girlfriend."

Obiefuna stared at him. Senior Kachi leaned back on the bed and lay with his buttons undone, exposing his bare chest to Obiefuna. Obiefuna rose to his feet. He had a feeling in his stomach that he recognized as the early onset of nausea, and he found himself suddenly overwhelmed by the foul taste of Senior Kachi on those nights when Obiefuna had gone on to his knees, his head held securely in Senior Kachi's hands. One time, he had been daring enough to ask Senior Kachi if he liked the feeling and Senior Kachi said no. "I only let you do it because you want to, but I don't like it. I am not like you."

Obiefuna walked out of the room, to his house. In front of his room, a quarrel had broken out between Festus and another boy; Festus had his hand wrapped around the boy's collar, thrusting his slightly bent head in the boy's face as he dared the boy to repeat the bad word he had called him. Obiefuna stood awhile watching them. He had always had a vague fascination, devoid of attraction, for Festus. His flamboyance was laced with confidence. He responded to mock-catcalls with an exaggerated batting of the eyelids, and the occasional taunts of "homo" were met with a swift "Your dad taught me." He was once whipped for painting his nails with ink. Everyone used Vaseline to protect their lips from the harmattan, but Festus's application was shiny enough to draw stares. He laced conversations with words of endearment. Once, he asked Obiefuna to pass him "a notebook, darling" and Obiefuna snapped, "I'm not your darling." In the silence that followed, with heads turning from every direction to stare, Festus looked him in the eye with a calmness that chilled Obiefuna. He could tell that Festus saw through him, and he panicked for a second that Festus would say something. Obiefuna remembered how, once, Festus had been walking down the house corridor and a group of boys had begun taunting him as usual. In a move that seemed at once spontaneous and premeditated, Festus turned to one of the boys and said, "Even you, Oscar? After last night?" and before Oscar could launch into a swift denial, Obiefuna saw a momentary look of panic flash across his face. Although the other boys tacitly laughed off the situation, Obiefuna did not fail to notice the contrived ring to the sound, the awkward silence that followed, the slight distance they kept from Oscar on the railings afterwards.

For one full week, Senior Kachi did not show up at his corner. Obiefuna lay awake on most nights, longing for the sound of those light footsteps and the laboured warm breathing on one side of his face, the hesitant tap. On the eighth day, he rose from his bed right after inspection and made his way to the prefect quarters. The night was brightly lit by a full moon, and its glow lent the room an ethereal appearance. Without Senior Kachi leading him, he felt less sure, more apprehensive. At the door, he took a breath before he stepped in, wondering whether to loudly excuse himself in case one of the other seniors happened to be awake. Senior Kachi's door was slightly open. Obiefuna inched forward when he heard the shuffling of feet. Perhaps Senior Kachi would be coming to him tonight after all. He turned around to go, but something made him pause and crouch behind a cupboard, waiting to see what would follow. He didn't have to wait long, it seemed, as barely seconds later a figure that was not Senior Kachi emerged from the door. Obiefuna took in the flutter of his wrist, the slight sway of his hips as he walked. He turned around briefly at the main door, and Obiefuna caught a glimpse of the face. It was Festus, and, as expected, he looked extremely pleased with himself.

ELEVEN

Uzoamaka thought, as she sat in the waiting room of the hospital, about whiteness. The hospital walls, the ceiling, the tiled floors, even the uniforms of the doctors and nurses that swished past were blindingly white, the kind of shade that made her eyes hurt. She could understand the deliberateness of the choice, and yet it felt odd somehow—all that pureness, the immaculate promise of perfection for a place where hope was ultimately dashed as much as it was restored. Uzoamaka had been waiting an hour now, but she did not mind. She had made peace with the fact that her case was not an emergency—that she was already late.

"If only we had reached a diagnosis earlier," the doctor had said, exactly five months ago now, though it felt like longer. His tone had been almost apologetic, as if there was any way he could have figured it out before she presented herself at the clinic. And yet, in those early months when she still had enough rage in her, fuelled by disbelief, fuelled by denial, she had heard a tone of blame in his voice when, retrospectively, there had been none; and she had raised her voice, called him a liar, demanded a second opinion, broken down weeping before strangers. Now, after two surgeries and multiple sessions of chemotherapy, she had too little strength to be annoyed. She accepted things the way they came—with as much grace as she could muster.

"Uzoamaka Aniefuna," someone called.

Uzoamaka put up her hand. She followed the nurse down the hallway that led to the cramped room of the doctor's office. It was a routine she was accustomed to by now—the brisk walk of the nurse, stopping at intervals to let Uzoamaka catch up, trying bravely to smile, her impatience ever-so-slight. Uzoamaka could have suggested she skipped the process—she knew the location of the doctor's office; she had memorized the doctor's tight smile when he saw her, the too-bright, false-hearted cheer in his tone when he said, "Madam, how are you feeling today?" The first time, she had merely looked at him, struck by how easily perfunctory he could be. But by now she had learned to return his smile and nod. Sometimes, she drily joked that she felt like she would die soon. She wasn't sure she was being funny because he never really laughed at that one.

"Your husband isn't here today," the doctor observed after she sat, looking behind her, towards the door.

"No," Uzoamaka said. She had told him she felt well enough to go alone today. She didn't have the heart to say that his presence made her worse: the way he sat tensed and jittery, glaring at the doctor in an almost confrontational manner. She found herself holding her breath when he was around.

"Is that a good idea?" the doctor sounded concerned. "Madam,

I don't like the idea of your coming alone. This treatment could make you very weak. You would need help getting home."

"I took a taxi here. I can take one back."

The doctor looked unconvinced, but he shrugged and proceeded. He didn't give her any new information, and Uzoamaka looked at the illustrated diagrams of human anatomy on the wall of his office as he spoke. They still believed chemotherapy was the most viable option they had. The surgeries had bought her time, but the cancer had spread rapidly since her last biopsy. Uzoamaka nodded without quite comprehending. She sensed the onset of the usual dizziness she often developed at the hospital, and to distract herself studied the pictures propped on the doctor's table. In one of them, he stood clad in his white coat, flanked by a smiling older woman and a younger boy. She wondered where the father was.

"I wanted to discuss with your husband the possibility of—"

"Is this your mother?" she asked, cutting him off mid-sentence.

He looked at her, taken aback. "Yes."

"When did you leave school?"

A longer pause. "Eleven years ago."

Uzoamaka nodded. She wouldn't have guessed. He looked too young. "Is she alive?"

"Who?"

Uzoamaka pointed at the picture. "Your mother."

The doctor stared back at her with an almost imperceptible frown. She thought for a moment he would not speak, and then he said, "Are you feeling any pain at the moment, ma?"

Uzoamaka bit down a smile, aware that she had been chastised. "I'm sorry," she said, "that was inappropriate."

But she thought about the picture on the drive home. She did not know why it left an impression on her, spurred within her a thousand curiosities. She wanted to know if the absence of an older male in the picture meant the father was no more, wanted to know where the woman was. The doctor had continued with his explanation after an awkward pause, in a neutral tone she found herself impressed by, although afterwards she noticed him darting glances at her, no doubt questioning her sanity. She imagined him calling his mother after she left his office, both laughing off the situation as one of those occasional oddities that came with the job.

Back home, she stepped into the shower first thing and remained standing even after her body was washed clean. The question had been about Obiefuna. From the moment she got the diagnosis, as she saw her world upended before her very eyes, it was her son that had come to mind. It had been more than a year since she saw him. How livid she had been when Anozie first told her, on that otherwise promising December morning fifteen months ago, that Obiefuna would not be coming home to her for his first and subsequent holidays, essentially confirming Uzoamaka's nagging suspicion—that the exile, such as it seemed, was not temporary. Every holiday since had been for them a shouting match: he threatened on one occasion to slap her if she talked to him like that again, and she instantly went mute, more stunned than terrified, at the kind of man he had become.

She recalled the incidents with humour at the irony. For it was she now, more than Anozie, who wanted Obiefuna to stay away. She had come to terms with her own hesitation in seeing him, or, rather, in letting him see her as she was. She had bounced back from the surgeries in good physical shape, still healthy-looking enough to beguile her friends and customers. But Obiefuna was no fool. He had only to look at her to see that something was wrong. And he never took these things well. She constantly thought back to a fall she had suffered when

Obiefuna was a little boy. She had lost her step as she mounted the stairs and had come crashing down. The injury was minor, just a few scratches on her upper arm from where she had hit the ground, but Obiefuna, when he saw the wound as she gave him a bath, had panicked so badly he developed a fever. For his sake, she had willed the wounds to heal faster, wearing longer clothes to conceal the bruise, and lied to him that she was better. She considered him her other half—he was, in a sense, eternally tethered to her. And, much as she despaired for her own life, it broke her heart even more when she thought of what the news would do to him.

TWELVE

The first thing Obiefuna noticed about him was his uniform—his crisp white shirt, ever-spotless and glistening when it caught the sun, neatly tucked into sleek, tapered trousers with razor-sharp lines running downwards, white socks and shoes that seemed never to have smelled dust or dirt. His name was Mordecai but everyone, for some reason, called him Sparrow. He belonged to the clique of the coolest boys in class, the boys who were known for their snobbishness; all six of them lived ostensibly easy-going, crease-free lives, free of the familiar hurdles, everything made much easier by the string of School Fathers who protected them and the teachers who adored them. They appeared elevated in a sense from the rest of the class, existing in their own exclusive orbit. They had the same things in common: they were always immaculately dressed and sported the best watches and sandals; they were always absent at functions; and they even had a bedroom to themselves, having arrived early or intimidated the original occupant into accepting an exchange. There was something curious about their power. None of them possessed any notable physical strength and yet they commanded an influence over even the strongest students. Their leader, Makuo, was a high-flyer, the second-best student in the whole class and a mathematics genius. He was also Sparrow's best friend, and with another boy named David, they formed a trio that appeared to inhabit an even more exclusive orbit than the rest of their group, relating to the other cool boys occasionally with a thinly veiled condescension that was apparent to a discerning eye. Obiefuna idly fantasized about becoming one of them, being revered without having to make any conscious effort. Most of all, he wondered what it would mean to be friends with Sparrow. He was aware that his existence went entirely unnoticed by Sparrow. In Obiefuna's time at the school, Sparrow had never spoken to him directly; there had never been occasion for their paths to intersect. And yet Obiefuna watched him assiduously, content with just observing, taken by his roguish demeanour, his life of clean lines, his loose-limbed, sure-footed walk. Sparrow possessed an arrogant swagger that Obiefuna found irresistible. He was one of the chapel instrumentalists, and sometimes, watching him strike the piano with long, lean fingers, Obiefuna would close his eyes and allow himself a fleeting fantasy of those fingers tracing patterns on his bare skin.

Obiefuna was in the second term of his SS2 year, and it went without saying, as the date for the prefect handover ceremony drew near, that Sparrow would be at the forefront. Obiefuna had considered applying, but the positions he fancied—health, agric or laboratory—already had people in the running, most of them recommended by their soon-to-be predecessors, and Obiefuna had neither the zeal nor the willpower to challenge them. Jekwu applied for the position of house prefect, and he was crippled with nervousness the day before the interview, failing the basic prep session Obiefuna had set up for him. By morning, he was still unable to recite his memorized lines of self-introduction, and he took whole minutes before he was due to be called in for the interview taking deep breaths.

"Maybe just ditch the speech and be yourself," Obiefuna suggested.

Jekwu looked at him in panic. "You think the speech is bad?"

"No. But you might be more convincing if you're not stuttering over half of the words."

Jekwu sighed, flinging the piece of paper to the floor. "I don't even know what I was thinking when I applied."

"Look, you've got this. You don't even have any competition. Stop thinking about it too much."

"That hasn't stopped them from disqualifying people in the past," Jekwu said gloomily. "Those people would persuade someone who isn't even interested to take up a post and disqualify someone who pined for it."

Obiefuna chuckled at the truth of it. The senior prefect in Senior Papilo's time was said to have been in class studying when he was summoned to the rector's office and had the post conferred upon him, with the entire horde of boys who had spent the whole day reciting manifestoes before the prefect committee overlooked. Senior Papilo himself had been repeatedly offered the position of sports prefect, even though he had not applied.

"Hey, can I have your tie?" a voice said. Obiefuna half turned to see Sparrow gesturing at Jekwu. How had he made an appearance so casually? The heady scent of his cologne filled Obiefuna's nostrils.

"What?" Jekwu said, astounded.

"I just heard I'm up next and I forgot mine," Sparrow replied breezily. The offence in Jekwu's tone was lost on him.

Jekwu said, "You think you're the only one applying for a post?"

"Are you?" There was a look of surprise in Sparrow's eyes.

"Yes," Jekwu snapped. He had caught the look, too, and appeared irritated. "You know there are other people who exist apart from you and your stupid—"

"You can have mine," Obiefuna said. They both turned to look at him, Jekwu with startled betrayal, Sparrow with puzzled surprise and, finally, a new look of recognition: Sparrow saw him. Obiefuna undid the tie from around his neck, avoiding Jekwu's eyes, and handed it to Sparrow.

Sparrow received the tie from him with a slight nod and wound it around his neck in a firm knot. Against Sparrow's white shirt, Obiefuna had never known his own tie to look so good.

"I won't forget this," Sparrow said.

HE WAS PLAYING a game of cards with Wisdom later that evening when Sparrow returned the tie. He was smiling his signature smile, but there was something clouding his eyes.

"Did it go well?" Obiefuna asked conversationally, surprising himself at the ease of his rapport, as if he were used to talking to Sparrow.

"Fairly," Sparrow said, but the worry lines did not disappear. He seemed to linger, reluctant to walk away. Obiefuna was too aware of his presence. He worried he would put down a wrong card and, worse than being penalized, draw odd stares.

"Are you reading this?" Sparrow asked suddenly, snapping up a book from Obiefuna's bed. He studied the cover closely, mouthing the title *Second Class Citizen*, his expression serious.

"Yes," Obiefuna said.

"What is it about?" he asked.

"Uh, you know . . ." Obiefuna never knew how to answer questions like this, and now, with Sparrow looking him in the eye, seeming very interested in what he had to say, he went blank. "A woman who goes to London to be with her husband," he finished, appalled at himself.

"Nice." Sparrow flipped to the back. "Buchi Emecheta. Sounds familiar."

"From *Joys of Motherhood*—do you know it?"

"I think so. The one about the slave woman?"

Obiefuna pondered a moment. "Two of her novels have slave women in them. But *Joys of Motherhood* is more popular."

"Okay," Sparrow said. He flipped the pages of the book, read through the author biography at the end and replaced it on the bed. "I'm impressed you read," he said. "I like people who read. I like to read, too, but I'm more interested in making money nowadays."

Obiefuna chuckled. He double-checked a card before putting it down. Sparrow was looking at him as if expecting a reply, and Obiefuna suddenly found the air around him too dense, too solid to inhale. Sparrow's words "I like people who read" rang in his ears.

"Okay, make I push," Sparrow said, getting up. "Thanks again."

"Are you friends with Sparrow now?" Wisdom asked after Sparrow was out of the door. He sounded envious and disapproving at the same time.

Obiefuna shrugged.

SPARROW LIKED HIM. It seemed incredulous to Obiefuna, almost surreal, and, as the days lengthened into a week, with Sparrow occasionally stopping by his room to say hi, easily striking up conversation with him when they crossed paths in public, Obiefuna anticipated that something would go wrong, something would snap and return things to their usual place; sometimes, unconsciously, he willed it. Once, as he ascended the classroom staircase, he made out Sparrow and his friends at the base and tried to walk past stealthily, not making it awkward for anyone, but Sparrow spotted him and called out to him, moving over to shake his hand in full view of his friends, and Obiefuna did not miss the puzzled glances they exchanged with each other. He wondered what they made of this new friendship, even as Sparrow took to stopping by his seat during prep to talk to him, sometimes throughout the night. It deprived Obiefuna of precious study time, yet he looked forward to those visits and worried when Sparrow was late in coming. Mostly, Sparrow talked about his relationships at home, the movies he loved, the song lyrics he knew by heart. They bonded over their mutual fascination for the *Lord of the Rings* series, disagreed over which Michael Jackson album was the best. Sparrow gave rapturous monologues on his adoration of Lil Wayne and his YMCMB crew. He dreamed of becoming a rapper like Lil Wayne, his body studded with similar tattoos, exuding a similar extravagance.

He sometimes complained about his friends. They were all the same, he said, bloody pretenders, the most annoying set of people he knew. They acted conceited when there was really nothing to be conceited about. It surprised Obiefuna, Sparrow's ability to criticize the conceited nature of his friends while being fundamentally enshrouded in the same conceit himself. But he listened all the same and made empathetic sounds of agreement, relishing the time when Sparrow said, "They think they are special but they are just blockheads. Look at you, for instance, you're very smart but you don't even make noise."

Sometimes, Sparrow turned up with exercises for Obiefuna

to solve, listening with vague interest as Obiefuna explained. He updated Sparrow's notes, thrilled when Sparrow complimented his clean, rounded handwriting. He liked it when Sparrow said, after he scored high in an assignment, with Obiefuna's help, "I don't know what I would have done without you, Obi."

On some nights, he taught Sparrow complex calculations, even though Sparrow never seemed to comprehend, waiting eagerly for a pause to chip in a random fact about Lil Wayne, a new tattoo idea he thought cool, the Illuminati.

"I don't know why we have so many 'masses' in this chemistry," Sparrow complained once as Obiefuna tried to explain atomic molecular mass to him. Obiefuna retorted that someone had once said he didn't know chemistry teachers were Catholics, what with all the mass—a lame joke, and so he was startled when Sparrow burst into laughter, his shoulders rocking back and forth from the force of the sound. Obiefuna was conscious, too conscious, of Sparrow's right palm spread out lightly on Obiefuna's left thigh and moving around without control the more he laughed. Obiefuna's own hands had gone to sleep and twitched almost painfully when he moved them. He wondered if Sparrow felt the same spark when he placed his palm on Sparrow's thigh. It was a stilted moment, mired in uncertainty, while they sat in silence after that laugh, feeling each other's thighs through their trousers, aware and yet feigning ignorance of their true intent. Sparrow's hand found Obiefuna's erection first, hard and aching within the tight space. He withdrew slightly as though it had been a mistake and Obiefuna was partly grateful for the dim light that hid his blush. They sat in silence for a long time, their hands still on each other's thigh, and then Sparrow found his erection again, and this time there was nothing gentle about the grip, nothing subtle or pretentious. Obiefuna's hands were slower, hovering around Sparrow's belt, fumbling unsuccessfully with the hook, until he felt Sparrow's fingers tapping the back of his palm. "Let's go to the house," he said.

Obiefuna found him on the staircase of Amadi House in ten minutes, the time interval necessary to quell suspicion. Sparrow pulled him close with a force that momentarily alarmed him, as did the expertise with which Sparrow undid all his buttons at once and yet somehow managed to leave them intact. But Sparrow gave him no time to process this—his hands were already tugging at Obiefuna's belt, his tongue making its way into Obiefuna's mouth. The sensation was new and consequently revolting and Obiefuna backed away, suddenly terrified by the thought of losing something of himself that he could not get back. "No."

Sparrow's hands hung for seconds in mid-air before he dropped them. His breathing was laboured and heavy. Even with his head bowed, Obiefuna was acutely aware of Sparrow's bewildered eyes on him.

"I'm sorry," Obiefuna said. He wished Sparrow would say something, but he was quietly buckling his belt and humming under his breath. Obiefuna expected him to walk away afterwards and not speak to him again, but he moved over when he was done to help Obiefuna button his shirt, his hum becoming louder.

It became a routine. They would slip out of class simultaneously, midway into prep, to meet under the staircase, rubbing up against each other for long minutes in the dark, until Obiefuna succumbed to the electrifying force that led to the stickiness in his underwear. Sparrow laughed every time this happened, prompting Obiefuna, himself unsure about what was particularly funny, to laugh along. Sparrow had an intoxicating effect on him; he felt with Sparrow a delirious happiness that sometimes made his eyes spin. He looked forward to the nights when he would melt into Sparrow's hands. The noises that came from him on such nights were loud and strange to his own ears, and Sparrow would clasp a hand around his mouth sometimes and later ask him, teasingly, if he was trying to get them caught. And they did get caught, on a rainy Saturday night. They had braved the rains to meet and had arrived at the spot dripping water, laughing together.

"See how I just got myself wet because of you," Sparrow said, and Obiefuna laughed harder. He felt a light-headed sweetness, as though he had just got drunk on sweet wine. Sparrow drew close to cover the space between them and placed a hand on the side of Obiefuna's face to hold it in position, so that Obiefuna's eyes were focused squarely on his. It was not the usual frenzy they were accustomed to. This was the poignancy of two people who were beginning to fall in love; people who could derive satisfaction just from looking at each other. Sparrow's hands were on his chest, his waist, his arm, and when Sparrow slipped a tongue into his mouth, it left him breathless. Obiefuna's eyes were closed, as were his ears, so he did not immediately see the torchlight reflecting on his back, on Sparrow's face, did not hear the familiar voice that yelled from afar, "Stop there!"

In retrospect, Obiefuna would marvel at his own skilfulness. He ran before he could fully comprehend what had just happened, past the grove of plantain trees around the tap, past the mould of concrete blocks that lay in untidy heaps around the school compound, arriving, finally, at the classroom. They had been discovered. He heard footsteps behind him and turned sharply, causing the smallish junior boy to scurry away. Sparrow had not come with him. Sparrow had been apprehended. He would be taken to the disciplinary committee and made to reveal who the other person was. Obiefuna would be exposed to the whole world. He sat on a step and tried to still the trembling of his hands, the painful throbbing of his neck, the loud thudding of his chest. From behind him, the concerned voice of the junior boy wanted to know if he was all right. From upstairs, the jarring sound of the bell for prep dismissal filled the stairwell.

ONLY TWO DAYS LATER and the news of the two senior boys caught under the staircase of Amadi House having "unnatural intercourse" had become common knowledge. By now, Sparrow had become a poster boy for all that was immoral and outlawed. He was stalwart in the face of his humiliation, readily admitting to the crime, accepting the revelation that his case was spiritual, that he was possessed by a thousand demons and would need deliverance. But he would not say who he had been with that night. On that aspect of the interrogation, he maintained an unwavering silence. He had been made an exception to the rule banning flogging, had publicly received twenty strokes of the cane from Sir CY himself, had been threatened with expulsion, exposure in a popular newspaper. But he held Obiefuna's name sealed inside himself. Two days later and Obiefuna would waft through his classes and house, his movements slow and numbing, each step he took layered in fear and uncertainty. He looked desperately for a glimpse of Sparrow and would cower when he was finally sighted. He wished he were invisible, absent from school, dead. He would long for Sparrow to look at him, communicate with his eyes what he was feeling, and he would look away, wishing Sparrow would not look at him, when he finally did. He wanted to talk to Sparrow, what about, he wasn't certain, but Sparrow avoided him nowadays, staying away from the back seat as much as possible, and, although it was easy to think of the development as Sparrow's way of protecting his anonymity, he was no less wistful for what could have been, and when he met Sparrow at the top of the stairs one Wednesday evening after extra-mural classes, he expected him to walk away. His grip on Sparrow's arm was light, undecided, and Sparrow could have shrugged it off and gone ahead as he seemed to want to, but he stood still, his eyes on the floor.

"What are you going to do?" Obiefuna asked.

Sparrow was silent. He had his eyes on the lower stairs, studying the descent below. With his slumped stature, his slightly rumpled shirt, he embodied an innocence that broke Obiefuna's heart. There was no trace of the defiance he bore in public. He looked scared and confused.

"Please, don't mention my name," Obiefuna said.

Sparrow looked up at him just then, really looked at him, perhaps for the first time since that night, and Obiefuna saw something in his eyes harden with resolve. Sparrow opened his mouth to speak, and then, seeming to change his mind, he simply shook his head and shrugged himself free of Obiefuna's grasp, ascending the stairs without a backwards glance.

SPARROW'S CASE was the first to be called the following Thursday morning. The teacher who read the case, her face scrunched up in apparent distaste, looked up at the crowd when she mentioned "the unnamed culprit" in her report, and Obiefuna felt his blood congeal, certain her eyes were on him, as were the eyes of every other person in the hall. He could tell that the many speculations that had been trailing for days had formed around him, and every stare in his direction was layered with meaning. Everyone was surely only biding their time until it was convenient to unmask him.

The summoning of Sparrow to the podium resulted in an uproar and scattered mock-applause. He walked to the podium with brisk movements, his eyes set forward, his gait almost confident amid the catcalling, amid the tugging of his trousers by the senior students in front that nearly made him trip. He stood with his hands clasped behind his back, his eyes fixed stoically on the crowd—Sir CY would not let him look down—and remained that way all through the reading of his case and the inevitable subsequent judgement. He was being excluded. He had until the end of the day to leave with his personal effects.

The next case was something about stealing, and, as Obiefuna stood up to leave the chapel, suddenly needing to urinate, he worried he would fall and get dust on his shirt. The bathroom complex was empty when he got there; healthy-looking flies swarmed around the moulds of faeces littered around the floor. He stood at a corner with his eyes closed, his belt undone, his penis in his right hand. The urine would not come. He half expected Sparrow to walk in and slap him, hit him over and over until he was curled on the floor in a messy heap, or stare at him with that look so empty of emotion that it almost hurt more than fists ever could. He wondered if Sparrow thought of himself as brave, if the decision to protect him was born out of a sense of loyalty. Sparrow did not have to protect him—he had nothing to lose and potentially a lot to gain by giving him up. He had walked down from the podium after his fate had been decided with his eyes cast down, and, as he walked out of the chapel, Obiefuna imagined Sparrow would turn round at the door at the last minute and scream his name for everyone to hear. But he had gone without so much as a backwards glance. Sparrow had saved him.

And yet, despite his gratitude, he felt relief. Sparrow was leaving. He would not have the opportunity to change his mind and expose him at a later date. How cruel, how selfish and small-minded, to think, above all things, of his own safety. How monstrous to feel yet more gratitude that Sparrow was going away forever, that their relationship—such as it was—was finite, contained. The stench had become unbearable, and, coupled with the heat, it made him dizzy, nauseous. A few feet away, a swarm of flies buzzed around a small mould of faeces; they scattered when he spat, only to converge again soon afterwards. Obiefuna fleetingly envied them this simple ability, the ease of gliding through, this gift of wings. The old tap on the wall made a groaning sound and dripped brown water. Obiefuna leaned against the wall of the bathroom and imagined himself in flight.

For days afterwards, speculations remained. Festus was an easy target, even though many people could vouch for his whereabouts—in class, being particularly noisy—at the time of the incident. Makuo threatened to fight the next person who dared to mention his name again. He wasn't a faggot, neither was he friends with one.

"But how sure are we that the person is from our class?" a boy, Kayo, asked. "For all we know it could have been an SS1 boy."

"Sparrow?" Makuo said. "No way. It has to be someone from our class," he decided and his eyes momentarily rested on Obiefuna.

Later, Jekwu said, "What I just don't understand is how a fine boy like that can be a homo. When he can get any girl he wants."

"Maybe it's not his fault," Obiefuna said.

Jekwu said, "Are you defending him?"

"What? No. I'm just saying—"

Jekwu laughed. "I'm just joking, biko." He paused, studied Obiefuna awhile. "Obi, just because he was your friend for two minutes doesn't mean you know him. Don't support evil." He added, with a teasing laugh, "Who knows? He probably came after you because he wanted your ass."

Obiefuna managed a smile. He wondered about the contrived

ring to Jekwu's laugh. Something about Jekwu, about everyone, told him it was only a matter of time before he was exposed. And so, without consciously meaning to, he steeled himself. It was the wait that was the hardest, to be aware of his impending fate with no ability to stop it. And yet when, a week later, he was summoned to the rector's office, Obiefuna wished he had been given more time. He searched the face of the classmate who delivered the message, pleading with his eyes to be told what he already knew. As he walked down the corridor of the second floor to the rector's office, he looked over the railings, at the ground beneath, wondering just how swift his death would be if he were to haul himself over. He wondered how they had found out. Had Sir CY's memory finally crystallized enough to picture him? He could remember that Sir CY's torchlight had brushed past his face after all, briefly, but might that not have been enough to identify him? Or had Sparrow finally told on him? Perhaps he had been given the condition of a suspension if he named the other culprit and he had decided that Obiefuna was not worth saving.

The rector's secretary sized him up as he walked in, her face scrunched up in her signature irritation, as she motioned him towards the rector's office. He rapped at the door, dreading the baritone that asked him in. He had never been in the rector's office before, and he was instantly intimidated by the vastness, the gleaming white walls, the compulsive sense of order. Sparrow was nowhere to be seen, but on one side of the rector was Sir Okafor, the chairman of the disciplinary committee, with Sir CY on the other side. Obiefuna caught quick breaths. His ears felt like a radio that had become faulty, with that piercing whine. The thought came to him instantly that he should get on his knees and plead for mercy. He thought, also, of denying everything. It was, in the end, his word against Sparrow's.

He would burst into tears at the accusation, he would tell them that Sparrow had been stalking him and, because he refused him, this was Sparrow's form of revenge. His immaculate record would prove it. Sir CY stood at one end of the room, his carefully neutral face giving nothing away. Sir Okafor motioned Obiefuna forward.

"Are you Obiefuna?" the rector asked.

Obiefuna considered for a wild moment denying his name. He nodded.

"Can't you talk?" Sir Okafor snapped impatiently.

"Yes, sir. I'm Obiefuna."

"SS2 A?"

"Yes, sir."

"You are aware of the recent misdemeanour of a certain Mordecai Njemanze?"

Obiefuna swallowed. "Yes, sir."

"What do you think?"

He blinked. "Sir?"

"I want to know your thoughts on what he did," the rector said.

Obiefuna noticed for the first time how very small the rector's head appeared even for his small stature, giving him the look of a beanpole. He turned to Sir CY and Sir Okafor, who looked on with a careful impassiveness. There was a barely restrained excitement in their manner. Were they trying to trap him in his own words, prompting him into nailing his own coffin?

"Hmm?" the rector prompted.

Obiefuna took a breath. "Bad, sir, very bad."

The rector nodded approvingly. "That's right. And it goes against everything we stand for. We don't want those kinds of students here, and we will fish all of them out."

Obiefuna nodded again. He felt a strange surge of strength suddenly. He was buoyed by resolve. The subject was in the open now. He could afford to breathe easily.

"Anyway"—the rector's words snapped him back into the room—"Mordecai happened to be the sanitary prefect when he was here, and, following his exclusion, the post is now vacant. The prefect committee met this morning to deliberate on a replacement, and they all settled for you."

Obiefuna blinked again. "Sir?"

The rector did not acknowledge the interruption. "The position of sanitary prefect is a very important one, and we were quite impressed with your file." He paused. "Why on earth did you not apply for the post?"

Obiefuna looked from one face to the other. From beside him, the air conditioner hummed loudly without letting out cool air. He realized with a start that both the men were looking at him, waiting for his response. He almost burst out laughing. It had to be a wild joke.

"Obiefuna," Sir CY called him. "Are you okay?"

Obiefuna caught himself. "Yes, sir."

"We realize that this might be unexpected, but we are confident you will not disappoint us," the rector said.

Obiefuna nodded. He wondered what Sparrow would think. "Yes, sir."

The rector reclined on his chair, seeming pleased by the ease with which the task had been executed. "Good. We'll make the announcement at the assembly tomorrow and present you with your tag."

"Okay, sir."

"You can go," the rector said.

"Thank you, sir." Obiefuna turned to the door and let himself out. The secretary was asleep at her desk. Outside the office, he stood for a few minutes by the railings, gazing down at the vast fields of the school compound.

THE ANNOUNCEMENT was made at assembly the following morning. As Obiefuna mounted the stairs that led to the podium, he was buoyed by the applause and whistles. He stood with his back straight and his hands behind him as Sir CY pinned the tag to his shirt, and, as he looked down from the elevated podium, at the sea of eyes fixed squarely on him, he wondered if there was someone there, somewhere, who knew.

THIRTEEN

Obiefuna sat through the sermon awash with shame. The title itself, "A Reprobate Mind," made him chafe under its stern condemnation. The chaplain's voice was raised for most of the time, as though the amplification of the microphone poised at his lips was not enough to drive home his point. He read from the Bible, chilling verses that threatened God's wrath for the many vices listed. He was given to dramatic pauses, filled in on cue by the instrumentalists who relayed sombre sounds to the room. Obiefuna kept his head bowed through the chronicle of the backsliding children of Israel, the audacious transgressions of Ananias and Sapphira, but it was the verse about the men of Sodom and Gomorrah that made his eyes twitch. "Some of you here are just like that!" the chaplain screamed from the altar. "Desiring your fellow boys! Shame on you!" He spoke with a trembling vigour, as if about to dissolve into tears. Obiefuna half expected the chaplain to hurl the microphone at him. He was relieved when the chaplain asked them all to stand, signalling the end of the sermon. It was time for an altar call.

"If you are here and you know you are still caged in any immorality, there's hope for you. Jesus Christ welcomes all lost souls. Here's your last chance for salvation."

Obiefuna tensed. He could hear the mass shuffling of feet around him, of boys heading towards the altar, and yet he remained where he was. Even when the chaplain demanded all eyes remained closed, pointing out Ananias and Sapphira's fate as a consequence of disobedience and deceit in God's house, Obiefuna did not move. His guilt ate at him, but he stood still. The chaplain had not been specific. It could be any of the many sins listed. No one would figure him out. But Obiefuna stayed. He felt a lurch to be a defeat, and in response he pinned his toes hard to the ground until they hurt from inside his shoes. A small, hard fear like knots formed in his chest. The chaplain was concluding the prayers of forgiveness. It was his chance to step forward and be delivered. He was just a moment away. He opened his eyes and turned to ask the person next to him to excuse him, and then the chaplain said Amen.

For days, he did not sleep well. He jolted awake from nightmarish images of being in a steady, bottomless descent, his hands and feet bound, loud, sinister laughter about him. At bath time, the thought of touching his own body disgusted him. More than once, Jekwu asked him if he was okay. Something about the genuine concern on his friend's face made him long to tell Jekwu, but he had played out the inevitable outcome many times in his mind's eye—Jekwu flinching at the revelation, avoiding him afterwards. He resented the possibility just as he resented Jekwu. Most of all, he resented himself. His mother heard something in his voice over the phone and asked him what was wrong. "Obiajulu, I'm your mother. You can tell me," she said. And for that sole reason, for that earnestness in her tone, he had almost told her. It was his inability, ultimately, to frame the words, to give voice to something so despicably real inside him, and his inability to envisage and live with his mother's reaction that had made him say, "I'm fine, Mummy. I just have a little headache."

"Ewo. Sorry, inu? Have you visited the clinic?"

He said yes and changed the subject. Her naivety, born of trust, saddened him. He would see the chaplain, he had decided, that evening. Perhaps visit him at home. It was not a place where the students normally called, but the chaplain, when he listened to Obiefuna's reasons, would certainly understand the need for privacy. But what if the chaplain did not welcome Obiefuna's presence in his home? What if the chaplain sent him away in disgust, or worse, exposed him to the school for having lied all the while? Something about the chaplain's fiery hostility made this possibility more likely. The chaplain might also be incensed by his not having obeyed the altar call. Obiefuna dreaded to think of what would follow.

But he went. Skipping dinner, Obiefuna left the school compound and took the lone, tree-lined path to the semi-detached bungalow the chaplain shared with the school's bursar. The sight of the weathered building with peeling yellow paint in the distance filled Obiefuna with a numbing terror. His double raps on the wooden door were light, and he half hoped they would go unacknowledged. But he heard the lock turn from within and the door was slowly eased open. At first, he saw no one, and then he made her out, crouched beside the door, a section of her face the only part of her visible. It was the first time he was gazing at the chaplain's wife up close, and something about her face disconcerted him. He had a feeling his presence had ruffled her.

"Yes?" she asked, from behind the door.

"Good evening, ma. I want to see the chaplain," he said.

She came into full view then and took her time to blow her nose into a handkerchief, studying him all the while. "Is there a problem?"

He hesitated, debating whether to nod or to shake his head. "No, ma."

She gave him a long look. "The chaplain is not in at the moment." Her voice sounded hoarse, as if she had a cold, and she seemed to hold on to the door lightly, as though terrified of it while also deriving support from it. "You . . . you can come in and wait for him if it is very important," she said.

Obiefuna did not want to wait. But she had already moved away from the door into the house, leaving it ajar, and there was nothing else to do but to take off his shoes and follow her in. The narrow corridor led to a small living room, sparsely furnished. The windows were open, but the curtains were drawn, giving the room a blue-dimmed interior. A citrus fragrance, like warm oranges, hung in the air.

She gestured to a chair. "Do you want water?"

He shook his head. The seat was soft and felt cold to the touch. Something about the doleful, faraway look in her eyes, her distracted air, made him wonder if she was all right. When she disappeared through the curtains, he found himself leaning forward in his seat, straining for a sound. There was a forbidding aura about the living room that made it seem wrong to be there. He had the disquieting sensation of peeping through the keyhole of an elderly woman's bathroom, an intimate shame accompanying the thrill of it. He looked at the framed pictures hanging on the wall. Most of them were of the chaplain, sporting a grin in three-piece suits, sitting cross-legged in a graduation cap and gown, as a youngish man in Ankara-styled material. There were no pictures of their wedding. The only pictures of her on the wall were two photos taken with the chaplain: one in front of a banner with a revival theme behind them, the other of them sitting side by side in identical prints, her blank expression in sharp contrast with the chaplain's wide grin, her small hands extended forward and slightly buried underneath the chaplain's. With her slight stature, her round face free of make-up, he could have passed for her father.

"What's your name?"

Obiefuna turned with a start to see her standing by the curtains, her arms folded across her chest, gazing at him intently.

"Obiefuna," he said.

She nodded slowly, as though thinking deeply about the name. She covered the short distance between them and sat on the chair next to him. Her knees grazed his.

"Why do you want to see the chaplain?" she asked.

Obiefuna stared at her. There was something almost enigmatic in her carriage, in the way she looked right at him as if she could see through him. It brought a blood-curdling stillness to his heart. But the woman couldn't have known. He had been able to hide himself well.

"You can talk to me, Obiefuna." His name on her lips sounded firm, as if she knew him. He focused on counting the lined patterns on the blue carpet. It suddenly felt too warm against the soles of his feet, which might become scalded if left there a moment longer. He was startled by the sudden sound of the bell for prep. He rose.

"I have to go now, ma."

She stared at him a while longer before she nodded. As he headed for the door, she called out suddenly, halting him. "Obiefuna."

He turned to her. "Ma?"

"There's nothing God cannot do if you tell Him and believe in your heart that He will do it."

From where he stood, he could get a better view of her face. It was composed now, but whatever she had applied underneath her lids had not entirely concealed the puffiness. He wondered how long she had been crying, if she would continue after he left. She turned her back to him and walked through the curtains. Outside the house, Obiefuna stood in front of the flowers closest to the driveway for a long time, marvelled at, of all things, how quickly night had descended.

Obiefuna prayed. He signed up to join the Prayer Warriors' unit, dutifully attended every session on Friday nights, staying long after everyone else had gone, kneeling before the altar. The prayers for deliverance typically came last, related in earnest whispers. Sometimes he found himself in tears as he prayed, something within him expanding to bursting. The chaplain's wife's voice replayed in his head at odd intervals. She had seen him. Between them, a silent communication had passed, a mutual confidence without the need for words. He wondered about her. He knew she and the chaplain had been married for eight years without having had a child. Some of the boys in the junior class claimed to have woken on many nights to the sound of her voice all the way from her home, praying. Obiefuna also wondered if her husband beat her. It was the imagery that quickly came to mind, the chaplain as large and severe-looking as he was, his wife lissom and fragile. Did he use his fists or a leather belt? Did he cradle her in his arms afterwards, saying over and over that he was forced to hurt her until she apologized?

In some of his prayers, Obiefuna slowed down to a conversation, and he imagined God flinching at the terse enquiries about why He would create him this way knowing it was a wrong way to live. Other times he begged, reasoning that God would be willing to engage with him if he were contrite and docile, if he simply asked for forgiveness. His understanding of God, after all, was that He was a person who forgave mistakes. Sometimes he believed that God had answered, and that he was changed, that something had snapped free in him, a weight had been lifted, a newness born. And sometimes he could feel God's silence hanging over him, his prayers and occasional crying mere pathetic sighs in God's ears. On one such night, he woke to find himself on the floor of the altar. It was past midnight; the side of his face ached from being pressed to the hard floor for too long. He pulled himself up and stood with his hands in his pockets, in the dark, on the altar of an empty chapel, far away from home. And then he brushed his clothes to get rid of the dust and went back to the house.

FOURTEEN

Obiageli had lived a fascinating life. As a young girl, she was convinced she would become a famous singer, subjecting Uzoamaka to long sessions of make-believe stage performances which ended with Uzoamaka applauding with all her might because she did not have the heart to tell Obiageli the truth. In secondary school, she had decided she would become a nurse, joking about inflicting the same pain of injections on others as she had received in her life. After three JAMB failures in a row, she finally graduated with a second-class lower degree in agriculture, much to their parents' disappointment. She had worked at the post office, taught for a few years at a secondary school and held a position at the local government office, a job secured for her by the man with whom she was in a relationship for nine years, a man whom she had believed was a childless widower. When she learned of his living wife and thriving marriage, his four children—the first nearly as old as she was—she broke it off and declared herself eternally celibate. God and godliness were her thing now.

Uzoamaka did not know why she had decided, of all her options, to go to Obiageli. Anozie had informed her of Obiefuna's scheduled return for the session holidays. Anozie's sister was unavailable for the duration, away in Lagos to care for her daughter and newly born grandson. "And frankly, Uzoamaka," he added, "this is becoming ridiculous. You can't keep on hiding this from him. He'll find out one way or another."

Uzoamaka had toyed with the idea of staying. She had gone over the conversation in her head, pictured his face when he heard the news, crafted alternative scenarios, and, in the end, two days before his arrival, she called Obiageli. She expected to be turned down, and when Obiageli paused after she asked, Uzoamaka prepared her apologies in her head, but Obiageli said, "About time. It's been too long, Ada nnam."

Uzoamaka liked the house. She liked the sparse orderliness of the living area, the spacious balcony where she sat on most evenings to receive fresh air. She liked most of all the fact that she was often alone, her mind permitted to freely wander. Obiageli left for work in the mornings before Uzoamaka woke up. When she returned home in the evenings, she busied herself around the house without paying Uzoamaka any mind. She went for vigils on Fridays and returned in the morning tired, her eyes crusty from sleep. Still, Uzoamaka could sense Obiageli watching her, her curiosity nagging at her. Sometimes, she asked Uzoamaka what was wrong.

"Why do you think something is wrong?" Uzoamaka retorted one time.

Obiageli scoffed, shrugging in a way that said, wasn't it obvious? "Because even if you try your best to avoid me, whenever things get really bad, you run to me," she said.

Uzoamaka stared at her in wordless surprise. Distance made it so easy to think of people with fondness and forget what made you leave them in the first place. She felt her anger amass slowly within her until it solidified into a blinding rage, propelling her to march into her room and gather her clothes from the hangers to fit into her bag. Midway, she remembered she had some clothes on the line from her morning laundry and so she put off leaving until the next day. By evening, the worst phase of her anger had subsided, and she was able, finally, to set aside Obiageli's spite and admit the truth of her words.

THEY HAD BEEN such good friends as children. There was a time when they could easily tell what the other was thinking. But Uzoamaka had spent most of her teenage years apart from Obiageli, serving as a housekeeper for their maternal aunt, who, in turn, paid for her secondary-school education. She had returned home after five years to meet an uncouth Obiageli, who picked random, unprovoked fights and talked back at her with a new viciousness, disregarding the three years' birth gap between them. Their parents' deference to Uzoamaka had only further incensed Obiageli. Uzoamaka could not point at a reason that made sense; it was difficult to grasp the possibility that Obiageli envied her. Obiageli was lighter skinned, conventionally prettier, and she had her university education, a privilege Uzoamaka had been denied. Uzoamaka sometimes found herself in the odd position of having to downplay her small, inconsequential victories, allotting undeserved credit to Obiageli, if only to positively improve their parents' perception of her, and in turn improve

Obiageli's own perception of Uzoamaka. But, in the end, there was no appeasing Obiageli.

Still, there were instances when Obiageli had been able to surprise Uzoamaka. Only Obiageli had supported her decision to marry Anozie. Her parents had disapproved of him even before they met him. Although he, too, was Igbo, they did not like the fact that he was not from their own state, and when they finally met him, furnished with details of his job as a trader, and his one-room apartment in a run-down part of town, they asked her if she had been bewitched. "He looks like he really needs you," Obiageli told her later, surprising her. "See the way he was looking at you. As if he will die if anything stops him from marrying you." She laughed. "Biko, follow the man o! Let someone's blood not be on your head."

For a whole year after the wedding, her parents spoke little to her. It was Obiageli who stayed close, sending sackfuls of foodstuffs, and lending money whenever Uzoamaka asked, even if she also gleefully reported the situation to their parents. When the miscarriages came, her parents had declared themselves vindicated. It was Obiageli, after the fourth, who had showed up one morning unannounced and dragged her off the bed where she had lain nearly unmoving for a week, willing herself to die, to Obiageli's own apartment, where, over the next few weeks, she nursed Uzoamaka back to health.

A FEW DAYS AFTER Uzoamaka decided to stay, Obiageli came home from work with a plastic bag and a mischievous smile. "I got you oka and ube from the vendor down the street. She's my customer and she reserves the best ones for me."

Uzoamaka almost smiled back as she extracted a cob of corn from the bag Obiageli extended. The heat burned her palms through the newspapers it had been wrapped in. Obiageli was pouring hot water into a plate to soften the pears, with which the corn was to be eaten. It was the closest to an apology Uzoamaka would get.

"I'm sick, Obiageli," Uzoamaka said.

Obiageli looked up. "Ewo, sorry." She felt Uzoamaka's temperature with the back of her palm. "How's it doing you?"

Uzoamaka shrugged herself free. "It's not that." She took a breath, steeled herself. "They say it's cancer."

Obiageli laughed then. The sound was without mirth. It was cackly, frightened. "Oyibo! You're just unwell, Uzoamaka."

"I'm on chemotherapy treatments," Uzoamaka said. She had the feeling of pressing down on an unhealed wound, watching for a reaction. "The doctor said I don't have much longer."

"Who would you rather believe? God or the doctors?"

"It's late stage, Obi—"

"Just shut up, Uzoamaka!" Obiageli shouted, rising. Her legs caught on the foot of the wooden table before her and it fell to the floor, cobs of corn landing around Uzoamaka's feet. Obiageli went to stand by the window with her back turned to Uzoamaka. She stood for a long time with her shoulders hunched forward and her head bent. Uzoamaka imagined she was crying silently. But when she finally spoke, her voice was clear. "You'll go with me to my pastor. The devil is a big liar."

THE PASTOR was a small man with a clean-shaven head. Uzoamaka had spent so long imagining his features from the many stories Obiageli told of him that she was slightly disappointed, sitting across from him. Obiageli introduced her as "the only family I have left." The pastor nodded piously. Uzoamaka prepared to go on her knees and have him lay hands on her, but he told them to extend their hands, and he said the prayers from where he sat. He accepted the envelope Uzoamaka passed across with a tight, sympathetic smile.

"He didn't even touch me," Uzoamaka said to Obiageli on the bus ride home.

"What?"

"Your pastor. I saw the way his hands were shaking when he took the envelope from me. He made sure our hands did not touch."

Obiageli gave her a long look, and then she sighed. "This isn't going to work if you don't believe it will, Uzoamaka."

NOW, AS OBIAGELI sat beside her in a taxi headed for the market, her sister hummed under her breath. There was something different about her now. Even as they prayed every night of the week, holding hands together, Obiageli binding and casting demons from generations back, Uzoamaka sensed Obiageli's terror. Three nights ago, Obiageli had broken down sobbing in the middle of their prayers, and Uzoamaka stood there watching, thinking about how grief had a way of humbling even the most uncharitable. She knew then that she had made the right decision to come here, to put off telling Obiefuna in the meantime. Let him have a few more months of blissful obliviousness; let him not have to watch for long as she slowly faded away.

"Do you remember Achalugo?" Obiageli said, startling Uzoamaka.

"Who?"

"Achalugo naw," Obiageli pressed. "From the village. The one that used to dress like a woman."

"That plays the ogene?"

"Gbam!" Obiageli said.

"What about him?"

"Hmm? Nothing o. I've just been hearing his songs in my

head all day." Obiageli laughed. "Remember I used to dance for him?"

Uzoamaka chuckled. How could she not remember? Obiageli would never let her live down that memory. She said, "I wonder where he is now."

Obiageli shrugged. "Last I heard, he was still in his little hut in the village. Such talent going to waste!"

Uzoamaka nodded agreement. Memories of him flooded her mind: she could picture him in his low-cut blouse and skirt, his solid headgear. His make-up was unparalleled. There was no one she knew who could match his abilities as an entertainer. His touch on the ogene was second to none, his talent as mysterious as his own life. He was a favourite of the village chief, who often invited him to perform at the palace, and sometimes in the village square. Uzoamaka had once tried to join his dance crew. She had never been one to dance, but she had followed Obiageli to the audition. She remembered now that the costume allotted to her had been too tight around the chest and made of a kind of fabric that grated on her skin. She had failed at the dance, getting the moves wrong and persistently lagging behind until she was asked to leave. The other girls laughed, loud enough for Uzoamaka to disappear into the bush and break down in tears. Midway, she heard leaves rustling, the sound of footsteps approaching, and she straightened up, wiped her eyes. It took her a moment to recognize Achalugo. With his mannerisms, his beardless, heavily made-up face in the waning evening light, he could have passed for any other woman around.

"Why are you crying?" he asked her. He had a serious look on her face.

She dug her heel in the soil without responding.

"So you don't know how to dance, eheh? Is that the end of the world? If you're not good at one thing, you find your strength in another, oburo ya?" His voice had a funny-sounding high pitch, or maybe it was simply not what she had come to expect from men. "Wipe your eyes, biko. Come outside and join in the fun!"

He held her hand and led her out, back to the square. His kindness had allowed her to return to the audition as a spectator without feeling shame, to brush aside Obiageli's gloating after she was selected for the crew. It had been a lifetime ago, and the memory of the encounter was dim—but it had come back to her once in 2005, when she arrived home from work to the sound of music coming from the sitting room. She was aware by then of Obiefuna's gift, his fascination for P-Square, the group of identical twin brothers whose songs dominated the radio. (She sometimes watched while Obiefuna, only thirteen, tried to imitate their dance steps. He would use Ekene as a substitute to replicate the group, and she observed with amusement as Ekene fumbled through the dances, utterly perplexed as to why he was doing them anyway.) Anozie, with his austere taste, disapproved of the songs, changing the station whenever they came on, and he forbade the boys from listening. That day, she peered through the window of the living room and suddenly, powerfully, Achalugo was brought to the fore, made stark by the sight of Obiefuna dancing, the sweat coating his bare skin as he moved from one end of the room to the other, screaming the lyrics of the song "Bizzy Body." He was disobeying Anozie; he could get in real trouble if found out. But he was dancing, doing with ease something Uzoamaka could only dream of. Something about the joy on his face, the sheer freedom, made Uzoamaka remain where she was a moment longer. He made a smooth forward-backward move, twisted his waist to both sides with impossible flexibility, and twirled without effort in the air. In that moment, she caught a glimpse of his smiling face, bearing witness to the absolute happiness he radiated, and, against her conscious will, Uzoamaka found her heart singing.

FIFTEEN

The car radio was tuned to a Highlife station. Next to him, from the driver's seat, his father nodded along to the track. Obiefuna pressed his face to the window, observing the slow-moving traffic, the hawkers navigating their way through the cars to advertise their products. He had almost forgotten what the bustle of a thriving city looked like. Ekene was sprawled across the back seat, asleep, his snoring loud enough to be heard above the music. They had taken him by surprise. He had risen that departure morning with every intention of heading for his aunt's. He was familiar by now with the route to her house and no longer needed to be picked up by his father. So when he had been informed, as he got dressed, that a man and a boy who looked like him were requesting to see him, he had reacted with disbelief. But Ekene had turned up himself on the second summons, and he added that their father at that point was gradually losing his patience. When they arrived home, it was dark. His father made the sign of the cross, got out of the car and turned round to get Obiefuna's bag from the boot. Obiefuna followed him up the front steps. As his father fiddled with the keys to the door, Obiefuna turned to Ekene. "Is Mummy still at work by this time?"

It was his father who responded. "Obiefuna," he said, "your mother is not home."

EKENE DID NOT KNOW where she was. He had returned from school one afternoon and she was gone. He guessed she was visiting their aunt Obiageli. He did not know when she would be back. Obiefuna was puzzled by the strangeness of it. Why was he here now? Why was his mother away, at this of all times? His father offered no answers, snapping at him the one time he pressed too hard. In that moment, Obiefuna searched his eyes for clues, to ascertain if he had told her. As he drifted off to sleep, he was jerked awake by flashes of his mother shoving him off a cliff, renouncing him as her son. When, a month later, he turned eighteen, she did not call to sing to him as she always did. The occasion, usually monumental in Obiefuna's imagination, went nearly unacknowledged by everyone, except for Ekene's belated remark, two days later, "Your birthday was the day before yesterday abi? Happy birthday in arrears o!" It could have been the saddest birthday ever, except, the following week, his father surprised him by coming home with a package which he handed to Obiefuna without ceremony, as if the Nokia phone, which was in vogue, was a mere, uninteresting present.

Obiefuna was swept up in the glee of reconnecting with his neighbourhood friends. And, with the phone, he could keep in contact with friends from school. Ekene probed him often for stories from his house, and Obiefuna indulged him, flattered by his interest, embellishing most of the stories for effect, enjoying the thrill in Ekene's eyes. He idly thought about Aboy from time to time, wondered about him. After that first visit, Aboy had not reached out to him again—not that Obiefuna, in truth, expected him to. Follow-up visits had been made by his father, brief visits that seemed to end as soon as they had started, with crisp precision. Once, while on an errand to get fuel for the generator, he ran into Dibueze at the petrol station.

"Are you not Oga Anozie's son?" Dibueze asked, sizing him up in exaggerated wonder. "How did you grow so big?"

Obiefuna smiled good-naturedly. When he asked after Aboy, Dibueze frowned slightly. "No one has seen him since he moved out."

"He moved out?"

"Yes. He no longer stays with us." Dibueze paused. "He ran into money and moved on."

Obiefuna tried not to dwell on the bitterness in his voice. "Do you know where he is currently?"

"Not where he lives, no. But he sells building materials along Ikeokwu," Dibueze said. Obiefuna listened as he gave the directions. It surprised him that Dibueze could keep such close tabs on someone he was no longer on good terms with. It surprised him, too, that Aboy had chosen a location not too far from his father. He wondered if they had run into each other in the last few months—very likely, as the market was so small—if any words had been exchanged, how awkward the encounter would have been. He set out for Aboy's the next day. Dibueze had described a woman who sold roasted plantains on the corner, and she pointed him to Aboy's shop. A large, flat piece of wood was mounted in front of the door, studded with nails and from which hung brushes and saws and other building materials. He found Aboy inside the shop. He had changed remarkably, with sprouts of hair on the side of his face. He was sitting on the only chair in the shop with a girl on his lap.

"Obiefuna?" he called out with a high-pitched note in his voice that immediately struck Obiefuna as phoney. Where had his self-assurance gone? His smile showed all his teeth.

"How are you?" Aboy asked. He half rose from the chair, seeming to forget the girl, causing her to half slide off his lap, but he stood beside her, his left hand wound around her lower back.

"Long time no see!" Aboy said, with that animated glint still present in his eyes. "How have you been?"

"Fine," Obiefuna said flatly. It had been a mistake. He shouldn't have come.

"Come and sit down," Aboy said, motioning him to the chair. "How is your father? And your mother? What will you drink?"

But Obiefuna kept his eyes on the girl. Her eyeliner had smudged her small face. She had about her the cautiously extravagant air of a girl just learning to explore her sexuality. It was perhaps her first time sitting on a boy's lap. She seemed to avoid Obiefuna's eyes, and he wondered if she understood exactly why he was looking at her. Aboy was out of the door. Obiefuna could hear him shouting instructions to someone next door to bring a bottle of Pepsi quickly. "Cold o!" he emphasized.

Obiefuna turned to the door.

"Ah, ah, Obi!" Aboy called out, half running the short distance to catch up with Obiefuna. He grabbed Obiefuna's wrist. "Where are you going? Come in, let's talk naw. It's been so long!"

Obiefuna found himself looking into those eyes that had once been so shy when he first opened the door that evening in October to let him into the house. What surprised him—for anger would come later—was not that he had been betrayed, but that Aboy seemed blithely unaware of the betrayal. He had a shop now of his own, moderately stocked with goods. He was, finally, living his dream. All around them, commerce thrived, traders loudly calling to customers, and Obiefuna knew they would begin to attract attention soon. He fleetingly imagined Aboy getting on his knees right there in public to beg him to come back, ordering the girl out of his shop, explaining away the scene, calling it a random fling. But he could already feel Aboy's grip slackening—perhaps he, too, was aware that people were starting to stare—and Obiefuna knew that there would be no kneeling, no ordering to leave, no explanation. Soon the grip was slack enough to allow Obiefuna to ease away his wrist, and he turned to go, hearing the last words he would ever hear from Aboy: his name, "Obiefuna." But he did not turn back.

THE BOYS AT THE FIELD were divided over which club was likely to clinch the year's title in the Premier League. It was the beginning of the season, with only a few matches under way. The general consensus was that Manchester United would likely continue its already impressive three-time streak from 2008/9. Obiefuna had watched the first match at the viewing centre with Ekene, where Chelsea beat Hull City 2–1, and with Drogba's increasingly admirable skill, he thought not to rule Chelsea out as a potential underdog. He said as much midway into the discussion. A sudden silence settled in following his contribution, with some of the boys nodding in surprised agreement. And then Chikezie said, "If people are talking, you'll talk, too?"

The boys laughed their mechanistic laughter. In the midst of it, Ekene's voice resonated in Obiefuna's ears. The sun was at its brightest, and he could already feel one side of his face burning up. With his eyes on Obiefuna, Chikezie received the cigarette that was being passed around, looking amused as always. Obiefuna glanced across at Ekene. He, too, had that relaxed smirk on his face that followed a good laugh. Perhaps the joke had indeed been funny. Perhaps he would also have laughed had he not been the subject of ridicule. Obiefuna rose from the grass and rounded the half-circle, stopping beside Chikezie, aware that all eyes were trained on him.

"I want you to repeat what you just said," Obiefuna said.

Chikezie tilted his head upwards to squint at him. There was part-surprise, part-amusement on his face.

"What now? You want to fight me?"

"I just want you to repeat what you said."

Someone whistled. Chikezie pulled a face. He seemed to hesitate a moment, unsure, but the silence that had ensued was dense with expectation, and so Chikezie equally rose from his sitting position. He took his time to brush off the stalks of dead grass that clung to his shorts. "I said you don't know anything about football. You are only sitting here with us because of Ekene. You should be at home playing Oga with your yard girls."

The group of boys cackled, made spurring sounds. Obiefuna breathed through his mouth. Chikezie was looking him in the eye; he could tell even then that Chikezie wanted to avert this confrontation as much as Obiefuna did. Still, he had not backed down, confident in his belief that Obiefuna would. Perhaps it was this sole crude fact, perhaps it was the culmination of slowly building rage from all the years before. Or perhaps it was the sound of Ekene's voice as he laughed, almost indistinguishable from the others, that made Obiefuna lunge a sudden fist at Chikezie. He struck bone, his fist aching right away. Chikezie staggered back, momentarily dazed. A look of surprise had appeared on his face, even as he assumed a fighting stance and lunged back at Obiefuna, striking him squarely on the chin. The fight was brief; soon enough Obiefuna felt hands prising them apart. He looked across at Chikezie, struggling to wrestle himself free from the grip of the boys who restrained him. Obiefuna walked back to the grass to retrieve his slippers. He straightened up after he had put them on and turned to leave, wondering for the first time where Ekene had gone. The other boys stood around, watching him with an alarmed expression, and he followed their gaze downwards to the large droplets of dark stains on his sky-blue shirt, felt the bridge of his nose and saw his fingers come back red with blood. He looked up at Chikezie again, and there he was, dutifully wearing his boots, attempting to go back to the game. Obiefuna took off his slippers. He charged without thinking, unsure of his intent, only becoming aware of himself when Ahmed intercepted him halfway, the searing pain in his shoulders from the force of Ahmed's grip nearly causing him to black out. Ahmed was barking into his ears, ordering his indefinite suspension. Obiefuna felt nauseous. He looked across at Chikezie again and, through blurred vision, amid the commotion, he felt, finally, a small victory at the fear that had formed behind Chikezie's brow. His heart thumped painfully against his chest; he felt woozy from the heat. Obiefuna eased himself from Ahmed's grip and turned sideways, on impulse, and there was Ekene, arms on hip, looking at him in quiet wonder. Obiefuna spat on the grass and took his slippers in one hand. He did not stop walking until he got home.

For days, they sidestepped each other, saying very little outside the most unavoidable interactions. They carved out unspoken territories in their shared room, avoiding each other's space. On the night of the fight, as they ate dinner together, Ekene reached across to touch Obiefuna's jaw, jutting it upwards to check the extent of the damage; Obiefuna slapped away his hand, and then he rose and exited the room, to stand by the balcony overlooking the yard. It was unreasonable to expect anything from Ekene—

his intervention, if anything, would have made the humiliation worse. Still, to observe how easily Ekene had sat there and laughed with strangers, to picture how indistinguishable he had appeared from the others. Obiefuna recalled moments from their childhood when their mother would entrust him, as they set off for school or the playground, with the responsibility of looking out for Ekene. "You know he's your baby brother," she would remind Obiefuna, a redundant piece of information, and yet demonstrating her easy confidence in his ability to protect. In the end, of course, Ekene had never needed looking out for, carelessly gifted as he was in securing friends, in belonging fully and without effort. Obiefuna did not understand how it came so easily to Ekene, why his body seemed naturally attuned to something that was a complicated science to Obiefuna.

Watching Ekene head to the field alone in the coming weeks, arriving home just before dinner, Obiefuna found himself feeling something that was almost like relief, knowing that Ekene would not be burdened by his presence. He remained holed up in their bedroom, pretended to study. He missed his mother. He did not understand how, but he had the sense that her presence at that time would have made it better. He lazed about the yard, watching from the balcony as the younger children in the neighbourhood played games of Swell and Oga. He had discovered a small ant colony by the wall of their apartment, and he spent the evenings watching the trail of ants ascending and descending, fascinated by the brief stops they made in the process to communicate with each other. It was there Ekene found him every evening, their stares brief, and, although Ekene never said a word to him, Obiefuna wondered if the knotted lines on his brow were disappointment.

❖

One evening, the day before Obiefuna's school holiday was over, Ekene returned from the pitch, ball in hand, and offered to teach him how to jog.

Obiefuna rose from the floor to match his height. He still had a modicum of reserved rage from the fight, which made him want to punch the wall sometimes. In that moment, Ekene's face seemed like the perfect wall. He could feel his heart pounding against his chest, his fists clenching and unclenching of their own accord, as if possessing a separate will from the rest of his body. "Don't insult me, Ekene. Please."

"I just want to teach you how to jog properly," Ekene said. "You know, without looking like a chicken." He had his eyes averted. His smile was awkward, untypical of his usual confident self. Obiefuna realized then that this was an apology, in the only way Ekene knew how to form it. They went out in the yard and jogged. Obiefuna watched with as much focus as he could muster as Ekene demonstrated, his slightly curved toes lifting the ball with delicate grace. There was grace, too, in his smile, in the almost seraphic gentleness of his face, and in the way his arms danced around his sides as he moved without effort to maintain balance, sometimes swapping feet, sometimes turning backwards, but still managing somehow to sustain a seamless rhythm. Obiefuna was less successful when he tried. The ball would not bow to his mind's will and stay on the tip of his toes as it did for Ekene, and he wobbled in his quest to maintain balance, twisting dangerously at one point so that he almost sprained an ankle. Ekene told him to be less forceful, less quick to put a foot forward, to take his mind off the process and go with the flow.

"I'm trying!" Obiefuna snapped once, kicking the ball with all his might. It bounced across the yard, landed in a ditch. Obiefuna descended to the ground and sat with his knees drawn to his chest. His head had begun to throb.

Ekene ran off and returned with the ball, bouncing it on the floor to rid it of the slime that clung to it. He lowered himself to sit next to Obiefuna. His bare shoulder was warm against Obiefuna's.

"I'm useless," Obiefuna said.

"Come on, it wasn't that bad," Ekene said.

Obiefuna gave him a side eye.

"Okay, it was bad," Ekene admitted, laughter bubbling in his throat. Obiefuna leaned away to spit. It was late evening, the sun uncomfortably warm on his skin. Ekene was dangling a water bottle between his fingers, but there was too little water in it, and Obiefuna knew his thirst would only get worse were he to take a sip. He did not have the willpower to rise from his position and go into the house.

"Do you remember back in the day when you used to win all those prizes during dance competitions?" Ekene said. "God, I used to envy you so much. I thought: 'How does he do it?' I looked like an idiot trying to imitate you."

Obiefuna turned his head to look at him.

"Why don't you dance anymore, Obi?"

Obiefuna exhaled. He remembered the moments Ekene spoke of, struck by the luminosity of the memory. Some of the events had taken place right there in the yard. There was a time when he was the star of the show, when onlookers roared his name like a chant. He recalled the delight in his mother's eyes as she pointed him out to the other parents, as she placed yet another gift atop the refrigerator where anyone could see. He remembered, too, his father's disapproval, the flat palms coming down on his face, instilling a shame that had stayed with him ever since.

Obiefuna felt himself now in an involuntary ascent—Ekene was pulling him up. "Just dance, Obi," he said. "Come on, show me you still have it."

Obiefuna grabbed Ekene's hands and set his feet down to halt Ekene's swaying movement. He shook himself free. He felt woozy, light-headed. His eyes had begun to spin. "We're too old for this foolishness, Ekene," he said. He could not help smiling.

"There's no one watching," Ekene promised.

"I've forgotten most of the moves."

"Anyhow you do it is fine with me."

"There's no music—"

"Why do you have me?" Ekene said. He began to clap his hands and stomp his feet to provide a makeshift beat: "Onye ga gba egu iya! Ga gba egu iya! Obiefuna ga gba egu iya!"

At first Obiefuna laughed—at the choice of song, Ekene's comic posture, the absurdity of the idea—but Ekene kept at it, undeterred, and so Obiefuna put a foot forward and then another. His steps were ungainly, awkward, a poor imitation from memory. But he was conscious, too, of a loosening in his limbs, the wind in his ears, a familiar feeling of freedom. He danced, oblivious to the heat of the sun rays, to the windows that were flung open, curious heads peeking out to observe. He danced until his knees hurt and he collapsed on the floor, laughing and struggling to breathe. The late-evening sun stood above him, its glow so warm and radiant it made his eyes ache. And yet he was reluctant to sit up or turn over. Ekene hovered above him, glugging water from the bottle and smiling a smile of accomplishment. Obiefuna thought for the first time how wonderful Ekene was, how brilliant and bright and beautiful everything was. He felt a delicious swimming in his head; the air that floated about him dried the sweat on his skin and calmed him. Later, Ekene splashed water on him and called him "chicken" and laughed when he mock-frowned. By the time Ekene pulled him up to a standing position, throwing a hand over his shoulder and leaning close to whisper, "Well done!" it was dusk and Obiefuna was filled with a sense of wonder at the world's perfection in that instant, and he was tired and sleepy and thirsty. Up above, he could hear the sonorous singing birds.

SIXTEEN

Uzoamaka sat by herself on the long bench in the waiting room. The other benches were fully occupied, hers vacant save for herself, but twice now someone had walked up to the seat beside her, and then changed their mind halfway and diverted. More than once, she had toyed with the idea of going to the bathroom to study her reflection, see what made people so scared of her, but it was too much of an undertaking, and in another minute Anozie would emerge from the doctor's office armed with a new list of her medications, information on lifestyle adjustments health-wise, and his determination to see her get well. His attitude towards her nowadays made her feel, at times, as though she were being courted. There was an alertness to him that she had not always been aware of, an instinctive desire to assist her, a penchant for patience she had almost forgotten he had.

"Your husband is different," a nurse said to Uzoamaka on one of their visits. In the next room, via a see-through glass door, they watched Anozie note down something the doctor was slowly enunciating.

"How do you mean?" Uzoamaka asked.

"Well, you know, he's present," she said. "Not many of them are."

Uzoamaka continued to give her a questioning look. The nurse hesitated, seeming to weigh her words, before she proceeded. "Most times, when we give these diagnoses, the person who's always hovering and falling asleep on a chair and disregarding visiting hours and generally being a pain to doctors is the wife. Too few men stick it through."

"You think I should be grateful?" Uzoamaka said. She wished she had taken out the sharp edge in her tone.

But the nurse did not mind. "No. I just think it's worth noting that he is quite unlike the men I've encountered in my career years." She gathered up her tools and rose to leave. "And trust me, nne, it's a long one."

The nurse's words had stayed with Uzoamaka. She realized how easy it had been for her to take Anozie's loyalty for granted. It went without saying that she would do the same for him were the roles to be reversed, and it had not occurred to her to think of gratitude as something she ought to feel. And yet she knew, if only from prior knowledge, that the nurse was right. She was reminded of an old neighbour they used to have, a pastor whose wife had died while birthing their ninth baby, conceived because the pastor's family had insisted on a boy. Her death had shocked the neighbourhood; it was the first time Uzoamaka saw herself actively mourning the loss of someone she knew only vaguely. A few weeks after the funeral, the pastor was seen going out with another woman, whom he later married, and for many months the neighbourhood opinion was divided between people who believed he'd had a direct hand in his wife's death and those, including Uzoamaka, who absolved him of any illegality but derided his lack of love for her in the first place. Later, Uzoamaka would wonder about exactly what she had found obscene. Was it that the man had remarried despite the circumstances surrounding his wife's death; or the ill-timing of the marriage, demonstrating the man's ability to bounce back from a tragedy that staggering in such short while; or that he had remarried at all?

She had begun, lately, to wonder about Anozie. He seemed to her now as a lost sheep; there was no doubt in her mind that her demise would break his heart. She could not picture him taking a new wife merely weeks after her death. But if there was one thing she knew by now it was never to think for one moment that she truly knew how a man's mind worked. They had been married for exactly twenty-two years, built enough memories to fill a room. How much longer till memories of her faded, till those twenty-two years wasted away and left him with nothing, finally unbound, able to gaze at another woman with desire?

Time had after all been kind to him. He still had the fine lines of youth. She was able, even now, to look at him and experience a rush of desire, the same way she had felt when she first saw him twenty-two years ago. She was the new girl in training at the salon, and he was the newly settled apprentice on his way to establishing his own business, and somehow this mutual newness became for Uzoamaka an auspicious sign. His shop was down the road from where she worked, but close enough to the mama put where the girls at the salon got their lunch. Uzoamaka volunteered to run food errands, and she would say hello to him as she passed by his shop, carrying that brief, ordinary glimpse of him with her for the rest of the day. He was unmindful at first, almost dismissive, of her crush. She gathered that, at only twenty, she was too young for him—he was eight years her senior—but it did not stop her from pursuing him headlong, doggedly, sometimes surprising herself with her own desperation. Nothing had mattered to her, not his apparent pennilessness, not his strong rural accent, not even the fact that he had a girlfriend at the time—an older woman Uzoamaka sometimes saw around. She had sent letters, even if he never really responded, had taken to randomly stopping by to chat, until he asked her to dance at the downtown club one evening in April, which ended with her waking up in his bed the next morning, a little sore between her legs, but buoyed by a ridiculous sense of accomplishment.

She knew she ought to love him for this—his faith in her improvement, his insistence on a fantasy of their growing old together, his refusal to imagine the situation otherwise. Still, occasionally, she felt a flutter of impatience at what seemed to her an uncharacteristic weakness, a propensity for self-denial, a tendency to daydream. And when he told her, "If you keep thinking you won't survive this, then you won't," she would hide a smile because since when did he become a person who engaged with trite motivational thoughts like this? "And maybe that's what you want, isn't it?" he would persist, determined now to get a reaction from her, which she would not give, would not even know how to give. "You think dying makes you better somehow abi? Go ahead and die, then!"

Later he would apologize and tell her he was just terrified, and she would sigh without speaking because there was no way to make him understand that it was comforting sometimes to think of her death as a choice she was making, rather than as an inevitable fate she could not get round.

SEVENTEEN

The flowers were in full bloom; the trees, recovering from the shedding of the previous season, sprouted tender, green leaves. The session was new, the expectation fresh after the holiday. Around campus, for many of the boys in SS3, the feeling was a palpable sense of breathless euphoria, high off their soon-to-be-graduate status. For Obiefuna, it was different. He sailed through the next terms with a staying, nebulous sense of unease. He had "arrived" in a sense, as he was now in the most senior class at the seminary, his final year, but he felt none of the elation he had expected to feel, no anticipation of what was coming. He watched with a feeling of remove in the months that followed, as his classmates counted down to their last days, as they laid out their strategies for WAEC, compared notes on the girls from their sister school who would be coming over to join them for the exams. Most of the boys had smuggled in their phones, and midnights now were spent on long calls with the girls. Nicknames were scribbled on the walls, new uniforms were bought and stored in boxes, to be unearthed on the first day of exams.

Obiefuna was still unused to being called "senior" and not having to submit to someone else, to being the first to rise and exit the chapel at the end of service, to being regarded as "in charge." Everyone but he had moved on—his class was spoken about now in the past tense. In March, they handed over their prefectships to the succeeding class. Obiefuna had passed on the honour of being asked to recommend a successor, but he approved of the eventual selection—a quiet, decent boy he knew only vaguely. The boy shook his hands and told him thank you, his smile so full and filled with promise that Obiefuna had to excuse himself and go to the toilet, where he leaned against a wall and burst into tears.

The stories had found their way to him somehow. Senior Papilo had yet to be admitted to university. Senior Kachi had performed so well in his WAEC exams that he received a scholarship from a university in Cyprus. No one knew anything about Sparrow. "Probably in prison being passed around," Jekwu joked, the one time Obiefuna dared to ask.

The problem with graduation was the nagging prospect of confronting the future, of having to answer the question: what next? Obiefuna did not know. He was set to write the external exams in May, and he hadn't a clue what he wanted to study at university. He had no knowledge of what was out there. The seminary had been easy: its threat had become familiar, the trick for survival learned with time. And it was easy here, clad in a uniform like a hundred other boys, to hide. Obiefuna was reminded of something his father would say to make a point about secrecy. "Every lizard lies on its belly, so we cannot tell which one has a belly ache." In a few months, Obiefuna would become a graduate, ushered out into the world; he would be like a lizard forced to lie on its back, inviting the world to take a peek at his aching belly.

On some nights, the voice of the chaplain's wife came to him; her words "There's nothing God cannot do if you tell Him and believe in your heart that He will do it" brought a brief, floating comfort. Once, as they walked back to the house from evening classes, Obiefuna veered off the pathway, giving a vague excuse to Jekwu, and headed for the chaplain's house. His parked car in the driveway indicated he was home. Obiefuna reached out to knock, but the door gave way under his knuckles, into the hallway. Obiefuna looked around before he stepped inside, savouring for a moment the coolness of the house, and that faint citrus scent. The living room was in mild disarray, as if someone had abandoned it in the middle of putting it in order. Or someone had ransacked it. Perhaps the house had been robbed. Suddenly, in quick sequence, Obiefuna took note of the cushions strewn across the floor, the human absence from the room, the queasiness in his gut. He turned to the door, his heart hammering in his ears, and for a wild moment he imagined the chaplain's wife, or worse, the chaplain himself, apprehending him at the door. He could picture the resulting chain of events: the chaplain's shock at finding him there slowly turning to alarm when he saw the state of the living room, hasty conclusions drawn. He was halfway down the hallway when he heard the sound. Obiefuna froze in his steps and listened for it again. He stood waiting for a long time until his legs went to sleep, and he wondered if he had imagined it, and then it came again. It was like the grunt of someone in pain. Obiefuna crouched on his knees. He could feel the heavy pressure on his bladder. He should have gone on ahead with Jekwu. Perhaps the chaplain had been shot by the robbers in his bedroom. Were they still here? Would they come out and shoot him, too? He gazed longingly at the slightly open door of the corridor, conscious of an instinct to bolt through it and not stop running until he was far away from here, and yet knowing he would never get his body to do that. He listened for footsteps, nursing a fleeting, foolish hope that the corridor was dim enough to hide him. When none were forthcoming, he crawled towards the bedroom, hating the brightness of the living room. He could already see the chaplain in his mind's eye, sprawled on the floor, drawing his last breath, in a pool of his own blood. He could picture himself in front of the chapel, being extolled as the decisive, resourceful student who had saved the chaplain's life. He was one knee away from the bedroom door when he heard the grunt again, followed by raspy breathing. He stopped and turned to the door from where the sound had come. It was the bathroom. With his heart hammering in his ears, he got to his feet and looked through the slightly open door. The chaplain was standing in the middle of the bathroom, one hand holding on to the hand-tub, the other lathered in soap and moving furiously up and down his erect penis. There was something about the way his face contorted, as though he were in intense pain. He let out a final grunt and leaned on the wall to catch his breath. With his eyes closed, his breathing becoming more measured, his gradually deflating penis held securely in his palm, he looked unsettlingly at peace. Obiefuna wanted to back away and run, but he realized almost immediately that he wouldn't be able to move even if his life depended on it. And so he didn't—even as the chaplain turned on the tub to wash his hands and face, even as the chaplain wiped himself clean with a towel, even as the chaplain opened the door wide moments later to find him standing there.

❖

He wondered if the chaplain would kill him. It seemed easy enough for the man to leap at him and strangle him with those massive hands, or bash his head with something heavy until he was unconscious, burying his body somewhere in his garden. A simple case of a student gone missing. It wouldn't occur to anyone that their own chaplain had done it. In retrospect, he would wonder why it had not occurred to him to be scared, how easy it had been for him to sit there on the soft cushion at the chaplain's order and to watch the chaplain dress, walk the length of the living room to shut the main door and finally settle down next to Obiefuna.

"You didn't see anything," the chaplain said. Up close, Obiefuna could see how tiny his eyes were, bloodshot and uncanny, eyes that were capable of killing. And so he nodded. Feeling had returned to his legs, but he accepted, with a calm resignation, that he could not leave. The chaplain looked at him for a long moment and then he closed his eyes and exhaled, that single act appearing to completely drain him of energy. When he opened his eyes again, they were bloodshot still but tired; the murderous look in them had gone.

"What is your name, my son?" he said.

"Obiefuna."

"Obiefuna"—the chaplain rolled the word around his tongue—"sometimes the devil attacks us in our weakest state and forces us to commit sin, even when we don't want to."

Obiefuna nodded again. The only thing he could think of was how badly he needed to urinate.

"You see," the chaplain continued, his hand outstretched as though to touch Obiefuna, and then he paused. For seconds, his hand was held in mid-air, and then he brought it to his own face and began to weep. Obiefuna recoiled at the sound: a harsh, choky noise that seemed to come from the pit of his stomach, catching in his throat.

"I'm so sorry, my son. I'm so sorry," the chaplain said between sobs. He seemed so small now, the huge, fearsome man Obiefuna was familiar with almost a wispy memory. He wondered if the chaplain would be alarmed if he got up and walked to the bathroom to urinate. The chaplain lifted his face after a while; slick mucus trailed from his nose, and he made no effort to wipe it away.

"I can't stop myself. I want to stop. I can't do it," he said.

Even in the dim light, Obiefuna could make out the desperately pleading look in the chaplain's eyes. Obiefuna knew desperation. He was familiar with the feeling of blanching under a weight larger than oneself. Obiefuna leaned forward and touched the chaplain's arm. "Tell me," he said.

Beneath his palm, he felt the chaplain go rigid. He finally swiped at the mucus trailing down his noise, smearing it all over his chin, and Obiefuna instantly wished he had simply let it be. Through tear-stained eyes, the chaplain stared back at him. Obiefuna imagined the chaplain was attempting to regain his composure, and he half expected the man to recover long enough to ask him to get out. Or finally to give in to his instinct to kill him. But the chaplain told him. What had started out as a group exercise with a few friends when he was young and ignorant was now an addictive habit. Once, he had touched himself to climax from behind an altar as he preached the night's sermon. The more he tried to stop himself, the greater the force propelled him. And he tried. He had fasted for weeks, and he only used devices that were not connected to the internet. He had burned his hands.

"The pain kept me from doing it for a full week," he explained to Obiefuna. "I did it the following week, before my wounds properly healed."

The thought came to Obiefuna then, small but insistent, nagging at his mind. What had been the title of the chaplain's sermon that Sunday? He searched in his brain for the word the chaplain had used, surprised at how entirely it eluded him. It had been a single, simple word, otherwise inconsequential, but one that had haunted him for months. He realized now, with a sudden jolt, that the chaplain had essentially been speaking to himself that day. He could recall how tearful the chaplain had been on the altar, as though personally affronted. The turn of events was too absurd; he wanted to laugh.

"I think God led you here, my son," the chaplain said. "He needed someone else to remind me of my shame."

Obiefuna kept his head bowed. He had come here to confess to the chaplain. He had come burdened with remorse, expecting to be at the receiving end of absolution. He had been thrust into a position for which he was unprepared and unworthy. God had to have a weird sense of humour.

"My son"—the chaplain touched the hand Obiefuna had placed on his arm—"you can't tell anyone what you saw."

Obiefuna looked up at him again. It was too dark to see his face, but there was something desolate about that voice that broke Obiefuna's heart all over. He wanted to tell the man that he would sooner throw himself from the top floor of the classroom complex than say a word to anyone. But he said, "I won't."

"Thank you, my son, thank you," the chaplain said over and over. He leaned across to Obiefuna as if to embrace him, but he buried his face in Obiefuna's shoulders instead, quivering as he wept. The chaplain's head was heavy, and soon Obiefuna's shoulders ached under the pressure. His bladder, unbearably full now, was beginning to throb, but with the weight of the chaplain's head on his shoulder he could not move. He stared ahead at the miniature vase on the centre table, devoid of flowers, as his collar grew damp with the chaplain's tears and mucus. He needed to get up and make his way to the toilet to urinate. He needed to let himself out through the door and never come back. But Obiefuna did not move. He remained where he was.

EIGHTEEN

The phone rang in the middle of dinner. It was Uzoamaka's policy to ignore it, because she knew it was Obiageli, who called every so often now to "check in and see how you are doing." The last time they spoke, Obiageli talked about planning a trip to the mountain with her pastor for a one-week fasting and prayer session for Uzoamaka. She asked if Uzoamaka wanted to join them, and Uzoamaka replied she would rather not expend her limited living energy on a tiring prayer session. She had intended to be funny, but Obiageli did not laugh.

After the third ring, Uzoamaka rose and went to the living room to take the call. She knew Obiageli meant well. It was just easier sometimes not to have to deal with her depressing air. She took the call, bracing herself for the litany of moot-voiced concern from the other end.

"Did you hear that Achalugo is dead?" Obiageli asked after the first hello.

The phone slightly slipped from Uzoamaka's hand, and she gripped it more tightly with both hands to keep it in place. "Which Achalugo?" she asked, even though she had known just one in her entire life.

"Which other? The one you know!"

Uzoamaka buried her head in her hands. Behind her, her family carried on with dinner, and the sound of spoons hitting plates filtered into her consciousness. She pictured a sudden flash of bright-red nail polish, an old but well-maintained wig, a sonorous voice singing. Over the phone, her sister's voice trailed off. "They said he was sick for a very long time," she said. "Probably AIDS. Who knows?" She made a spitting sound. Uzoamaka could hear a finger snap. "He was never going to end well."

Uzoamaka breathed evenly. It was just like Obiageli to be emotionally obtuse. They drifted to Uzoamaka's health, and as she gave breezy updates about her doctor's appointments, she was distracted by the sound of singing, a clear sound of sharp laughter ringing out. After she hung up, she remained sitting, silently staring at the ground.

"Is everything all right?" Anozie asked from the dining room.

Uzoamaka closed her eyes and exhaled. She shook her head.

Later, as Anozie emerged from the shower to join her in bed, she told him about Achalugo. As she spoke, she was struck by her inability to sum up his life. He had been too many things all at once, so that everything she said, every aspect of his life she related, felt merely like scratching the surface. She could not think of him without thinking of the tinkering of his ogene, the sultriness of his voice as he beckoned all to dance to his melody. No one knew for certain how he had come by his style. For as long as any of her peers could recall he had been there, just the way he was. She believed that he was an orphan, having lost both his parents in the Biafran War. She knew of one of his uncles, a wealthy businessman who had tried many times, unsuccessfully, to have him checked into a psychiatric hospital, knew that the futility of this action was largely due to the village's intervention. They stressed that he posed no danger to anyone. He lived alone in his tiny hut near the village square. When he was not performing, he was a smallish man of nondescript bearing, bore no resemblance to the larger-than-life figure that made even the most unfeeling detractor throw an unconscious foot forward in homage to the sound. He had possibly died alone in that hut, with no one by his side.

"You're really affected by this," Anozie said.

She told him about the dance auditions, his words to her about finding something else she was good at.

He nodded absently and lifted the bed-covers to join her in bed.

"Every one of us cannot be good at the same things. Life is about variety. It's a major principle," Uzoamaka said.

Anozie lay still. He was quiet for a long time, and she wondered if he had drifted off to sleep, but then he said, "This is about Obiefuna, isn't it?"

Uzoamaka said, "To send him away, Anozie. To shut him out at first instinct without a second thought."

"Everything I've ever done was for his own good."

"Telling yourself that many times does not make it any truer."

"Now what is that supposed to mean, Uzoamaka?"

"Do not use your good intentions to justify your deeds. There must have been a part of you that wanted to singularly punish him—to help him maybe, but to punish him first of all."

He stared at her. Even in the dark, she could see his eyes as they travelled quickly along the contours of her face, searching for a meaning in her statement, and then she saw realization dawn on him, saw the skin of his face relax in mild astonishment. "You knew."

She sighed. "He came from me, Anozie."

"You knew," he repeated, as if she had not spoken, as if he could not believe his own discovery.

"All this while you defended him and made me look like the enemy and you knew?" he said.

She wondered if he were going to cry. There was a part of her that wanted to hug him and tell him it was all right. You are not the worst father. No one taught you how to love a son that was different.

"All this while I used to think, 'If only she knew, she would understand.'" Anozie said. "I gave you the entire benefit of the doubt. I assumed you of all people knew what was right and wrong. So tell me, do you think having a homosexual for a son is ideal? You think it made me happy to have to send him away?"

Uzoamaka exhaled. She wondered if Ekene could hear them from the boys' room. How had she taken so long to do this? What kind of a mother was she? "Frankly, Anozie, I don't care how you feel. At the end of the day there's only one person truly suffering here and it's not you—or me."

"But he's my son," Anozie said, the tone of his voice falling to match hers. "It's my job to be tough on him."

"A child does not scald his palm with burning coal placed on it by his chi," Uzoamaka said. "You have to know when you start playing God, Anozie."

"Oh, so now it's all about me and what I do. But what about you? You won't even see him nowadays!"

Uzoamaka drew back. She had the feeling of having been struck in the face.

Anozie said, "I didn't really mean that. I'm just not thinking well right now." He reached out a hand to hold hers. "Please don't be angry."

But she didn't even have it in her to be angry. What she felt these days was tired.

Later, just as she drifted off to sleep, she felt Anozie nestle close to her. He said, with a voice nearly as low as a whisper. "I don't care for him less than you do, Uzoamaka."

Uzoamaka closed her eyes then and said, without turning, "It's one thing to love a child, but it's an entirely different thing for the same child to feel loved. The boy is young. He'll get a lot of 'buts' in his lifetime. A home is the last place a child should feel conditionally loved."

NINETEEN

From his very first day of resumption, more than two years ago, Obiefuna had marked the second week of March 2010 in his mental calendar as significant. The inter-house sports competition at the seminary occurred only once every three years, and, in the months leading up to it, the boys could talk of nothing else. Obiefuna figured that among the many reasons for this was that it was a rare opportunity for contact with the girls from the sister campus, who were invited both to partake as well as to observe the boys. Coerced by Jekwu, who was the outgoing prefect of Blue House, Obiefuna participated in the preliminary hundred-metres senior-race category—and, to his astonishment, he was selected to represent the house. He spent long evenings practising with his teammates under Sir Offor, who was the housemaster, and even longer hours practising on his own with a stopwatch. He had been informed that one of his opponents was from Yellow House, an SS2 boy named Wole, who, in classic Usain Bolt style, was said to derive fun from delaying a start during practice, only to beat his opponents all the same. The week before inter-house sports, Obiefuna practised non-stop until his knees and back ached and Sir Offor ordered him to hold off until Friday, concerned he would overwork himself and come down with a fever. On the morning of the event, he watched the preceding races from the sidelines with Jekwu. He rejected the water Jekwu offered him, holding Wole's eyes across from him the whole time. The girls from the sister school had arrived ahead of the race and were now gathered around a canopy, watching the games under the stern eyes of matrons. Finally, it was time for his race. Obiefuna strolled towards the track, hating the smile on Wole's face. The other three boys from the remaining houses filed through. Obiefuna crouched on his knees on the coach's instructions and looked up at the lane stretched out in front of him. When the sound of the whistle went, he was acutely aware, and in a sense relieved, that Wole had not assumed his customary hesitation. Obiefuna felt his legs trudge on beneath him, disconnected from his mind. For a while, he was aware of nothing, only the sense of his running. In front of him, there was no one. Behind him, he could hear the heaving of breath as the other runners tried to catch up. He was going to get gold. There were just a few metres to go. And then, from the corner of his eyes, he saw Wole catch up with him and speed past. Obiefuna put in a last-minute effort, but Wole seemed possessed by a spirit. Obiefuna finished a close second. He could see his housemates' jubilation. From around him he heard loud calls of his name, and he thought he could make out Jekwu's voice. He shrugged off the glucose that was offered to him as he went ahead to receive his medal. He liked the firm weight of the medal against his neck. The next round of athletes were already taking their positions. Obiefuna shook hands with the housemaster and house prefects before proceeding to the tap near the house to wash his feet. He was bent over, scrubbing, when he sensed someone hovering around. He looked up to see Wole.

"Good run," Wole said.

"Thanks. You too."

"At first I thought you were going to win, and I wasn't going to have it, so I . . ."

Obiefuna stood upright and looked Wole in the eye.

Wole caught the look. "Erm, I'll go," he said, heading off.

As Obiefuna walked back to the sidelines to watch the remainder of the races, he heard his name again, this time in a feminine voice. He turned in the direction of the sound and was mildly alarmed at the sight of a group of girls clustered around the laboratory. From afar, he could spot the famous Bee occupying the centre of attention, as expected. Who could possibly know him? He stood watching, until one of the girls emerged from the group and began to move towards him. It took him a moment to recognize Rachel. Obiefuna smiled. How much she had changed in just less than two years, from the slight, unassuming girl he had seen that day with Senior Papilo to a rounder, fleshier young woman. Not the prettiest of girls, but she held her own. Her name wasn't unknown on the boys' campus.

"Rachel," he said, resisting the urge to hug her, aware that eyes watched them from all over.

"Ha, Obi! You've grown so tall!" She was laughing her cackling laugh, looking at him in wonder. Even her shyness was gone. "You don't ask of me again."

"Haba, Rachel."

"Eziokwu," she snorted. "You don't look bad at all. With your small bia bia." She reached out to tug at the sprouts of beard on his jaw. "I was just telling my friends how wonderful you were on the track."

He chuckled, pleased. "Thank you."

"How are you?" she asked.

He shrugged, trying to sound at ease. "I'm better now that you've asked to see me."

She pulled a face. "Oh, but it wasn't me who asked to see you," she said, tilting her head slightly in the direction of the group, her eyes twinkling with mischief.

Obiefuna looked over at the group and almost smiled at how swiftly they averted their gaze. He tried to guess from their body language who had asked to see him, but they all seemed identical to him, or maybe he was no good at reading these things. When he looked for too long, Rachel slapped his arm lightly.

"Ah, Obi. Be a guy man. You don't stare at a lady so openly."

"Which of them?" he asked, returning his gaze to Rachel.

She clucked her tongue playfully, enjoying her role as the potential matchmaker. "The one in green."

"There are three girls in green, Rachel."

She rolled her eyes. "The beautiful one."

Obiefuna looked over at the group again, laughter bubbling in his throat at her insinuation, but it died down when he saw what she meant. Even from a short distance, he was awestruck by the roundness of the girl's face set in a fixed smile as she listened to Bee, her hair cropped close to her head, her slender curves outlined in her sportswear. How could he not have noticed her earlier? He saw now that it was she, not Bee, who commanded the group's attention. The mini-circle seemed to have formed itself around her.

"So . . ." Rachel dragged out the word. "You want me to go talk to her?"

Obiefuna cleared his throat. The sun burned the back of his neck. "Sure."

Rachel winked at him and headed off. Obiefuna felt a rush of gratitude for having applied generous deodorant that morning before the race. Even though he was soaked with sweat, he still smelled good. He watched as Rachel spoke to the group, her back turned to him. She gesticulated intermittently, not turning to him once. None of the girls glanced at him as she spoke, until he began to wonder if she was even talking about him. He did not understand the need for a lengthy explanation when everything was supposed to have been prearranged.

Finally, the girl did look at him, and from afar he felt a weakening in his knees. He took steady breaths for when she would walk over to him, but it was Rachel who turned and walked back to him, half jogging the distance. "She has agreed to talk to you."

He stared at Rachel in blank confusion. The realization came to him gradually. Although the girl had sought him out, she needed to feel chased. She was giving him the hint to take the first, major step.

"Okay, please ask her over here," he said.

Rachel gaped at him. "No! You are supposed to go over to her."

"In the midst of the others?" The thought filled him with terror.

Rachel said, "Have you never done this before?" She was watching him with an open, teasing expression. But he could make out a genuine puzzled curiosity in her voice. He wanted a drink of water.

"They'll give you privacy if you ask nicely," Rachel assured him, heading back to the group.

Obiefuna exhaled. He brushed at his arms to lay his arm

hair flat. He waited until Rachel was settled within the group before he advanced, deliberate in his strides, worried that the calculated, laidback slouch he leaned into as he walked was too laidback. As he approached, he wondered if the girls' sudden laughter was directed at him. He stood a few feet away from the group and tried to keep his back straight.

"Hello," he said, but the girls went on conversing as if oblivious to his presence. He caught Rachel's eyes and she gave him an encouraging nod. He cleared his throat and tried again, louder, "Excuse me."

The girls looked at him. Their expressions were one of faint puzzlement, as though they were seeing him for the first time. Only the girl kept her eyes averted. "Hello," he said again generally, and then addressing her specifically, "May I speak with you briefly, please?"

She looked at him. "Me?"

"Yes."

She hesitated, wanting him to know that she had hesitated. She glanced around the group as if seeking their approval. Obiefuna had the sensation of precious sand slipping between his fingers.

"All right," she said finally, stepping aside from the group to join him. He walked her towards the mango tree closest to the laboratory, acutely aware that, with his hands criss-crossed behind him, the figure he cut was more of a chaperon than a potential date. Her fingers, small with closely cut nails, played with the hem of her top. She smelled a heady floral perfume. Obiefuna wondered if she would flinch if he reached out to intertwine his hand with hers. What could he possibly say to her? What lines would dazzle her without coming off as slick? He wished Jekwu were here with him. Jekwu would know what to say.

"Where are we going?" she asked suddenly.

He came to an abrupt halt and looked at her in bewilderment. He glanced backwards and saw that they had walked past the mango tree and had gone a distance.

"Erm." He cleared his throat again. "I don't know, taking a walk hopefully?"

She chuckled. "A really long one," she said. "I promised my friends I'd only go a safe distance."

"You're safe with me," he said, surprising himself. She looked into his face, her eyes mysteriously sombre, and then she smiled what he could only interpret as a pitying smile. She had heard that one before. Was she repulsed? Did she find him disappointingly shallow? He considered apologizing, but even the thought of it seemed ridiculous.

"You ran well today," she said.

So she had watched him. He suddenly wanted to return to the race and snag the gold medal. Wole or no Wole. "Thanks."

"Can I see?" she asked, gesturing to the medal around his neck.

"Sure." He took it off his neck and held it in his hand for an awkward second, uncertain whether to hand it over to her or place it round her neck. As if sensing his dilemma, she smiled her sweet smile and bent her head towards him. Obiefuna almost laughed, flushed with warmth, and slid the medal round her neck. His fingers lightly brushed her chin.

She held the medal in her hand, twirled it this way and that, and the only thing he could think of was his sweat resting on her smooth, clean neck. "It looks real," she murmured, studying it carefully as he watched her. When she looked up, she caught him staring, and he darted his eyes, embarrassed. "So, Mr. No Name . . ." she began. She tilted her head sideways to watch his face, wanting him to know she was teasing him.

He smiled. “Obiefuna.”

She returned the smile. “And I’m Sopulu.”

The name took a moment to click. Obiefuna’s felt the smile fade from his face. So she was *the* Sopulu. The same one Jekwu had talked about, the same one everybody seemed to be talking about. There she was, right before him, twirling his medal round her neck, inviting him. He wondered if this was a crude prank, a dare perhaps. He imagined her bursting into sudden laughter at his raised hopes. He imagined the other girls running over to them in uniform amusement, awed and impressed at how far she had gone to play her part.

And when, just in that moment, they were interrupted by a hiss and Obiefuna turned around to see the girls waving at Sopulu, he panicked that his fears had been proved right. But Sopulu did not laugh. She seemed, if anything, disappointed. Obiefuna realized then that the signal had been a warning: the matrons were now on active prowl to apprehend errant girls. Sopulu turned to him with an apologetic smile.

“Bad luck,” she said. “Maybe next time.”

She reached round her neck to take off the medal, and he extended his hand to receive it from her, and, in doing so, his hands brushed her elbow, and she paused in her movements and looked at him. Obiefuna dropped his hands to the side just as she let go of the medal and he watched it settle back on to her chest as if it had always belonged there. He could feel a rumbling in his stomach and he wondered whether to touch her, but she had already turned away from him with a small wave, and so he settled for a final nod, watching her saunter back to her friends.

THE SWIFTNESS with which the news spread before morning astonished Obiefuna. By breaktime, a horde of boys had crowded his desk, seeking details of his encounter with Sopulu.

Did he know her from home? Were they perhaps related? Did they share the same school, father or mother at some point? It was as if they simply refused to entertain the possibility of a more intimate scenario.

"Probably some ex-school-prefect stuff," Philip said, half questioningly, his tone a dare. Obiefuna had heard the story of how he had pined for Sopulu from their junior days, adamantly refusing to acknowledge her rejection year after year.

Obiefuna ignored them all. The earnestness with which they probed him annoyed him, but in a way he enjoyed their speculation, the air of mystery he now seemed to have acquired with his continued silence, and the quiet understanding that he now belonged. He was one of the boys, not just because of an entanglement with a girl from the other campus, but because it was with the most sought-after girl. It was why, when he received the letter from Sopulu two days later, delivered by a junior student in a sweet-scented envelope, he let the boys around him see the name written on it in her elegantly slanted handwriting.

"Maybe you wrote it to yourself?" Philip said to general laughter, although Obiefuna could tell even Philip did not quite believe that himself.

He read the letter under the cover of night, the crickets outside the window and an occasional snore from one of his roommates the only sounds to be heard. She had used a fancy pen, and the ink sparkled when it caught the light from his torch and gave off a sweet floral scent.

Obiefuna,

What an interesting name. I'm thinking: Obim efugo, and you would have to return it to me. I remember seeing you in our campus when you came to carry bunks, and I had to ask the girls around. I wasn't surprised to learn you joined us in SS1. I would have remembered your face from Junior WAEC. I like your eyes. I like you. Write to me.

Sopulu

He folded the letter and put it in his box. On second thought, he took it out and put it in his cupboard, placed underneath his bag of sugar, where Wisdom or any of the other boys would not be able to get to it without his key. He remembered the day she spoke of. The week before prefect handover, he had gone over to the girls' campus across the road when Sir CY had instructed him and Edet, the labour prefect, to select and supervise a few junior students, who were to be tasked with replacing the broken bunks in the boys' section with unused extra bunks from the girls' section. How had he not seen her that day? How was he the only one unaware of her existence? And how had she, out of all the boys in his class, chosen him? Jekwu said the only one she had ever dated in the past was Makuo, a brief fling during their Junior WAEC that fizzled out over the long holidays. How could she settle for him, an obvious step down from Makuo? He wondered, too, what her friends thought of him. Although they had related to him that day, Obiefuna had sensed an unvoiced uncertainty that leaned towards disapproval, except for Rachel. How could he hope to impress a girl like Sopulu when he essentially had nothing to offer? Not money, not terribly good looks, not even charm. He could picture the benefits of becoming associated with her: an escalation of his status among his classmates, a renewed respect in the eyes of the Big Boys. They might not welcome him into their clique, especially considering Sopulu's history with Makuo, but they would be forced nonetheless, however unwittingly, to acknowledge his acquired worth. And there she was, the absolute prize. He thought of her in the following days, her sweet smile flashing before his vision as he walked to class, as he did his laundry, as he sponged himself in the bathroom. Her voice swarmed in his head, invading his thoughts at random. And he stepped into rooms, aware of the eyes that looked up and held him, aware of the whispers that trailed his exit. Sopulu brought him recognition among his own peers. It seemed as if with her—or with the idea of her—his own classmates finally saw him, and he was at once grateful for, and resentful of, her power. One time, he looked up from browsing through a shelf in the library to meet Makuo's eyes on him. The cold rage in them puzzled Obiefuna. The version of the story he heard had painted the break-up as a mutual affair, with Makuo bragging afterwards that he had initiated it because he discovered she wasn't all that, no doubt enjoying the unspoken message: he was the only one capable of hurting a girl like Sopulu. Obiefuna wondered now if there was more to the story. Had Makuo been dumped? Was this mildly terrifying look he shot at Obiefuna jealousy because he still wanted her? Or was it simply disappointment at her choice of replacement, and how it reflected on his own worth?

Obiefuna reread the letter often, savouring the warmth of each sentence, a tingling sensation coursing through him to his toes. He wished it were longer. He wished it could go on forever. Her request that he write back to her filled him with vague terror. What would he write? What could he possibly say to her? He considered requesting Jekwu's help. He could see Jekwu coming up with an appropriate response in one go. But he knew also that Jekwu's response would be a superficial, lovey-dovey gimmick. Obiefuna wanted something different, something unusual. He wanted to give her something to think about for days on end.

A full week passed and her letter remained in his locker,

unanswered. Often, in the dark of night, he crafted responses to her in his mind, tossing them away immediately for being too long or too short, or not sincere enough. Once, he woke up before dawn with the thought of her on his mind and reached for his notebook, scribbling without pausing to think. It was on his reread that he realized what he had done, what he had been doing all the while. The other letters in the book, dense with melancholy and weighed down with longing as they were, slightly accusing, had all been written to Aboy. The absurdity of it stunned him. He was holding in his hands a letter from one of the prettiest girls he had ever seen and all he could think about now was Aboy's face up close to his, smiling in his sleep. Obiefuna balled Sopulu's letter in his fist and put it in his mouth, chewing until it was near-mush to prevent anyone from picking it up from the bin. He made peace with the fact that he would never write back to her.

As the days went by, he half expected a second letter from her, saddened by the prospect. And then he laughed at his presumptuous foolishness. Of course she would never write to him again. Her pride had been wounded by the fact that, probably for the first time in her life, she had been ignored. For this, she would hold him forever in her heart, in a space reserved for those for whom she harboured the most intimate ill-will.

But when he saw her again, nearly a month later, standing at the door of the rector's office in the company of a matron and a few other girls, her expression portrayed none of the disdain he had anticipated. It held worse—a blank unrecognition, as if she did not see him, as if, for her, he had simply never existed.

OBIEFUNA WAS SURPRISED at how quickly the time sped past. It seemed to him one moment they were writing mock-preparatory exams, crowding around the notice board to check the results, hoping to do equally well in their main WAEC exams, and the next it was the last week of April and they were submitting their subject listings to the dean, counting on one palm the days to final exams in May. He spent one dull Thursday afternoon in the small office of the Guidance and Counselling Unit, which was crammed with books and smelled too strongly of camphor. The counsellor, a slight man with thinning white hair and a full beard, tiny eyes peering from behind thick-rimmed glasses, seemed as though he were in need of guidance himself. He repeated the same basic questions over and over and took a long time to understand simple things. So Obiefuna did not tell the man about the confusion he felt about his actual choice of study—medicine, which would impress his mother, or engineering to please his father—or his lack of a preferred institution. He told the man he would study biology at the state university in Port Harcourt, instantly regretting it, as it launched the man into a long-winded lecture about how with his grades he could do better.

The first day of WAEC filled him with anxiety. He had spent the whole night reading and yet felt even more unprepared by morning. At the physics practical, he kept glancing over at the girls' row until the invigilator asked him if he needed a skirt to join them. Later, he hovered around the purifier, leaning in to tap it lightly when he felt a dull smack on his buttocks. He turned to see Rachel. He had spotted her earlier that morning and half expected she would do something like this before long.

"Hey," he said.

"You know she's an arts student, right?"

"What?" he asked.

"Oh, please." She rolled her eyes. "Don't think we didn't notice all those glances you were shooting across. At some point I was worried you would mix the wrong things and set this whole place on fire."

Obiefuna laughed. Even in his tense state, Rachel could make him feel light.

"She's not here, Obi," she said after a while. "You'll see her when we write our first general paper on Monday, mathematics?"

"Oh," Obiefuna said. That was almost a week away. In total, they would write only four mandatory papers together. He didn't know whether to feel relief or disappointment.

Rachel was watching his face. "I expected better, Obi," she said.

"Rachel, I'm really sorry. It wasn't what I planned at all."

"What do you mean?"

"I mean, it was just too much," he offered, sighing. He knew he wasn't making any sense. How could he ever get her, anyone, to understand? Rachel was looking at him, her head angled slightly to one side, ready to take in his explanation, but he said nothing else, merely kept his eyes on the floor, until her friends called out to her and she gave a final, disappointed exhalation, and went ahead to join them.

The following Monday, Obiefuna watched from his seat as the girls arrived, easily spotting Sopulu in the crowd. The seat numbers were scribbled on the desks in chalk, and she walked down to the front, where she settled down without fuss, and he was stricken with a strange longing for what could have been. He wished she had not sought him out. And then he wished more rationally that he had been built in such a way as to be able to acknowledge and act on the affection of a pretty, dreamy girl beyond simply feeling flattered. He cared for her. He just wished she understood that it was not in the way she wanted.

❖

THE LAST DAY came too soon. Obiefuna spent the night revising his civic education textbook in a silent hall packed full of his classmates, and he felt half sleepy just before the exam. He found the questions easy, common-sense questions on corruption and citizenry, and he shaded in the answers quickly, passing on the test paper scribbled with his answers to the seat partner behind him who had been nagging him all along, inwardly amused at the irony. Finally, the bell went off for submission and a sudden scream rang out, hurting his ears. All around, the boys were drumming on their desks and dancing, the girls laughing and hugging one another. Obiefuna felt light-headed. It had finally come to an end. His three years of being here had shored up enough memories to last a lifetime. He felt a sudden calm envelop him, overshadowing his wilder instinct to scream, to rip his shirt, to mount the desks and stomp hard until they cracked under his sandals. He felt a tap from behind, and when he turned Jekwu wrapped him in an embrace so tight his airway was temporarily severed. Jekwu smelled faintly of deodorant and sweat, and Obiefuna found in this a burgeoning nostalgia that made his eyes water. Jekwu eased the hug and held Obiefuna's jaw with both hands, laughing into his face. "We did it, Obi!"

"We did it," Obiefuna repeated in a lower voice. What was wrong with him? This was the moment he had lived for; one that he had dreamed of from the very first day. He was happy to be done, to be moving on to a new, auspicious phase of his life; and yet he could only manage words in a whisper. He would miss Jekwu. He would miss Wisdom. He would miss this place, with its strict rules and crowded dormitories and putrid toilets. Jekwu leaned forward as though to hug him again, but he held his shoulders and whispered in his ear, "She's coming, Obi."

Obiefuna tensed. He took a deep breath before he turned. Sopulu was walking towards him with her usual grace, his medal in her hand. He could see her friends clustered in a corner, watching. Jekwu gave him an encouraging tap on the back and walked away. Sopulu stopped in front of him.

"Hi," he said.

"I just came to return this." She extended the medal to him. Her expression was impassive.

He reached out to take it, and then held on to her hand. She looked at him, her eyes steely, but he could feel her arms slacken and he knew she would not pull away.

"I can't tell you how sorry I am, Sopulu."

"You didn't even have the decency to reject me to my face."

"I could never reject you."

"Right," she said. He could tell she was annoyed, but determined, as always, to maintain her poise. She would not let him see her break a sweat. "I guess your letter got lost on the way? Or you didn't receive mine, maybe?"

"I did. It meant everything to me, and I tried to write back. I just . . ." He faltered, breathed evenly. "I couldn't."

Whereas he had felt a slackening earlier, what he felt now was a grip. She was looking at him with eyes that were no longer steely. "Why?"

For the earnestness in her voice, for the firmness of her grip on his palm, and for her trusting, sympathetic eyes tracing the width of his face, it felt right to tell her the truth, to unburden himself, regardless of the consequences. "I don't really . . ." he began, and then his courage failed him and he dropped his eyes. "There's . . . someone else."

"Oh," she said simply. Obiefuna kept his gaze on the floor. It was absurd. How often did a girl like Sopulu show interest in someone like him? She was not the kind of person who needed to compete. He was filled with a stupid, delirious urge to laugh.

"From home?" she asked.

He looked up at her and nodded.

She smiled at him then and he thought again how unreal it was to have to navigate life looking as she did, with the smooth, caramel-coloured skin of her face, the curly hair framing her forehead.

"That's really lovely," she said. "Good thing we're done with exams, right? You'll get to see her again."

For a moment, he was puzzled, not certain who she was referring to. And then it occurred to him that Sopulu had assumed whoever he was missing had to be a girl.

"No, she . . . left." He finished with a sigh. It sounded so apt. Left.

She eased her hand away from his and brought it to his chin. He wondered fleetingly if she was going to lean close and kiss him. For one second, he willed her to. He was aware of her friends looking at them, aware that everyone was looking at them.

"I'm really sorry, Obi. I did not know."

He wanted to tell her it was all right, but he could feel the tears clogging his throat, making his eyes twitch, and so he simply nodded and placed a hand over hers on his chin. She caressed his face, smiling at him, and it was when she swiped his eyes that he realized a tear had slipped out.

"Come on, be a man," she teased with a light laugh, and he couldn't help but smile. Finally, she pulled away from him and waved him goodbye. He watched her walk back to her friends. He could make out a scowl on Bee's face. As they exited the door, Rachel turned to him with a wink.

TWENTY

As soon as Obiefuna opened his eyes, two things became apparent to him. The mattress beneath him was uncomfortably springy, with an impersonal, albeit familiar smell. As he pulled himself up to a sitting position, he was hit with a splitting migraine that made his vision temporarily blurry. He held his head in his hands; his tongue had a clammy taste. Around him, the loud buzz of intermingling voices penetrated his skull, further aggravating his headache. Obiefuna fell back on the bed.

"Olodo, you're finally awake," a voice said.

Obiefuna opened his eyes to behold Jekwu's face smiling down at him. His mouth smelled of cigarettes. Obiefuna leaned sideways to retch.

"Hey, none of that. You already made too much mess last night," Jekwu said.

Obiefuna looked at him. "Last night?"

Jekwu laughed. "My God, you don't remember! You were drinking like a tank. My roommates were so impressed."

Obiefuna leaned back once more into the bed. His tongue had the feel of sandpaper.

"What time is it?"

"12:46."

"Oh, God."

"Which reminds me," Jekwu said, "Ronald will be here soon to get the mattress. So get up."

Obiefuna frowned. Ronald was Jekwu's School Son, a small, smiling boy who often offered to do Obiefuna's own laundry. "We're leaving tomorrow, Jekwu. What will you sleep on tonight?"

"I'm leaving tonight, actually," Jekwu said.

"What? Why the hurry?"

Jekwu was silent.

"Jekwu?"

"I just need to be home today. My father insisted."

Obiefuna sat up to look Jekwu in the eye. "Jesus, you're lying through your teeth."

Jekwu rose from the bed with an uncomfortable chuckle.

"What's going on?" Obiefuna asked.

"What? Nothing!"

Obiefuna reached forward to grab Jekwu's wrist. "You no longer trust me?"

Jekwu gave him a look and sat back down. "We've got something planned for V-night," he said after a moment.

"What?"

He exhaled. "Festus."

Obiefuna looked at him, eyebrows raised.

"He's had it too easy, man," Jekwu said with a shrug.

"What do you mean?" Obiefuna asked.

Jekwu looked around the room to rule out eavesdroppers, before he leaned in close. "We want to teach him a lesson. Maybe break a few bones, you get? Keep him in check."

Obiefuna let go of Jekwu's wrist and leaned back in bed. Variety nights were the closest the seminary came to lawlessness; with departure scheduled for the next day, civil codes were unofficially relaxed, and, in the few hours before holiday morning, long-held scores were settled, crude pranks pulled: Obiefuna had witnessed a boy's eyes and mouth taped shut with glue as he slept; another had all his clothes soaked in water; but, while occasionally overdone, there was a general, fundamental sense of non-cynical, if extreme, humour—nothing intended to permanently scar.

"You're with me on this one, Obi?" Jekwu said, a question that was not a question.

Obiefuna stared at his hands. He remembered Festus's face in the dark night, illuminated by the moonlight, in what seemed now like a lifetime ago. He had gone on his knees, humiliating himself, to give pleasure to someone who would not touch him with a stick in public. Still, ironically, it had been for him a sort of victory.

Jekwu was looking at Obiefuna, his frown deepening, new questions forming in his brows. "Obi?"

Obiefuna nodded.

Obiefuna stood still, his back held straight. It was a busy night; the roar of voices could be heard from a distance. Still, enclosed in that small space between two guava trees, hidden from view by tall blades of grass, Obiefuna felt sealed off from the world. He wondered if the other boys felt the same way. Although he could not see them, he was aware of their presence, lurking in the dark, awaiting their prey. Obiefuna could no longer remember what the plan was. He regretted not wearing his watch. A long time had passed and his legs had almost gone to sleep when he heard the soft squelching of wet grass as footsteps approached. He heard Festus's husky "Are you sure?" It was too dark to see from where Obiefuna stood, and he held himself still, pausing his breathing even if it was probably not loud enough to be heard.

Then, Jekwu's voice: "Take off your clothes."

A giggle. Festus said, "Take them off yourself."

More giggles. The sound of a metal jingle as the belt came off. Obiefuna closed his eyes. He experienced a rush of urine to his bladder, the unbearable urge to ease himself. His head felt oversized, swollen to bursting. He bit down hard until he could taste blood. And then, without thinking, he stepped out from his cover. The boys had stripped off their shirts, and only their white singlets were immediately visible. They jumped with a start when he emerged, and each scurried to a guava tree. It was easy to tell them apart by their features, even in the dark: Jekwu's showed irritated surprise, Festus's sheer bewilderment and terror. The next few moments proceeded in a swift sequence. The other boys charged forward from their hideouts; while ruffled, they were still intentional, bent on their purpose. Obiefuna counted six of them. He stood several feet away and watched as they took Festus down with a clean sweep. He watched as the first blow landed on Festus's face, followed in rapid succession by multiple punches and kicks. He watched Festus resist, his frail arms thrashing above his head, his cries ringing out clear. They beat him until he no longer resisted, until his cries had been reduced to a whimper. Jekwu did not participate. Like Obiefuna, he, too, watched, arms folded across his chest, a smile on his face. And when the beating stopped, it was he who led the way back. Obiefuna followed in their wake, but midway he turned to look at Festus on the ground. In the faint light from the stars, he seemed odd, curled in on himself like a tortoise. The sound of crickets and frogs pierced through the night's silence. Obiefuna walked back to where Festus lay and squatted over him. His eyes were closed, but he opened them after a moment, and they rested on Obiefuna's form, deadpanned. Apart from his soft breathing, Festus did not make a sound. He allowed Obiefuna to wipe the dirt off his face, brush away the sand that stuck to his hair, fit him into his shirt. He did not resist when Obiefuna tucked an arm underneath his armpit to help him up. And when he was finally standing, Festus drew back to take a long inhale and spat in Obiefuna's face. It landed in one piece on Obiefuna's chin, the force of it, the unexpectedness of it, causing Obiefuna to stagger backwards, lose his balance and crash to the ground. He touched the slime on his left chin, repulsively warm against his skin, too stunned to speak.

"You tell yourself you're one of them," Festus said. He lowered himself, his face inched so close to Obiefuna that he could smell his breath. "You call them your friends, but it could very easily have been you today, Obiefuna Ani."

Obiefuna continued to look at him. From where he sat, under Festus's glare, Obiefuna felt smaller, weaker, as if it were he, and not Festus, who had endured the group beating. He waited for Festus to kick him, in an attempt to get back his pound of flesh, but Festus, smiling a small, eerie smile, simply turned round to retrieve his slippers from the ground, and then stumbled his way out through the grassy path.

PART

THREE

TWENTY-ONE

PORT HARCOURT, 2010

He looked the same, the smile just as she remembered, the perpetual sweat formed around his brows, the way his eyes glowed as he stared down at her. Her boy. She had woken that morning with a knot in her stomach that stayed even after the sun came in the sky. She spent the day on the balcony, overlooking the yard, feeling her heart soar and sink simultaneously at the slightest sound from the gate, an odd blend of relief and disappointment when it revealed someone else. Then she had dozed off, his face in her mind, clear, and suddenly there he was before her, rocking her shoulder in a gentle motion, his sweet smiling face staring down at her.

"Mummy," he said.

Uzoamaka looked at him. It had been way too long. She received him in her arms, nestled her nose in his neck. He had a few scars on his face from a recent breakout, and she was unable to pinpoint that unfamiliar scent on him. He pulled away from her to study her up close. She could see the questions in his eyes. She caressed his face. "I'm just tired, nnam. There's food in the kitchen for you to eat. Go and keep your bag inside."

He nodded, straightened up. "Where's everyone?"

"Your father went to the shop. No one ever knows where your brother goes on a Saturday."

Obiefuna laughed. How much she had missed that sound.

"I'll check the field," he said. "I should surprise him."

She nodded. As he changed indoors, she listened for the sounds. He emerged from the room in a simple pair of shorts and a jersey. He had lost a lot of weight, but he seemed taller somehow.

"I'll see you soon," he said.

She nodded, watched him head for the door. As he made to leave, she called out, "Obiajulu."

He turned to her.

"Welcome back," she said. He seemed momentarily confused, and then drew a slow, puzzled smile, nodded with enthusiasm and bounded down the stairs. She watched him sail out of the yard in a short sprint, the wind billowing about him. She had never seen him freer.

HE WAS CHARACTERISTICALLY an early riser, but nowadays Obiefuna was curled in bed, deep in sleep, hours after Ekene had left for school. Uzoamaka surmised it was the inevitable effect of the change of environment. Still, it bothered her slightly to note this significant change in his routine, wondered if it hinted at something larger. He had grown up away from her, just as she had with her own parents, and she had the nagging feeling now of being just one step removed from truly knowing him. She watched him watch her, saw the questions in his eyes accumulate. She offered breezy replies when he asked, knowing even then that he did not buy them. She asked him for details about the seminary, and he indulged her curiosity, describing his escapades at school. She was reminded, as he spoke now with a familiar gusto, of the way he would recount an event in his childhood as they walked home from the salon, his insistence on re-enacting the scenes down to the impressions, as if determined to transport her into the actual moment, remembered how it had always been a highlight of the day for her. So she played her part and humoured him, exaggerating her elation at his having been made a school functionary, her sympathy when he described a race he had lost, her disgust as he went into details of the over-crowded houses and putrid toilets.

"What about your friends?" Uzoamaka asked him. "Did you make any?"

He told her he was friendly with everyone.

"So no close friends?" Uzoamaka pressed. She was treading on slippery territory. Once she had voiced it, there would be no way to take it back. She could already see the hairs on his arms standing on end.

"Close friends?" he asked.

She could have laughed it off then, veered into a light-hearted conversation, saved him, and herself, from having to discuss it. Uzoamaka sat up instead, steadied herself. "Yes," she said. "Like Aboy."

She watched him retreat, pressing his back into the seat behind him as if he could disappear into it if he tried hard enough. She thought she saw his face drain of colour; she wondered if she ought to get him a glass of water.

"Mummy . . ." he said.

"It's okay," Uzoamaka offered, when he did not continue. She considered reaching out to touch him, but the part of him that was closest to her—his right knee—was not within reach, and she had a feeling that any overt movement from her would be interpreted as violence and alarm him. So she settled for a smile. "I understand."

He began, unsurprisingly, to avoid her. He was stealthy, or at least he tried to be, exiting rooms the minute she stepped in, taking his meals in the kitchen only when he was sure she was absent, holing up in his room for whole days at a time. The few times she chanced on him, he would not even look at her. He was polite but evasive, responding to her with gestures and awkward body movements, and in instances where words were absolutely necessary, he offered them in stuttered monosyllables. Uzoamaka had thought herself prepared for it; she thought she understood his fear, the shame of being what he was, and especially his feeling of having disappointed her. Yet it made her sad to watch him sink into himself, think of her as anything but primarily on his side, her heart breaking the one time she overheard him communicating his boredom to someone over the phone and he had used the words "trapped at home." In September, a month after his nineteenth birthday, he told her he had been admitted to the University of Port Harcourt and would need to move out very soon; and she took in his smile, heard a tone of relief in his voice, and, in spite of her pride at his achievement, she was wounded by the thought that he considered his exit from home, from her, as a kind of freedom.

Two weeks after the conversation, as she stood peeling potatoes on the kitchen worktop to make porridge for dinner, Obiefuna spoke from behind her.

"Do you hate me now?"

Uzoamaka tensed and dropped the knife. He knew better than to startle her like that. She turned around to face him. "Only if you've done something wrong," she said carefully. He had his body turned away from her; he was gripping the door handle with his right hand, steadying himself for more. Uzoamaka turned back round and picked up a potato.

"You weren't here the last time I came home," Obiefuna said. She heard an accusation in his voice.

"I went to see your aunt Obiageli," she said.

"You left the day before I arrived," he said. "Ekene told me you came back three days after I returned to school."

Uzoamaka closed her eyes and drew in a breath. She realized she had been wrong. What she had heard as an accusation was indeed despair, fear, an apology.

"It's me, Mummy, isn't it?"

Uzoamaka turned round again to look at him. He had moved away from the door and was now squarely facing her. It was always such a surprise to gaze upon his features nowadays. His sheer growth astonished her. And she realized that in her fixation on his physical aspects, she had let his emotional side slip past her. She had crystallized him in her mind as her little boy of a time past, so simple in his disposition. But that boy did not have the ability to look her in the eye and demand answers, had simply accepted things as they were. The one standing before her, this nineteen-year-old who looked only vaguely familiar to her, would not shy from the truth; he would not cry himself into a fever over a few bruises on her arm.

So Uzoamaka said, thinking about the present Anozie had given him for his eighteenth birthday, and what she had now to give him: "I have cancer, Obiajulu. It's late stage. I might have just a few months left."

❖

EVEN THE HOUSE HAD CHANGED. Their once-wide living room that had always seemed to have unending space seemed so small now, furniture crammed together and getting in his way, so that during the first few days after his arrival he had kept bumping into things. The room had lost its sparkle, peeling paint coming off the walls and sticking to his shirt when he leaned back against them. The window in the bedroom was broken, half of the glass having shattered in the last storm, Ekene explained, and in its place now was cardboard that let in a little water whenever it rained. Ekene had grown taller in the past year, towering a foot above Obiefuna, sprouting fuzzy hair on the side of his face, bubbling with laughter at every turn. Obiefuna could no longer picture the gangly, dour-looking boy he had left at home, nursing an ever-stern expression. On his shoulder was a belt-inflicted scar from where their father had whipped him after he arrived home from the field late one night, smelling of liquor. Obiefuna could not envisage Ekene handling alcohol, but he could no longer tell with Ekene anymore. The once easy-to-read boy he knew was gone; in his place was an emerging adult, every inch a cut-out of their father. He was banned from the field now, even though, Ekene complained, he had impressed the coach the last time he had played, and an academy in Ghana were almost on their way to signing him. The liquor incident had been the last straw in a series of mishaps, and their father would not hear of any signings.

"But you can talk to him, Obi," Ekene begged; "he might listen to you."

Obiefuna said, "Why on earth would he listen to me?"

"Oh, but you're the good son now," Ekene said. "He talks these days as if you walk on gold."

Obiefuna sniffed, looked away. Now that Ekene had voiced

this observation, it seemed more real. He had imagined that the courtesy with which his father treated him nowadays was all in his head. It seemed like a reluctant affection, responding to his greetings with a certain fondness. When his WAEC results were released, a decent mix of As and Bs, his father had smiled so broadly that Obiefuna feared the skin of his face would remain permanently altered, and afterwards he had spent over an hour berating Ekene on what a far cry he was from his elder brother. Because of this, and because of the desperation in Ekene's eyes, and because he was aware that Ekene would resent him forever if he didn't at least try, Obiefuna approached their father with the request on Ekene's behalf, adding the promise of personally making sure it would not affect Ekene's preparation for WAEC the following year. Their father seemed to give it only a moment's thought before he said yes. Obiefuna accompanied Ekene to the pitch on the first day, receiving the handshakes of the boys and giving breezy replies to their enquiries about school. Ekene lagged behind on the first half, making several wrong passes and wildly losing a penalty kick, until the coach threatened to remove him from the pitch and place him on the bench for many matches to come. By the second half, Ekene was back on form, employing the many skills he was known for, losing three defenders with a single dribble and sliding a winning goal between the posts. In the uproar that followed his victory, as he was hoisted on to the shoulders of his teammates, Ekene looked across at Obiefuna with an expression that Obiefuna could only interpret as love.

He had felt at home, truly happy to be back, until his mother had talked about Aboy. As he had sat across from her that day, his chest hurting from the force of his heartbeat, the one question in his mind had been when she had found out, and how. But when she smiled in the end and told him it was all right, he got his reply in her eyes. Of course she had always known. He had done his best to hide, to protect her from the disappointment. Yet she had known all along, had still referred to him as her son. How much their time apart had changed her, both softened and hardened her at the same time, made it easy for her to casually accept him, and even easier to relate the news that would forever alter his life and sense of direction.

AND JUST LIKE THAT, his life changed. His mother's revelation became real, a hulking, malevolent thing, always present in the room, taunting him, terrifying him. Obiefuna lay awake for long hours, even as crickets' noise filled his ears. He listened to Ekene sleep, snoring without care. Ekene had known. "I wanted to tell you, Obi," he confessed later. "I swear! But you know, she made me promise."

Obiefuna said he understood. But he did not understand at all. He had always thought the way people dealt with tragic news in the movies unrealistic—the way they carried on with their lives, their routines unaltered. He did not understand how Ekene could bring himself to head for the field each day and dazzle everyone with his skill, possessing the information he did, did not understand how their father summoned the motivation to rise every morning and head to the shop for another day of sales, as if everything were normal. And his mother. He lived now in a state of perpetual surveillance. He watched her as she set about her day, making breakfast and lunch and setting the table herself, all while humming a Chinyere Udoma song that expressed gratitude for God's many surprised blessings—striking in its irony. He imagined the cancer eating her from the inside out, he imagined her body failing her. It was the worst form of betrayal. He wanted to be close to her, he wanted to help her to fight what was coming, to put it off somehow, and at the same time he could not bear to be around her. He found her forced enthusiasm suffocating, felt irritated, and then guilty, because of her contrived cheerfulness, her easy resignation. And, while he pitied her, a part of him almost resented her. For, after all was said and done, her inability to help it notwithstanding, she was going to leave him alone to deal with the world.

His friends reached out. Obiefuna had not planned to say anything. By now he had perfected the state of dual personalities, and with Wisdom and Jekwu, as much as he treasured them, he knew not to let himself be vulnerable with them, to control the aspects of himself they had access to. Still, somehow, Jekwu had heard something in his voice and pressed him until Obiefuna told him. Jekwu told Wisdom, and now they called him often to check up on him. He hated talking to them, hated the tone of commiseration in their voices as they spoke to him. His mother was still alive, able to walk unaided, even carry out some household chores, which she insisted upon. Sometimes, looking at her, he considered the possibility of a misdiagnosis, a doctor's cynical exaggeration, her own ploy to orchestrate a crude prank on him. Sometimes, when they all had breakfast together at the dining table, someone would share a joke, and, in the moment they laughed, Obiefuna felt, if only temporarily, at home. And then there were the days when the house had an echoing silence, and the cancer seemed at its strongest. Obiefuna took to running to clear his head. The swift rush of wind past his ears, the curious stares of passers-by, the occasional blaring of warning horns made him feel alive. Once, he returned home to find the door unlocked, his mother asleep in her room. He took off his running shoes and headed to the bathroom to have a wash. Naked, he hovered over the bucket, looking at the pool of water that reflected the blank expression on his face. His heart thumped softly against his chest. Obiefuna felt a stirring in his groin. He pictured Aboy's lips curving into a sleepy smile. He recalled the soft feel of Sparrow's clean hands on Obiefuna's skin, the warmth of his breath as he moaned Obiefuna's name. He remembered Senior Papilo, his graceful, sinewy torso, smelled the cool, woody scent of his cologne. From next door, he could hear his mother's breathing, sounding to his ears like a pant. His penis felt warm and hard against his palm, and at first his movements were slow, undecided, and then, after he lathered his hands with soap, they became faster, more intentional. He felt himself swell to bursting. And just at the tip of his climax, he fell against the wall, descending to the tiled floor. And as he sat quaking from the force of his sobs, the chaplain's voice came to him, the word floating without effort into his memory after all these months of searching: "Reprobate." How nice-sounding and yet so chastising. How crisply damning.

TWENTY-TWO

The university campus had a vastness that unnerved Obiefuna. Used to the smallness of the seminary, the recent quiet of home, he found the university to be like a rowdy village, the real world in every sense of it, a large, unquantifiable, unknowable country, pathways trailing on and on until his legs ached. Obiefuna spent the first few weeks struggling with adjustments, trying to memorize locations, to tell faculty buildings apart without looking at signs, to discover where to board shuttles. He was yet to fully process the implications of being there. His admission itself had come as a surprise. It was Rachel who informed him that the list was out, interrupting him in the middle of a Saturday clean-up. She had called, distraught, to say she had missed out, and Obiefuna held on to the phone long enough to console her, his heart hammering in his chest at his own prospects. He took a bus ride to the university campus, and spent several minutes hustling and shoving at the crowd of fellow aspirants swarming around the notice board; but there his name was, boldly displayed at No. 12 under the Department of Optometry, next to his UTME exam number, announcing his new status.

His mother stared at him blankly when he stood in front of her with his suitcase. Then she said, "You're leaving?"

"It's for university, Mummy," Obiefuna said. "Remember?"

"Of course." She looked away from him for a moment, and turned back to him with a smile. "I'm so proud of you, my son."

Now he was here. It had been hard to come. As he put his things together, as he looked at the available campus accommodation, as he boarded, on that final day, a bus headed for university, he thought endlessly of his mother. He pictured her face during lectures, her patient smile, heard the steely, determined voice with which she promised him she would be all right. She was seeing a doctor at the public hospital in Mile 1. He had gone with her to one of her appointments, and she held his hand all through the consultation, her head leaning sideways on his shoulder, as if needing to draw her strength from him. He felt the dull ache on his shoulder from the weight of her head, oddly reminiscent of the chaplain's—a person begging to be saved. And, although he had promised himself not to, he burst into tears in the taxi on the way back home, and she just sat there staring ahead, unmoved.

At university, he tried to lose himself in a new routine: he walked long paths to class, he read his books in the library, and he availed himself of the free tutorials provided by the second years. After contributing the most to a class presentation on common eye diseases, he was elected the class representative. He amassed new friends; was elected secretary of a new Igbo organization; became accustomed to running into a familiar face whenever he stepped out, even on that large campus. Yet, as much as he tried to distract himself, he thought of his mother, worried for her. She told him, in a voice that almost sounded chastising, to worry instead about a good grade, as she would be all right. For the first few weekends, he dutifully boarded a bus from campus for the half-hour journey home to see her, until his father had finally intervened, on his mother's request, and instructed Obiefuna to stay at university and study on the weekends instead. She assured him she was taking care of herself; she was trying out some new medication now and already felt improved somehow, she said, and he willed himself to believe her. Initially, he called every day, holding his breath for when she would answer, awash with relief when her tired "Obiajulu" came on from the other end. But soon, as the term picked up pace, his calls grew increasingly fewer. He received an odd sort of succour from his roommates—eleven boys slumming in a space originally made for six. They readily shared their provisions with him, involved him in their activities and took him along for small campus parties, even though he found himself having to step out midway. One of them, Mike, introduced him to a girl, and they talked awhile before the vibe stalled; his replies to her texts and calls became more infrequent; and then he ran into her one evening after class, walking hand in hand with a boy he recognized as a senior. She called him later that night, and when he ignored it, she delivered the break-up news via text.

Obiefuna stared at the message awhile before he deleted it and went to bed. The next morning, he woke with a funny feeling in his stomach and a headache. In class, he sat perched, staring without comprehending at the lecturer. His phone buzzed throughout the class—a call from his mother. Finally, he stepped out to take the call, but it was only Ekene on the phone.

"Obiefuna?"

He sighed. "I'm missing an important lecture. This better be important."

Silence.

"Ekene?"

"Obiefuna," Ekene repeated, took a breath. "It's Mummy."

PART

FOUR

TWENTY-THREE

The room was square and small and without character: brightly lit with white fluorescent bulbs, chic chandeliers hanging from the ceiling, enhancing the small, framed colourful paintings that lined the white walls. Obiefuna stood to the side with a glass of undrunk wine in his right hand and his left sunk in his pocket as he stared at the painting before him, conveying, he hoped, the amount of melancholy appropriate for a discerning art lover. He felt overdressed in his immaculate starched white tunic and leather shoes, next to the casually dressed strangers who nodded approvingly at the paintings, gave into sudden exclamations, their words and activities a fuzzy blur. Patrick had insisted on picking out the clothes for the occasion, too swept up in the elation of finally being allowed to show his work at this gallery.

And Obiefuna had deferred after a brief argument, just as he had known he would.

Now Patrick stood at the far end of the room speaking with the gallery owner. Earlier, Obiefuna had watched as he led potential buyers to the wall where two of his works were displayed, speaking animatedly about the paintings, one of them a line drawing of two dancing figures, the other a nude portrait of a headless female body. They listened with polite smiles, nodding as if his words held the most significance, and then they turned away. As the night progressed, Obiefuna sensed that Patrick's acquired charm was dissipating, as he became unable to hold up the act any longer. He would step out in a minute or two, on the pretext of getting fresh air or using the restroom, and then stick a needle into his arm, or smoke a wrap of marijuana, and he would return wasted, and the night for him, for both of them, would be over.

THEY HAD MET ON 2GO. Obiefuna had not considered Patrick attractive, with his lanky frame, teeth yellowed from drugs. But he had been relentless in his pursuit of Obiefuna, who found himself driven to curiosity about him. It wasn't meant to last. Just a minor fling, a way to get his mind off things. Yet, oddly enough, that was the very reason he had stayed. His mother's death, only a year prior to meeting Patrick, had left a hole in his heart, and, numbed by tragedy, humbled by grief, he demanded little from life. More than that, he had been haunted by monotony. Every breath he took felt like a taunt, every face he saw, every voice he heard, was too familiar, too reminiscent of what he had lost, reminding him too much of how altered his life had become. So that to have Patrick, unassuming and eccentric as he was, felt like a refreshing distraction. Through the eight chaotic months afterwards with Patrick, even on the worst days, when he genuinely feared for his safety around Patrick, Obiefuna was in a sense grateful to him—to the warm nights he created with weed and alcohol, the much-sought-after escape from reality.

The funeral had taken place without event. Obiefuna had found himself dry-eyed in the days leading up to it, staring, with a sense of remove, at the procession of people who came to deliver their condolences. They were a mix of people he was familiar with and those he knew nothing of: their neighbours, a few of his parents' friends, his mother's customers from the salon. They were friendly and sympathetic; they said kind things about his mother, referring to her in the past tense. On the day of the funeral, Ekene had declined to go in to see her one last time, and Anozie had suggested Obiefuna skip the process, too, but he had insisted, the act appearing to him in that moment to be the most important thing in the world. He lingered at the casket, watching her. She was dressed simply in a blue gown and headgear made from a pretty, butterfly-patterned Ankara fabric, a gift from Anozie. Up close, she looked merely asleep, her lips set as if about to break into a smile. He wanted to reach out to touch her, but his father nudged him gently from behind and he realized he was holding up the line. Obiefuna pressed forward, his father's hand on his shoulder, preventing him from turning back, as if shielding him from the situation; and once they were out of the room, the curtains fluttered closed and Obiefuna stood there, staring.

He had pulled through the service with an appropriate amount of stoicism, offering a grateful smile to the sympathizers who squeezed his shoulders and told him to deal with the loss like a man. He had almost made it through. But right at the graveyard, just as he was offered a spade to scoop the earth and throw it in the grave in fulfilment of the dust-to-dust rites, he felt his acquired manhood slipping. The weight of the spade in his hand, the sound of the red earth hitting the coffin, the sea of doleful eyes on him, had felt too much. It was from Ekene, weeks later, that he learned of his own descent to the ground as he handed over the spade to the priest, his violent wriggling on the ground while their father tried to restrain him, the mud that clung to his clothes and hair even as his father pulled him up and held him tightly in an embrace.

Now, nearly two years later, he was still getting accustomed to grief, to the fact that he would never see his mother again. He had made peace, too, with the reality that his life would never return to what it was. There was something mindless and weird about loss—it never really got better; it never really went away. It surprised him sometimes, the intensity of the pain, sometimes physically manifesting in the form of a chest ache. It had a way of lurking, just slightly removed from his consciousness, suddenly springing forth without warning, often at inappropriate times. Sometimes it caught him in the middle of laughter, reminding him that he could not share that happiness with the one person he had loved most in the world; and, in the space of a moment, he succumbed once more to that tumbling feeling of drowning and drowning, never quite hitting the bottom.

"SPECTACULAR SIGHT, NO?" a voice said now from behind him.

Obiefuna half turned to see a middle-aged man in spectacles. He had both hands stuck in his tight trouser pockets, so that he walked as if slightly dragging himself.

"I noticed you've been admiring it awhile," the man said. His voice was firm and yet lilting, as if he could issue orders and break into singing in the same breath. He stepped forward into the light, and Obiefuna realized he had misjudged his age. "Handsome" might have been too much of a reach to describe him, but he was the kind of man you would let your eyes linger on just a moment longer.

"Yes," Obiefuna said, although he had barely noticed the painting at all.

"You have a good eye," the man said. His tone was admiring. "Tell me, what do you think about it?"

"It's beautiful," Obiefuna decided.

The man nodded slowly, a placid smile on his face, as if disappointed by Obiefuna's shallowness. He began to talk about the painting, the simple and yet breathtaking concept of it, the careful attention to detail. He thought the painting strikingly expressive. It was the kind of art with the potential to appreciate in value over time, if you were more into that side of things.

"Would you buy it?" Obiefuna asked.

The man paused. He looked slightly taken aback. "I mean I would. But you seem to like it."

"Oh, I have no use for it," Obiefuna said.

"You don't like art?" He sounded personally affronted.

"Not as much as you, it seems."

He laughed then, the suddenness of the act taking Obiefuna by surprise. He took off his glasses and wiped the lenses with a tissue-like material and then fixed them back on. Obiefuna had never known anything more seductive.

"So what's your thing?"

Obiefuna said, "I study optometry. Third year."

"Ah, the eyes," he said, with a fond mock-impression, giving Obiefuna a casual once-over. "Optometry student and wanna-be art lover? You could do much worse."

They laughed together, and then there was silence.

"It was nice to meet you . . ." the man said, prompting.

"Obiefuna."

"Obiefuna," he repeated. "Tell you what," he began, sliding

over to cover the small space between them, "why don't you pass me your phone number and allow me teach you one or two things about art?"

His name was Miebi. He had grown up in a village not too far away, but had moved to the city for university as a young adult and stayed on. He lived alone, in a two-bedroom apartment just outside the main city. The house had a quiet, understated charm to it, surrounded by a thick fog of trees and flowers that drew tiny, multicoloured birds to the front yard.

"It's where I come to get away from the craziness and high cost of you people's city," Miebi said on the first day of Obiefuna's visit, with a light laugh. Behind the house he kept a small farm, consisting of a poultry cage and several mini-ponds in plastic containers housing varying sizes of catfish. On the first day, they sat side by side on the sofa in Miebi's living room, talking art and politics and their favourite TV shows, laughing at the similarities of their interests, and then they were leaning in to cover the already small space between them, tracing patterns on the backs of each other's hands, the heat radiating off their bodies. The kiss, when it happened, left Obiefuna breathless, and he slid off his shirt with an ease that surprised him, reaching for Miebi with a desperation that felt alien. In bed, they explored each other's bodies; bursting with desire, but fully naked, they stalled, hesitant, unsure how to proceed. They had not, up until then, discussed sex, and it felt awkward to begin now. They lay on their backs next to each other, their breathing slow, in a hollow but satisfying silence, until Miebi laughed, seeming nervous, and mumbled, "Too fast, eh? Let's give it time."

The second time, Miebi was out of condoms and so they lay astride on the wide mattress, stripped of their shirts but with their trousers on, their heads touching as they looked up at the ceiling.

"I don't really feel it," Miebi said.

"Feel what?"

"Sex. Penetrative, that is. I'm more of a make-out guy." He laughed his nervous laughter again. "I'm weird, I know."

Obiefuna pulled himself up to a slightly sitting position, his elbows supporting his weight, and he half turned to look down on Miebi's face. It had to be love, this syncing of likes and dislikes, of qualities, of sexual preferences. He kissed Miebi's nose and said, "I guess I'm weird, too."

In the following weeks, weeks he spent in Miebi's apartment when he was not at university, he grew accustomed to Miebi's life, seamlessly fitting into the fringes, unable to imagine himself elsewhere. The first night he spent in Miebi's house, he slept through Miebi's jarring alarm, waking up a few minutes past 11 a.m., to find Miebi in the dining room, typing on his laptop. "Morning," Miebi said when he saw him. "I was beginning to worry you had died." He laughed. "You slept through my alarm and yours."

Obiefuna smiled. He sat across from Miebi at the other end of the table, which was set for one. It was a Saturday morning. He could not fully recollect the events of the previous night, but the sleep had left him clear-headed, fully refreshed. The floor was cool against the soles of his feet, and he felt the pleasant fatigue that came with a good rest. Miebi watched him as he scooped scrambled eggs into his mouth. Obiefuna could get used to this.

After that, he spent more nights there, and soon he was taking the bus to university from Miebi's. Slowly, his personal effects started to accumulate in Miebi's home, and after a few of the increasingly rare weekdays he spent in his dormitory, he returned for the weekend to find a whole wardrobe section cleared for him, bare hangers for his use, a small reading table assembled in a corner of the room where he could work. Obiefuna slept for longer, studied alone in absolute silence, scored higher in his tests. Miebi rose earlier, before dawn, to go running, and then devoted an hour or two to the farm before taking a shower and heading out for work. Obiefuna readjusted his alarm to sound a few minutes after Miebi's, so he could observe Miebi from the window as he worked. At first, Obiefuna offered to help, but it quickly became apparent to him that Miebi, accustomed to a routine perfected over time, was more efficient alone, and so Obiefuna settled for watching as Miebi paced about the backyard with single-minded purpose. He seemed attuned to his surroundings, collecting newly laid eggs to fit in the crates in the kitchen, letting the chickens out of their cages to roam around, occasionally picking up a squawking chicken to inspect it more closely. He included Obiefuna in other ways: asking Obiefuna's opinion on certain procedures, dropping random trivia and interesting facts about the animals he domesticated, mock-frowning when he spotted something unpleasant in the farm, which sent Obiefuna into giggling fits. He fed the fish last, the simple act of assembling their feed and dispensing it into the water as they hustled endlessly, flapping their fins and spilling water about, seeming to Obiefuna like art. He learned titbits from Miebi. He explained how important it was to change their water constantly—at least thrice in a week—to reduce the possibility of their consuming their own waste, which would hamper their growth; he extolled the wonders of a simple salt-solution treatment as a local remedy in the event of a minor disease outbreak. More than the new knowledge being conveyed, Obiefuna was moved by the light that came in Miebi's eyes as he detailed a fascinating concept, the new cadence of his voice as he demonstrated his remarkable knowledge of the animals. For this reason, Obiefuna came to love the little farm. But more than that, he loved the idea of it. That Miebi, an electrical engineer with a Master's degree, kept a meticulously run farm and nursed larger dreams of expanding in the near-future, going into full-time management and considering a second Master's degree in animal husbandry, reflected something in his character, something sustainable and ultimately wondrous which Obiefuna loved. He loved, too, the air about him, the ease to him, his life of clean lines, his playfulness. All along Obiefuna had never felt like he was searching, but with Miebi he felt the peculiar relief of having finally found. All those long years of stumbling uncertainty, and there was Miebi, with his kind, trusting eyes, his easy manner, his soft and earnest way of speaking.

Occasionally, Obiefuna thought of Patrick. The night at the gallery had been the last time Obiefuna saw him. He still had some personal effects in Patrick's room, and sometimes, on his way to university, as the bus pulled past Patrick's neighbourhood, he flirted with the idea of alighting. He let Patrick's calls ring unanswered, deleted his text messages without reading them. He allowed a few weeks to pass before he deleted Patrick's number. For a few days, Patrick did not call, and then Obiefuna's phone rang one afternoon. He was in the hallway outside a classroom, waiting for a lecture to end, and for a distracted second he did not recognize the number, and so, with one hand placed over his left ear to block out some of the noise, he asked who the caller was. "You've really moved on, haven't you?" Patrick said after a short pause, and then he stopped calling.

Obiefuna told Miebi about Patrick. He held nothing back, describing the nights of marathon smoking sessions; the one time he woke up late in the night soaked in his own sweat, overwhelmed by nausea and convinced he was going to die. They were nestled in bed, Obiefuna's back pressed to Miebi's chest, Miebi's breathing warm on the side of his face. "You're fine right here," Miebi said, in a voice Obiefuna believed. He felt, with Miebi, a lightness of being, a tendency to laugh more, a state of permanent smiling. Sometimes, he caught himself staring at Miebi, smitten, just as he had been on that first day. Miebi would catch him staring and make a wry face, or raise a playful eyebrow to ask, "What?" Or sigh dramatically, and say, "I know. My beauty is breathtaking, abi?" at which Obiefuna laughed. It seemed as though Miebi had waltzed into his life just at the precise moment the door was held open; and in occasional misanthropic moments, sitting next to Miebi as he drove, or beneath the sheets, or across a dining table, he tried to conjure up alternative scenarios, of what he could have been doing with his life otherwise, none of which looked good. Once, Miebi asked him what he was thinking, and he said, "I feel as though you saved me," and, after an awkward pause, Miebi laughed, as if Obiefuna had been joking.

It felt to Obiefuna as though Miebi had been waiting for him. Miebi was used to living alone, and yet he easily made room for Obiefuna, creating a space so seamless and wide for him that Obiefuna did not have the disconcerting sensation of a major shift in his life. At first, he held on to his allocated room at the dormitory, panicked at the thought of giving it up, of the implication of it—that he, for the first time, fully belonged to someone. In the end, the decision was not left to him, and the next time he stopped by on a visit he discovered the room had been occupied by squatters, his roommates having received the impression that he had moved back home. Later it would occur to him that he had not bothered to correct their assumptions. For he thought now of Miebi's house as home. The house was warm and welcoming and oddly familiar, giving him the sense that he had always lived there. In the mornings, he stayed in bed long after Miebi had gone to work, reading a book, or playing games on Miebi's iPad. The house had a quietness to it and glistened from the thorough cleaning of the drop-in housekeeper, a strikingly dark-skinned boy named Moses who arrived every morning soon after Miebi left, letting himself into the house with his own keys. Aside from a polite good morning to Obiefuna, no other words were exchanged as he went about his chores, moving from room to room with a robotic stealth, letting himself out as soon as he was done, leaving the house in an airy state of lavender-scented calm. Obiefuna spent the rest of the day bingeing shows on DStv and riding Miebi's bike down the narrow, sloping streets, enjoying the swift brush of air that glided past his ears and the people who shot one uninterested glance at him and went about their business. In the evenings, Miebi arrived home from work, his tired eyes lighting up at the sight of Obiefuna, eager to get out of the car and into his arms. There was, to him, a hovering attentiveness, ready to spring into action at the slightest prompting. Miebi's life was defined by order. He walked around the house with an easy yet courteous familiarity, as if he himself were only a visitor. He cleaned up after every meal and put away his clothes the minute he took them off. He always dressed in casual clothes even when at home: soft, comfortable clothes that smelled like him. He kept the television volume low and squinted at the screen when the news came on, ultimately falling asleep, always, at precisely ten minutes into viewing, his head lolling to the side as he snored softly. In bed, he slept with both hands tucked between his thighs, curled like an embryo. He sang along to Bruno Mars and Adele and Onyeka Onwenu on weekends as he made breakfast, flipping pancakes in the pan and cheering when they landed on their other side in a perfect swing, his joy so childishly pure, so simple and unencumbered with bitterness, it made Obiefuna want to cry.

On Sundays, Miebi hosted a small gathering of his closest friends—he called them his ideal family—in his house. They arrived shortly after noon, often within minutes of each other, some still dressed in their church clothes, having made the drive directly from a service. Obiefuna was taken by the charming Tunde—a social worker with a sexual health NGO, with his perfectly oval face, and white teeth in sharp contrast to his dark skin—who announced, right after the first introductions, that he was a whore. "Just in case anyone finds that information useful," he said with a wink. Obiefuna paused before he laughed. It was a joke, and yet he looked up from time to time to meet Tunde's eyes on him, scrutinizing him somehow as though he were some exotic artefact. Obiefuna was just as drawn to Patricia. She was the only woman in the group and alternated between oversized T-shirts over boyish shorts and flimsy gowns that accentuated her figure. Her messy love life was playfully dissected at every gathering. Obiefuna marvelled at the wide range of her experience, the lurid details she gleefully provided—from the famous bank manager who liked to be pegged occasionally, to the young girl she had met online who physically stalked her for weeks, to the religious, funny-dressing youth leader at her now ex-church whom she had briefly had a sexual relationship with, breaking it off when he, on learning she also had sex with women, had spent a full hour quoting scriptures that promised eternal damnation for her soul.

"Didn't you say you guys were fucking?" Edward asked. His Ijaw accent coloured his words, and Obiefuna understood him only a few seconds after he had spoken. His loud insistence contrasted with the quiet and introspection of his partner, Chinedum, who seemed to be, discounting Obiefuna, the youngest in the group.

Patricia laughed. “Right! He couldn’t recognize irony even if it slammed him across his face.”

“Straight men are a different breed of absurdity, eh?” Kevwe teased. There was a general eye roll. He was, Obiefuna would later learn, the only heterosexual man in the group, and had a habit of putting up a disclaimer in the case of a perceived generalization or disparaging of heterosexuality.

“Give it a fucking rest, K,” Patricia said with a drunk laugh. They proceeded to other topics, drinking wine from tall glasses as they spoke, drifting from politics to Hollywood, pop culture to sports. They were completely at ease in Miebi’s home, more familiar with it, Obiefuna realized, than he was. They sat perched on the arms of sofas, cross-legged on the tiled floor, stood with their back to the wall as they ate from plates of food that they had served to themselves. Jabs were flung back and forth, subtle ridicule dropped in between sentences. They burst into sudden laughter at the hidden meanings of cryptic phrases, or a recalled memory from long ago. Obiefuna found it all difficult to follow, but he was content nonetheless to be swept up by the lull of voices, amused at the vigour with which they argued with news presenters on TV, their assessment of people’s fashion. They laughed at the fake accents of presenters, read aloud blog posts, bristling with animation, and commended or dismissed headlines.

“Obiefuna must really find us a bit too much,” Patricia said, smiling, as she reached for her glass on the table.

Obiefuna was startled, and then shy, as all eyes in the room were momentarily fixed on him. He sat upright, cleared his throat. “No. I’m actually having fun here.”

Miebi reached sideways to hold his hand, and, for once, in the midst of other people, he did not feel the conscious need to pull away.

"Where did you guys meet again?" Edward asked. The question was addressed to Obiefuna. It was the first time Edward had spoken directly to him since the first hesitant "What's up?" when they were first introduced.

It was Miebi who responded, smiling at Obiefuna as if speaking to him. "It was at the gallery opening in Trans Amadi. Remember, the one I got us tickets for and you bailed on me?"

"So he went with you instead?" Edward said, not acknowledging Miebi's joke. His eyes burrowed into Obiefuna's.

The room fell silent. Everyone looked at Edward. He had his glass poised at his lips; his gaze fixed on Obiefuna above the rim. His eyes were red but clear. From beside him, Chinedum leaned forward to place a hand on his knee.

"Obiefuna paid for his own ticket, Edward," Miebi said after a while, in a cool, level voice.

Edward paused and gave a slow, deliberate nod. He seemed on the edge of saying something else, and then he shrugged and took a sip from his glass.

LATER, CHINEDUM SAID, "I love your shorts."

"Thank you," Obiefuna said. They had drifted away from the others midway, Obiefuna needing to clear his head and Chinedum joining him on the balcony.

"I'm sorry about Edward," Chinedum said. "He gets that way sometimes, especially when it involves Miebi. Meant no harm to you, really."

"What do you mean?" Obiefuna asked.

"Erm . . ." Chinedum paused, unsure if the story was his to

tell. "Miebi can be very generous, sometimes unwisely so, you know? And it has had its consequences. You know, people who are looking to prey on his soft-heartedness. Like his ex—if I can even call him a boyfriend—Jeffery. He was a disaster. Nearly drove Miebi to bankruptcy while making passes at every one of us—including Patricia."

"Oh, wow."

"It was hard for Miebi. At some point, one of us considered moving in, just to keep an eye on things. He and Edward kind of go way back, you know? So Edward takes it a bit more personally than the rest of us."

Obiefuna nodded, seeing.

Chinedum watched his face. "But you, I can tell you're different. You have a good nose."

"Nose?"

"Yeah. It's perfectly shaped, not like that stupid bimbo with his bad skin and nose shaped like a bicycle seat. I never understood what Miebi saw in him."

Obiefuna laughed. Later, after the group had left and the house was quiet again, he took a cold shower and lay awake in bed. Outside, Miebi carried out a late inspection of the farm. Obiefuna followed the sound of his idle whistling, trying to guess the song. He was almost drifting off to sleep when he heard the soft ting of Miebi's phone. Obiefuna stared at it a while before he picked it up. He gained access to it without having to enter a password, surprised at Miebi's lack of privacy. It was a text from Edward, a concluding statement to a longer exchange. Obiefuna dropped the phone back on the bed and after a while picked it up again. The conversation was confrontational, Edward's end long and studded with disapproving emojis, with sparse, seemingly tired-out responses from Miebi. Obiefuna saw his name in one of the texts and sat up in bed. He scrolled up to the beginning of the conversation.

Not too bad. He's got a good build.

You think? He's so easy to love.

Lol, please. I think you mean you are too easy to fall.

Edward, don't start.

What? Am I the only one who noticed the boy looks like he went off breastmilk yesterday?

Okay, mister, I'll have you know that Obiefuna is twenty-one. And more emotionally mature than most.

Bet. And there's you three years away from forty and letting a child run you dry.

Lol, olodo. The boy hasn't asked for anything.

Does he need to? I bet my last dollar you give him everything.

Edward—

Look, I get it. You're starved of fun and the boy looks like he knows how to please Daddy. But when will you learn to leave it at that? To have him live with you within just two weeks of meeting? Come on, dude, it's like you've learned nothing at all.

I can't talk about this with you rn. Farm calls. G2G.

KK, whatever you say.

Obiefuna dropped the phone on the bed and stared at the wall. He felt strangely calm even though his hands had begun to shake. And then he felt dirty, like something without worth, placed on a chopping block and haggled over with no meaningful bargain in view. From outside, he could hear the sound of squawking chickens, Miebi's sudden laughter ringing out. It was needless to create a scene. He would not give Edward the satisfaction. He slowly, methodically, rose from the bed and went to fetch his bag from the wardrobe that by now felt like his own, the emptiness when he extracted his clothes odd and echoing. Only when he began to assemble his things in the bag did he realize how much he had in the room, and became overwhelmed by a sense of dread at the thought of never seeing this house again. He waited until his heartbeats had slowed, and Miebi had stepped out for a late run, before he got up and left.

In the days afterwards, shuttling between classes and the dormitory where he was now, essentially, a squatter, he was filled with a hollow sense of self, his skin crawling with self-conscious disgust. But more than that, he was filled with rage. It was unreasonable and unnecessary, to be fixated on the opinions of a mere stranger. But, try as he might, he was unable to simply shrug off the words. How dare Edward say those things about him? The man knew nothing about him. And how had Miebi been able to entertain the slander, offering only limp defences? He ignored Miebi's calls and left his text messages unanswered. At the dormitory, he was coolly polite, but evasive, with his roommates; the easy rapport he once shared with them had become strained. Soon, though, the worst of his rage dissipated, and he had nothing but longing for Miebi. He missed waking up to the sound of the crowing from the rooster. He missed the warm scent of Miebi's sheets, the cool floors and steady-buzzing refrigerator, the ambience of the living room. He missed the warmth of Miebi's body on his back as they slept, Miebi's breath on the side of his ear. He missed Miebi's food, his essence, the light in his eyes. He replayed scenes in his mind, of Miebi immersed in farm routine, his steps slow and deliberate, his routine methodical, his gait sure. In classes, the words of the lecturers were drowned out by his imagination, mingling with one another, amounting to nothing concrete, and at the end of each day he stepped out of the classroom and almost drifted towards the place where he would board a cab heading to Miebi's apartment; and then, remembering he could no longer go there, a lump formed that stayed in his throat. And so, on the day he walked out to see Miebi's car, while he had the momentary urge to ignore him and keep walking, he instead walked across to the side and got into the passenger's seat.

"I'm driving you to your dormitory to get your things so I can take you home," Miebi said in that gentle, slightly hoarse voice Obiefuna had missed.

Obiefuna, staring ahead, said nothing. He had almost forgotten the car's wonderful scent. Throughout the ride to the dormitory, he hummed under his breath, generally saying little except to point out a few directions. His bag was still unpacked. He threw in his toothbrush, a new pair of shorts and a few books and went back to Miebi's car. He could sense curious eyes peering at him from the dormitory's windows.

"Aren't you supposed to be at work?" Obiefuna asked.

"I took the day off," Miebi said, searching his face up close. His eyes looked pale. They said nothing after that until they got to a traffic stop. "Edward is coming over to apologize."

"That's not necessary."

"It is. He had no right to talk about you like that."

You let him, Obiefuna wanted to say. You didn't speak up passionately in my defence. But he said, "Why didn't you tell me about Jeffery?"

Miebi gripped the steering wheel and tapped it lightly with both thumbs. He did not look at Obiefuna or say anything in response, until they had driven up to the house, and he had let them in through the gate. "I should have told you." He paused, as if debating the next line, and then exhaled. "But talking about it reminds me of what a fool I was, and that's not a feeling I enjoy having." He reached for Obiefuna's left hand and brought it up to his right chin, forcing an awkward shift in their postures. "Also, I guess I was worried you would get the idea that I was some heartbroken thing in need of rescue. Cos I'm not, I think?"

Obiefuna did not want to smile, did not want to give the impression that he had let go so easily, that he was one to let go so easily, but Miebi was making that puppy face again that made him look ridiculous and childishly adorable at the same time, so that it was difficult for Obiefuna to keep himself from smiling, and then giggling, his shoulders rocking back and forth as Miebi stared.

"Really, babe, you're nothing he described and I'm sorry I let him say those things."

Obiefuna caressed his cheek. It felt fuzzy beneath his palm, like dried grass. From the backyard, he could hear the chickens squawking loudly, as if welcoming him home. He wanted to live in this moment forever. "Edward doesn't have to come tonight," he said. "Just the two of us is fine."

THE NEXT WEEKEND, Edward took him to one side. "I meant no harm by my questions," he said.

There was, Obiefuna could not help noticing, no direct statement of apology. But Obiefuna had learned by now—and made peace with the knowledge—that he and Edward would never get along. Their relationship moving forward would be one of unspoken antagonism. So he said, "Okay."

Edward frowned. He had perhaps expected a more enthusiastic reception. He studied Obiefuna awhile, before he proceeded cautiously. "Look, don't take this the wrong way, but, like, what's the deal here?"

"What do you mean?"

"I mean, look at you. You're a fine boy, intelligent—according to Miebi, young. Now we both know Miebi is not the most handsome man in the world, not to mention almost twice your age. It's hard not to suspect that the only attraction he holds for you is how much he has."

Obiefuna took measured breaths. It was pointless getting upset, especially since he sensed that was exactly what Edward wanted, and he had decided by now that Edward existed only to rile him. He turned without a word and walked back into the living room to join the others.

LATER, HE TOLD MIEBI, "I actually don't have to explain myself to him. Or to anyone, really."

Miebi clicked his tongue in sympathy. They were leaning on the railings of the balcony long after the others had gone. It was a good night. All evening, they had followed international news reports of President Obama's instructions to the US Supreme Court to strike down the Defence of Marriage Act on the grounds that it was discriminatory to gay couples. It had left Miebi in a jolly mood, drinking more than he usually would. Now he appeared flushed, with liquid eyes, his expression in a state of permanent smiling. He tried to look attentive, but Obiefuna could see he was far gone. The glass dangled precariously between his fingers.

"Edward's just jealous," Miebi said.

Obiefuna raised a brow.

"I mean, Chinedum is simply adorable. The best. But look at you!" He gestured, thrusting both hands forward in a dramatic flourish, the gentle force of his movements causing him to sway a little.

Obiefuna shook his head. If Miebi took another sip, he would drop the glass and soon enough be unable to bear his own weight. He moved forward and eased the glass, without resistance, from Miebi's grip. "Let's get you inside."

THERE WAS EVEN MORE news to celebrate by their next gathering. Together they pored over updates in Miebi's living room, learned that the US Supreme Court ruling was expected in the coming week and that there was, so far, cause for optimism. Despite protests by the Churches and a number of right-wing groups, popular opinion hinted at a possible positive consensus. A public poll showed a staggering number of respondents firmly backed striking the act. The friends toasted to a favourable outcome, and then they lounged lazily in the living room, drinking wine from cups until soon most of them were half drunk and drowsy, drifting from one pointless conversation to another, laughing randomly at unfunny things.

"When was your first kiss?" Patricia asked Obiefuna. She was sitting on the arm of the sofa closest to him, her body leaning slightly towards him. Her voice had been low enough, and yet Obiefuna felt the room go quiet as everyone waited for his response.

Obiefuna thought of Aboy. For some reason, it was the image of Aboy squatting to demonstrate he wanted to use the toilet that came to Obiefuna's mind, long before he could form the right words in English to articulate his needs, long before he had become accustomed to and at ease with city life. It had been a while since he thought of Aboy, and he was struck now by the lack of resentment in him. "That would be one of my father's apprentices, Aboy."

"Oooh, spicy," Patricia said. "I like the thought of an apprentice. When was this?"

Obiefuna chuckled. "Ages? I can't remember the details."

"Oh, come on," Tunde said, "Of course you can. Spill the tea, honey."

Obiefuna pictured Aboy's sleeping face that night, all those years ago, the dark spread of hair on his upper lip, the serene peace he radiated, and the curve of his lip in an ever-so-slight smile. But the details, even after all these years, felt too personal to share.

"Where's he now?" Patricia asked.

"I don't know," Obiefuna said. "My father caught us in a compromising situation, threw him out of our house and shipped me off to the seminary."

The room was silent. Everyone was staring at Obiefuna. Miebi leaned forward to gently tap his knee. Even he had not been told this. Obiefuna was surprised by the emotions that tore through him in that moment. He felt clear-headed. And yet something else. An urge to laugh and cry at the same time.

"So no one has a childhood love story with a happy ending, eh?" Patricia pressed, attempting to lighten the mood.

Tunde raised a hand.

Patricia rolled her eyes. "Tunde, for the hundredth time, we already know about your disgusting rendezvous with your Introtech teacher. The man should be in jail and you in therapy!"

"Well, I think in general love stories like ours don't tend to have such happy endings," Chinedum said. "It's like a story set in wartime. How much happiness can you get? Even the appearance of happiness is set against the backdrop of a larger sadness."

There was momentary silence. And then Kevwe said, "Of course there'll be Chinedum, with his grand-old-man wisdom."

Everyone laughed. Chinedum reached for a pillow and threw it at Kevwe, missing him entirely.

"No, but seriously," Chinedum said, when the laughter had subsided. "I often think of how much love is lost as gay kids grow up. We are robbed of the chance to experience the innocence of early teenage love. Because you spend all that time filled with fear, mastering your own pretence."

Patricia said, "Chinedum, save your grand analysis for later. Right now, we need happy gist."

Tunde raised his hands again.

"Tunde . . ." Patricia warned.

"Relax, it's not my teacher," Tunde said. His voice had taken on an uncharacteristic shyness. "I met someone."

Edward laughed. "What? Resident whore finally decides there's no more fun to be had on these streets?"

"A man needs to be settled at some point," Tunde retorted, batting a sarcastic eyelid at Edward.

"What's he like?" Chinedum asked.

"Well, we are yet to meet or make it official," Tunde said. He took a sip from his glass. "But, just so you know, you can expect an addition to this house soon."

ONE EVENING IN JUNE, Miebi returned home with a bottle of wine and in a bubble of excitement.

"They've ruled DOMA unconstitutional, babe!" he announced to Obiefuna.

"What's DOMA?" Obiefuna asked.

But Miebi was too excited to explain. He turned on CNN and together they watched the news anchors recite the words of the Supreme Court justices of the United States, affirming that the Defense of Marriage Act (DOMA) had been ruled unconstitutional on the grounds that it discriminated against LGBT people in America.

"You know what this means?" Miebi said, pouring out the wine in two glasses for himself and Obiefuna. "The most powerful nation in the world just declared visibility for our kind."

Obiefuna nodded. He did not grasp the full impact of the law, but he was gratified by Miebi's joy. He accepted his glass and toasted with Miebi. That evening, the friends arrived, a rare gathering for a weekday, and they watched the reports together. In one of them, a man openly proposed to his partner, to loud cheering in the background.

"When will we get this?" Patricia said, a look of animated longing in her eyes as she watched the screen.

"A pipe dream, my love," Tunde said with a laugh. "It's the worst nightmare of every Nigerian."

"We're Nigerian," Chinedum countered, with an emphatic tone that momentarily caused a general pause.

"Okay, not every Nigerian," Tunde finally conceded.

"Tunde's point stands, though," Edward said. "I don't see this becoming our reality. If anything, I can bank on the Nigerian government doing the very opposite."

"You never know!" Patricia said. "Wasn't there that anti-gay bill put forward many years ago? It was defeated!"

"Actually, it was just six years ago, Tricia, and it wasn't 'defeated.'" Edward said. "Let's just say there was a lot of politics going on at the time. I would argue that the prospect of its passage was as popular back then as it would be today."

"What was going on?" Obiefuna asked, speaking for the first time.

Edward paused. He seemed surprised that Obiefuna had spoken to him. "I believe it was around the time Obasanjo tried to amend the constitutional limits and extend his term indefinitely. Many feelings were hurt. The bill was an attempt to appease everyone. It was a clever distraction."

"I still don't see what we had to do with any of this," Patricia said.

Edward laughed. "Sweetheart, what planet do you live on? You should know by now that we're the, what's it called, go-to bones thrown at raging dogs to calm tempers whenever these idiots mess up. If there's one thing Nigerians will unite around, it's their hate for us. Obasanjo knew this too well."

"What about Jonathan?" Obiefuna asked.

"What about him?" Edward wondered.

"He does seem more enlightened than most," Obiefuna said. "It could be different this time."

Edward scoffed. His smile was slow and mocking: "Ah, the easy optimism that comes with youth. I almost miss it."

"Obiefuna has a point," Miebi said. "Plus, Jonathan must have his hands full with Boko Haram in the north. There's like a bomb going off every other day of the week. I don't see how Oga Jo is thinking about us amid all this."

"But that's the point," Edward countered, dragging himself to the edge of the seat. "The man has failed disastrously. Public rating is in the gutter. And you have general elections coming up in less than two years. What's the one thing you think he could do at this point to make everyone happy before election day?"

There was silence as they pondered Edward's question.

"In that case, I should probably get married to Vincent as soon as possible before it becomes illegal, right?" Tunde said.

"Who the hell is Vincent?" Edward asked, smiling.

"Oh, God. The man I talked about weeks ago!"

"Wait, that's for real?" Edward said.

Tunde looked at the group with mock horror, as if the realization just occurred to him. "You've really given up on me, haven't you?"

"You can't say we didn't try, honey," Miebi said, laughing. "All our attempts to get you settled haven't turned out well."

"Are you going to tell us what he's like now," Chinedum said, "or would you rather still hoard the tea?"

Tunde rolled his eyes. "When have I ever not told? I'll just have details when we meet in person."

"What's the hold-up?" Miebi asked.

Tunde took a sip from his glass. "Pretty busy guy."

"Or he's nothing like his pictures," Patricia chipped in. "Be careful out there, babes."

"We did speak on video," Tunde said. "He was okay."

"I never pegged you for an online date girly," Chinedum said.

"You'd resort to anything in my shoes," Tunde said. "Your long-term options are not so great when you're poz."

"Hey, stop it," Miebi said, reaching a hand towards Tunde's knee. "You're great. And this new mystery guy is lucky to have you."

For the first time ever, Obiefuna saw Tunde get misty-eyed. He tried, unsuccessfully, to laugh it off. "Well, you'll get the chance to tell him that soon, won't you?"

"Really proper timing, though, isn't it?" Edward said.

"Edward!" Chinedum warned.

"You know how I get with too much sentimentality," Edward said.

"Let's look on the bright side. Like Obi said, Jonathan seems enlightened. Wasn't he previously a university lecturer with a PhD?"

Edward laughed. "The man who introduced the first bill in 2007 was a lawyer who got his Master's from the London School of Economics."

"Edward . . ." Chinedum warned again, louder.

"Okay, okay," Edward said, throwing up his hands in surrender. "I hope you guys are right. By God, I really do."

TWENTY-FOUR

He thinks of his mother as a star. Sometimes, she manifests in his dreams as a small dot in the sky, the lone light that stays on even as the others fade. She doesn't speak, as far as he can tell, but he can hear her voice, singing a lullaby she used to sing for him as a child, something about comforting a child who was robbed of his belongings by a greedy world. Her words resound in his ears even as he emerges from the fog of sleep, and they stay with him for the rest of the day. He speaks infrequently with his father. Their communication is restricted to talks about his classes and grades and confirmation of his allowance. He does not need the money sent to his account every month, but there's no way to explain the "why" to his father. He receives letters in the post from Ekene in Ghana, spaced out over months. Ekene is, Obiefuna learned from the letter, finally getting the hang of the new country. The letters are mostly short, straight to the point. They provide updates on his new life. He has got used to the food, but he worries he is slacking in his skills. He is left on the bench too often. He suspects he is being treated unfairly because he is a foreigner. He has grown a full beard. He is in love with a pretty Ghanaian girl.

Obiefuna's responses are longer, suffused with a sentimentality he knows Ekene disapproves of. He mentions nothing of Miebi. He provides updates on their father. He still isn't taking the loss well. He seems to be losing his hearing, has Obiefuna repeat things to him nowadays. God, please keep this man for us; my heart cannot take the loss of another parent, Ekene writes back in the closing paragraph of his most recent letter, and Obiefuna finds himself nodding agreement.

ON THE MORNING the bill was passed, several of Miebi's fish died. He had observed, earlier in the week, the paleness of their colours, white patches on their fins, and the slowness with which they swam. They were unresponsive to repetitive salt solutions, and that morning they all lay afloat in the water, in their respective ponds, their eyes gorged. Obiefuna found Miebi hunched over one pond, staring in. He turned around as Obiefuna approached. Obiefuna counted twelve dead fish. Miebi's eyes were clear, his face expressionless.

"What could have happened?" Obiefuna asked.

"Some sort of outbreak, it seems," Miebi said. "I've called the vet. We'll know more when he arrives."

Later, after the vet arrived and administered the treatment in the pond, and spoke at length with Miebi, Obiefuna and Miebi ate breakfast in the dining room and remained seated afterwards, playing cards. In the living room, the television was on, the channel tuned to CNN. Obiefuna was winning. Miebi seemed distracted, his face focused on something behind Obiefuna, and he had to be reminded more than once when it was his turn to put down a card, but when Obiefuna suggested they stop, he pressed on. The words of the newsreader filtered in from the living room, and, once, perked up by something he heard, Obiefuna glanced at the television. The caption was bold, spread across the lower screen in menacingly capitalized letters: NIGERIA OFFICIALLY CRIMINALIZES SAME-SEX UNIONS.

The Nigerian parliament yesterday officially passed a bill criminalizing marriage and other forms of sexual relations and partnerships between people of the same sex. This comes on the heels of unprecedented recognition of gay unions recently in developed countries, most notably the United States. The bill, according to local media, was one of the fastest ever to be enacted into law, with a near-unanimous consensus among law makers, and carries varying sentences of between ten to fourteen years for both gay people and their allies. The bill has received widespread condemnation from the international community. By contrast, however, the bill has seen a mass support among the Nigerian populace, unsurprising in a country with ultra-conservative values.

The news gave way to clips of jubilation among Nigerians on the streets of Lagos, holding up placards on which were written the words NO MORE GAYS! FOURTEEN YEARS IN PRISON! JESUS LIVES HERE! Miebi had risen by now, inching too close to the television, almost obscuring Obiefuna's view, as if shielding him from the reality. His expression retained its blankness. Only his eyes, blinking too rapidly in a few seconds, betrayed his disbelief.

The newsreader went on:

Nigeria is not the only African country to outlaw gay unions. In fact, more than half of the countries that make up the continent have one form of restriction or another on relations between people of the same sex. However, Nigeria, being the continent's most populous nation, wields considerable influence among other nations, and it is speculated that this development might have possible spiralling effects on her neighbours' legislations . . .

Miebi switched off the TV and went into the bedroom. Obiefuna stood there awhile, staring at the blank screen. The ensuing silence was interrupted by the swirling of the ceiling fan. The woman's voice trailed in his brain: "with a prison term of between ten and fourteen years." He felt calm, too warm on the inside even though the room was cold from the residue of the January harmattan, and as he moved, his skin felt as though there were needles stuck into him. He had, in his ears, a long and sustained whining, and when he sat on the sofa it absorbed his weight with a little squeaky protest, as always. The living room seemed the same: small and square, welcoming in its warmth. Nothing seemed to have changed. Everything as clean and orderly as it had always been.

In the bedroom, Miebi sat upright on the bed, playing games on his iPad. He looked up when Obiefuna came in and his eyes rested on Obiefuna's face, as if studying him.

"It took them less than a day," Obiefuna said. "It's uncharacteristic of them to be this efficient."

"They're bastards," Miebi said. His voice was neutral, bereft of bitterness. He sighed and finally smiled, stretching out a hand to Obiefuna. "Come here, my darling."

Obiefuna strode across the room to Miebi, took his hand and lay on him. Two weeks ago, they had toasted to the new year,

Miebi leading a prayer for 2014 to bring only the best. Now he quietly hummed a song, and it took Obiefuna a moment to recognize the track: Onyeka Onwenu's "One Love," and, as he followed the rhythm in his head, Obiefuna wondered if it was a conscious choice by Miebi, a simple and defiant reaffirmation of their commitment to each other, illegality regardless.

THE NEXT DAY, Chinedum, down with an illness, was absent from the gathering. The rest of them sat upright on their seats, words tumbling out at the same time, their drinks hardly touched. They swore at news analysts on the screen, screamed at one another, took a swipe at the air. But even their rage was tempered with dismay, their demeanour cornered, disbelieving of their own ears.

"Who would have thought?" Patricia repeatedly wondered. "How jobless can the Nigerian parliament be?"

"It's the ripple effect from so much gay-rights recognition all over the world right now," Kevwe said. "Nigeria feels threatened. This is their pre-emptive way of making a statement."

"That's absurd," Patricia said. "We've never even demanded any rights to begin with. Where is the threat coming from?"

"It's the election, sweetheart," Tunde said. "Oga Jona had to take a stand, and those foreign governments weren't going to re-elect him next year, were they? It always boils down to the politics in the end."

"He's a bastard," Edward said. He had been uncharacteristically silent all the while, brooding, and now the coldness of his voice startled Obiefuna and, it seemed, everyone else in the room, as they all turned to him. "This is the best he can do? For someone who has appeared to be a colossal failure, he's got a lot of fucking nerve!"

"Well, you have to admit this one was smartly played," Kevwe said. “Look at the news. People have been singing his praises. And we’re talking about someone they couldn’t wait to drive away from Aso Rock. Suddenly, he’s the best thing to happen to Nigeria since independence.”

“If he thinks this is going to guarantee a win for him next year, even he needs to go back to kindergarten and learn the basics of politics,” Edward said.

“Still, even you cannot deny that this was not an injurious move for him,” Kevwe pressed. “Those major endorsements from approving religious groups won’t hurt. Nigerians are too easy.”

They turned back to the news. More and more clips showed people celebrating the law. A public-opinion segment anchored by an independent news channel, and sampling different demographics, revealed near-unanimous support for the law. An elderly man barked at the reporter who had asked him if he thought the bill was fair.

“Of course it is!”

“So you think gay people deserve prison?”

“Yes,” the man said.

“Why?”

The man leaned away from the microphone to glare at the correspondent, convinced she had lost her mind. “Because we have values here,” he responded finally. “We will not accept anything that goes against our lifestyle.”

Many more respondents echoed the same sentiments in varying tones, over and over, until Obiefuna felt drowsy from the monotony of it all. “It’s unnatural,” someone said. “It’s not in our culture as Africans. Anyone who wants to do that should go to America,” another said. A man, tall and dark skinned, with sharp-edged features like carved wood, when asked if he believed there were Nigerians who’d had no exposure to Western influences and were gay regardless, said: "Maybe. And I'm using this opportunity to tell them to count their days. We're going to fish out all of them and kill them one after the other."

Patricia gasped. "Did he actually say that on live TV?"

Tunde chuckled. "Oh, he knows there's nothing to worry about. He's completely safe. Nigerians are more concerned with fishing out imaginary criminals than apprehending a real one."

"And many of them agree with him," Miebi said. He sounded tired. "His use of 'we' was very intentional."

Obiefuna squeezed his hand and Miebi squeezed back before he got up to use the bathroom. After waiting awhile, Obiefuna followed him. The door would not budge. The shower was running from inside and Obiefuna contemplated knocking, but he did not, aware that Miebi needed that moment to himself.

Miebi appeared tired in the following days, even as his routine followed its usual course. He went running in the morning, tended to the farm and made Obiefuna pancakes for breakfast—the fluffy kind dipped in honey that Obiefuna loved—but something in his spirit had dimmed, the animation slack. He no longer watched the news, spending entire evenings in bed with his laptop. Even their intimacy had changed, becoming strained somehow. When they went out together, they instinctively walked apart, sitting side by side in restaurants rather than across from each other, and they had Patricia hang out with them more often nowadays. She had recently suffered another heartbreak, and they talked about it on one of the outings, Patricia moaning about the amount of the money she had spent on the girl. They laughed at her routine, teased her on her new hairstyle, suggested potential dates, but the sound was shallow, tempered, aware somehow of its own false-heartedness.

"How could they do this to us?" Patricia asked once, on one of their gatherings, and her question was met with silence.

TWENTY-FIVE

The news of the first arrests greeted Obiefuna two weeks later. It was a sunny Thursday evening; on his way home from university, he noticed the cluster of students around the public newsstand. Something about their postures, their bodies held still in self-righteous disgust, made him draw close to observe. It was the eyes he noticed first, bewildered and shining with a fear that was almost palpable. Before Obiefuna read the caption emblazoned beneath the picture, he knew. He picked up and paid for the paper and slid it into his bag, thinking throughout the long ride home about the haunting familiarity of those eyes. He took out the cover page, which consisted only of the headlines, when he got home and crumpled it in his fist; and yet, as he skimmed through the report, piecing together the oddly animated narration of a mass arrest of young men suspected to be gay, at a house party in

Kano, he found himself unable to blink those eyes away. It was the same feeling he would carry with him in the coming weeks, a nebulous sense of doom, imbued with a discomfiting awareness that his own reckoning was close. He stumbled through nightmares of sitting in the chapel as a booming voice read out Sparrow's verdict. Midway, Sparrow raised a hand to halt the verdict and pointed straight to Obiefuna, and, as a sea of shocked eyes swept in his direction, he was jolted awake, his clothes damp with sweat. He followed blog articles day after day about the gay-targeted rampage, the mass arrests in nightclubs of men dressed in "suspicious" clothes, the "clampdown" on effeminate-looking men in lower-income neighbourhoods, two young women accosted in their rooms as they slept naked in each other's arms and raped by the group of men who found them. Obiefuna read an opinion piece in the papers in which the writer made a case for the rape as a necessary lesser evil. He absorbed the terrors of the victims, as he pored over pictures—dazed-looking young men and women nursing bloodied wounds, their naked bodies scarred and exposed. But it was the comments that were most jarring. He read paragraphs about people affirming the treatment of the victims, some of them dissatisfied with the fact that the men were still alive. Each comment settled something hard in Obiefuna's stomach that sometimes made him feel physically heavy. He pictured those people as the boys at the seminary, who had been his friends and companions, with whom he had shared reasonable lengths of his life. Decent, friendly people who accommodated him. But he was struck now by a startling awareness that any one of them could easily be the people in the comments.

Miebi told him to stop reading the news. "All that paranoia isn't helping anyone," he admonished. Obiefuna still scoured for more, each news story feeling like a sharp probing of an unhealed scar; he found himself addicted, unable to stop, sinking into despair as he read, pausing in between reads to fill his lungs with air.

More articles were published, pictures of terrified young men splattered on the sites. When the friends gathered at increasingly spaced-out intervals, they talked about the raids. A friend of Tunde, on the grounds of being effeminate, had been forced off a public vehicle by policemen and subjected to a public body search, ultimately arrested when a lubricant was found in his wallet; another, a friend of Edward, had been arrested for being in possession of his lover's nude pictures. Edward had run down his own savings to secure his bail. Yet even he acknowledged it was a best-case scenario, the men privileged to be based in the south. The men arrested at the Kano party, mainly Muslims, were not as lucky. With their trials months away, under Shariah law, a guilty verdict could result in a range of punishments, from severe public whippings to death by stoning.

"An extreme form of BDSM, wouldn't you say?" Tunde joked, but no one laughed.

"Is there really nothing that can be done for them, Eddie?" Miebi asked.

Edward sighed, reclining on his seat. "We've exhausted our contacts, man. Unless a miracle happens, those brothers are far gone."

Miebi sighed. "But these raids are illegal. You can't just barge in on people's private spaces and arrest them without significant proof. Even the stupid law doesn't give the police these liberties. Surely someone can point that out to them?"

Edward chuckled. "Who'll bell the cat, bro? Everyone is too scared and embarrassed. It's a nightmare; they just want it over with."

After a moment's silence, Edward added, "You need to be careful, Obi. It's real chaos out there."

Obiefuna looked at him. Something about the concern in Edwards's voice moved him. He said, "Thank you, Ed. I will."

AND HE WAS CAREFUL. Or he tried to be. At university, he kept his head down. He attended classes, read books in the library, did his practicals in the lab, took the taxi home. He found himself looking at people longer, trying to tell them apart, to decide who was likely to be a commenter on those blogs. How could he get Miebi to understand that it was difficult to put the news behind him when the hate was like a giant rock right in front of him, immovable? He heard the bill being discussed in the taxis he took home, at the library, in class. On a Tuesday morning, a boy was being publicly harassed by the school security for "walking like a girl," pitting the majority student population against the scant minority who abhorred the treatment. Obiefuna sat in class trying to study. He had learned by now to listen without speaking, using an earpiece to make him seem unavailable. Most of the class was against a girl who admirably held her own on why the treatment was wrong. The others laughed off her arguments, jeered, insisted the boy deserved a worse treatment.

"Don't you agree?" someone had asked Obiefuna, pointing him out randomly from the crowd, and the sudden sea of eyes that swept in his direction, the silence that settled in as they waited for his input, had prompted him to blurt out, "Surely." A simple word. His response elicited approving murmurs, a few handshakes, renewed respect in the eyes of his classmates. Across from him, the girl stared, her eyes narrowed, and then she sighed, defeated. It was the first thing Obiefuna told Miebi when he got home. "They asked what I thought and I agreed. I was disgusting," he said.

Miebi looked at him. He was stirring eggs in a bowl on the

kitchen worktop, his hands doused with flour. "You were in a difficult position. You had to say what you had to say."

"I could have said nothing," Obiefuna said.

"You could have," Miebi agreed. "But then you shouldn't have been asked in the first place." He put away the bowl of eggs, sighed. "You're not the problem here, my darling."

Obiefuna retreated from him. He hated when Miebi talked in this glib, easy manner of his. He wished Miebi would not try to absolve him of blame. He needed to do something with this guilt.

Miebi followed him into the living room and enclosed him in an embrace. At first Obiefuna held his body still, thinking of the disappointment in the girl's stare, the soft pounding of his heart in his chest as he had waited for her to blurt out something salacious in response. Soon, he was lost in the rhythm of Miebi's heartbeat and felt himself relax. "I need you to know you're home right here, Obi," Miebi said. "The world might be going crazy, as it always has been. But you're home with me. Right here."

He wished Miebi would demonstrate a little fear. He wished he would worry a bit more about what his neighbours thought of a boy in his home, an unmarried man as he was, a boy whom they knew was not related to him. He wished he would have a few of those nightmares Obiefuna found himself having lately, of people barging in through the gate as they slept, into the bedroom, finding them entwined in each other's arms. But Miebi sailed through the days and weeks with his signature optimism: colour had returned to his face, warmth to his voice, animation to his movements. It was a quiet and forceful defiance. He possessed the bearing of a man who danced to his own beat, refusing to allow the world to set the rules for him, as if his life moved to an internal rhythm.

❖

UNTIL TUNDE was abducted.

It was a rainy morning in March. Obiefuna woke up to the sound of Miebi's voice. The light was on. Miebi paced about the bedroom with his phone pressed to his ear, seemingly frantic. He hung up after a moment and stood staring at the door.

Obiefuna said, "What's going on?"

Miebi turned around and walked towards him. "Sorry I woke you."

"What happened?" Obiefuna asked again.

"It's Tunde. He's been kidnapped," Miebi said.

Obiefuna sat upright in bed, the last traces of sleep leaving his eyes. "What?"

But Miebi said nothing else. He was already slipping into his trousers, bolting out of the door after a hurried kiss. Obiefuna stood up and went to the balcony, watching as Miebi drove out of the compound. In class that day, he was unable to concentrate, trying to make sense of the scenario, to conjure a possible motive for the abduction. A part of him willed it to be a false alarm, an exaggeration on Miebi's part. He wildly imagined Miebi getting abducted, too, detained for months. But he found Miebi when he arrived home after class. He was sitting on the floor of the living room, reclining against the sofa, his head turned away from the door. Obiefuna moved towards him, his heart pounding against his chest, and roused him gently. He turned to Obiefuna. His eyes were bloodshot.

"He was given nothing to eat for two days," Miebi said.

Obiefuna caressed his face. He had never seen Miebi this broken. "What happened?"

Miebi blew his nose into a tissue before he spoke. Tunde had finally gone out on a date with the mystery lover, who turned out to be a set-up, some lowlife on the prowl for gay men. He had been lured to a secret location and abducted. His parents, when contacted and informed of the reason for his abduction, promptly hung up. He had been released an hour ago after a ransom, raised mostly by Miebi and Edward, had been paid. He was taking shelter in Patricia's apartment.

"He was treated like an animal," Miebi said. He had snot seeping from his nose. Something about the way his legs were stretched before him, and his head lolled to one side, gave him an undignified air. "They stripped him of his clothes and made videos of him confessing to being gay. They beat him so badly he lost consciousness many times."

Obiefuna bowed his head. He remembered the soft cadence of Tunde's voice as he talked about the mystery lover, the pure optimism in his tone as he looked forward to their meeting. He tried to picture the exact moment Tunde realized he had been set up, the horror overtaking his typical mischievous exterior, his handsome face grotesquely swollen from the force of their hits, uncertain which blow to ward off, aware even then that something had changed forever. Obiefuna did not realize he had begun to cry until Miebi pulled himself closer and took Obiefuna in his arms, whispering, "He's stronger than we give him credit for. He'll survive this." And, somehow, the wonderful, nostalgic scent of Miebi's cologne, and the apparent certitude in his tone, suggesting that he had simply believed Obiefuna's tears were out of sympathy for Tunde alone, the easy faith he had in Obiefuna's goodness—all this made Obiefuna cry harder. He thought of Festus in the dark of the night, sprawled defenceless on the wet grass, receiving the blows that rained on him with the practised resignation of one who had seen it coming. He did not know why he did, but he began to talk about Festus. The smallest, incontrovertible details were the ones that had stuck to his memory: his uncanny manner of looking at Obiefuna straight in the eye, the glow of his pleasured smile in the moonlight that streaked in through the window, the warmth of his spit on Obiefuna's face. As he opened up now, confronting a past he had safely tucked away in the part of his mind he never visited, he felt a pause in time, acutely aware of Miebi's slow disengaging, his horror unmasked, until the distance between them was the size of an arm's length, until Obiefuna felt the warmth of Miebi's skin give way to a prickling cold.

"You scarred him for life," Miebi said, his voice unusually level and thick with disgust. "How could you do such a thing, Obiefuna?"

It was the first time in recent memory he was addressing Obiefuna by name, in a tone Obiefuna had never heard him use. For a while they sat staring wordlessly at each other, an invisible line drawn in each one's mind, with Miebi finally seeing Obiefuna for what he was. And then Miebi rose from the floor and exited the living room, the firm click of the bedroom door filling the silence in his wake. Obiefuna reclined on the sofa and stared at the walls lined with Miebi's prized art collection, a smiling picture of him in a Corps uniform. He was a perfect man—typically the kind of person to have had everything figured out from the get-go, to have learned early enough the principle of being comfortable in one's skin and shutting the world out. He would not have seen the need to attack his own kind just to prove himself to anyone. He would not have had a past like Obiefuna's.

Obiefuna woke up with a headache. He had a bitter, clammy taste on his tongue, and his limbs felt only loosely held together. Miebi held out a glass of water to him.

"All that crying leaves you dehydrated," he said. He tried

to keep a straight face and then broke into a smile. He inched closer, took Obiefuna in his arms.

"Do you know where he is now?" Miebi asked.

Obiefuna shook his head. Somehow, oddly enough, in all the discussions reminiscing about seminary experiences, in the many group chats created for the purpose, Festus had never come up, had never been a participant. Festus with his vivacious personality, his ability to fill up a room.

"You were a scared, ignorant teenager in a seminary," Miebi said, his arm around Obiefuna's shoulders. "You're nothing like them."

Obiefuna nodded. His eyes welled up with tears and he closed his eyes in an effort to hold them back. Even with Miebi's attempt to be kind, he could not make out the difference between himself and Tunde's captors. He wondered if there had been a person like him among them, one who had seen himself in Tunde, who had stepped aside as the sticks rained down, detached and terrified, but ultimately grateful for the chance to simply observe from the sidelines, held still by an intimate knowledge that it could very well be them on that floor. That night was the last he had heard of Festus, and now Obiefuna scoured the internet for him. It was not a difficult search. As soon as he got the surname right from memory, there he was. Festus's Facebook profile was available only to friends, and Obiefuna pored over the few pictures he could access, trying to make the most he could from the random unremarkable snapshots of Festus. He clicked on the "Add Friend" icon and debated a moment whether to send a message request along. What initial tone should he strike: a breezy catch-up or a straightforward apology? In the end, he settled for a bit of both. "Hi Festus, long time, bro! Could you leave me your number? I'd like to tell you something." And then he logged off and put his phone away. Later that evening he logged back in, nervously eager to read Festus's reply, to hear that high-pitched voice again, but he could no longer access the message, could no longer find the profile. He provided alternative spellings in the search bar but nothing panned out. Miebi suggested he try to access the profile using Miebi's own account, and when Obiefuna did so, there was Festus's profile, exactly as he had seen it originally. Their fifteen mutual friends included Tunde.

"He blocked me," Obiefuna said after a long silence.

Miebi held his hand, squeezed it. "No one could say you didn't try."

By the beginning of April, Obiefuna began an externship. He was assigned to a small eye clinic three stops from Miebi's apartment, so he woke up earlier to catch the morning bus. He was disorientated, at first, by the brightness of the wards, the smell of disinfectant, the claustrophobic feel of the cramped offices where he was to observe the chief optometrist seeing patients. The clinic was privately run, with an entire staff of four, and Obiefuna was one of the two externs who did not bolt after the first day. He saw patients rarely, spending most of his time in the waiting room studying, or watching a Nollywood movie on the old, loud television. It was there, two weeks in, that he watched the news of the abduction of over two hundred schoolgirls in Chibok. It was the latest in a series of brazen attacks by Boko Haram, which had by now all but taken over the north. Investigation was under way as to the girls' whereabouts. The government was seeking valuable information from the public, in order to help with what was a perplexing situation.

Obiefuna watched as clips of a ghost town were shown, smoke rising from some of the burned buildings. There was nothing to indicate that human beings had dwelled there only hours ago. The thought did not occur to him until he was halfway home on the bus that Rachel lived in the north. She had moved there two years ago for university. He could no longer remember the exact state she was in, but at that point, uncomfortably seated between two people in the crowded bus, he was only able to picture the north as one small village, with one act of violence spilling over. He rang her immediately he got off the bus, and it was not until he had lost count of his attempts to contact her, late into the night, that her phone was answered, and her voice filtered into his ears. She was safe, she said, scheduled to return to Port Harcourt that weekend. She was done with the north, prepared to abandon her hard-sought university admission for a safer prospect in the south.

"It's under wraps for now, Obi," she warned him at the end of the call. "Sorry, but it's just hard to know who to trust these days."

Obiefuna nodded and said he understood. After she hung up, he stood for a long time outside on the balcony. Because of the insurgency, air operations had been stalled—the state did not have a functioning airport. She would have to access the roads. The news said the military had been deployed to the region to beef up security. Still, Obiefuna could not stop picturing the worst: their vehicle breaking down in the middle of the road, gunmen waylaying them. It would be her first trip since she went off to university, the first time she would be travelling with no intention of returning. But there was a strength, a steeliness, in Rachel's voice on the phone that made him certain she would survive. It would be such a thrill to see her again, to hear the mischievous laughter he so desperately missed.

Obiefuna went into the bedroom, wanting to tell Miebi about Rachel, to repeat her assurance out loud. Miebi was sitting on the edge of the bed with his head in his hands. Obiefuna touched his back. "Are you okay?"

"Tunde's captors released the videos they recorded on social media," he said. "The police showed up at his parents' house to try to arrest him."

"Does Tunde know about this?" Obiefuna asked.

Miebi nodded. "Patricia phoned me at work. He's losing his mind." He turned to Obiefuna. "He's going to kill himself, babe."

"Shh." Obiefuna put a hand to his lips. He could feel the tremor building inside Miebi as he inched forward and took him in his arms. He held Miebi close as Miebi sobbed, brushing his palm flat against Miebi's back. "He's going to be fine," Obiefuna said. "Trust me, darling."

TWENTY-SIX

The room was quiet. Obiefuna lay stretched on a sofa, with his head on Miebi's thigh. The friends sat around the living room, surfing on their phones or staring into the distance. The long nights they had spent chasing mundane conversations seemed like a wispy memory now. Earlier, they had watched a live re-enactment of a public whipping of a gay prisoner by a bailiff in the north and watched clips of the judge extolling his own leniency in not pursuing the death penalty. It was a week after they'd moved the last of Tunde's things from his apartment, two weeks since he'd been smuggled out of the country to Cameroon, from where he was to seek asylum in the United States. He was currently held in a secure facility that seemed anything but, overcrowded as it was with people who were fundamentally unknown to each other and yet united by their horrors of flight, by the hope of a new, unknown future ahead.

"He was the best student in his class," Patricia said, breaking the silence. She had said little all day, dutifully nursing one half-filled glass of wine after the other, a faraway look in her eyes. "He devoted unreasonable hours to the kids he worked with, to his own detriment."

"What I don't understand is why they can't all be more careful," Kevwe said. "There's a law against this right now. There's no need to be reckless."

"What's that supposed to mean?" Edward asked.

"I care for Tunde, man," Kevwe said. "But it takes a level of recklessness to go on a date with a random stranger, especially at a time like this."

"You go on blind dates all the time," Edward said.

"You know it's not the same thing," he said. "As sad as it is, our realities are not the same."

"You're a bastard," Edward said.

But Kevwe stared back without flinching. "Getting needlessly emotional over an objective truth doesn't change the fact."

There was silence, fraught with expectation. Obiefuna held his breath, kept his body perfectly still, anticipating, and yet unsure of what to expect. He gazed at Edward, who seemed to be digesting the moment, taking it in his stride, and then suddenly Edward reached forward in one fluid motion to sweep a glass off the table and fling it in Kevwe's direction. It missed him completely, smashing to pieces on a portrait on the wall.

"How fucking dare you." Edward rose and advanced towards Kevwe. Miebi leaped instinctively to serve as a barricade, stalling his approach by placing restraining palms on Edward's chest. "What the fuck do you know about the risks we take?" Edward fumed from behind the restraint.

Across the room, now standing, Kevwe spoke in an unsettlingly measured tone. “I’m not the enemy here, Edward. Tunde was my friend as much as he was yours.”

“You fucking bastard.” Edward advanced again, trying unsuccessfully to wrestle himself free from Miebi’s grip on his wrist.

“That’s enough, Edward!” Miebi barked. And then to Kevwe, “Man, please. I’ll call you later.”

Kevwe did not argue. He took up his car keys from the table and let himself out.

“They never really get it, do they?” Patricia said after calm had returned to the room.

“The audacity,” Edward seethed.

“Edward, he meant no harm,” Miebi said.

“Perhaps,” Patricia defended. “Regardless, it’s not his place to decide what’s risky for us and what isn’t.”

Miebi raised a puzzled brow. “He’s our friend, Pat.”

“Yes. But he doesn’t go on a date and worry about being kidnapped and tortured specifically for what he is. He doesn’t have to run for his life just because he attempted to get laid.” Her voice was rising.

“He will never come back,” Obiefuna said. He held no particular affection for Kevwe, and yet he felt a sinking in his stomach, a weight that rendered him numb. Everything seemed so wrong.

Patricia said, “None of us are the same anymore, Obi.” She put down her glass on the table and brought her hands together, clutching them tightly as if each hand derived strength from the other. “It’ll never be what it used to be.”

Later, after the guests had left, Obiefuna took the glasses to the kitchen, merely rinsing them under the tap before putting them away. In the living room, Miebi stood studying the ruined painting. The glass had made only a slight dent, nothing irreparable, and yet there was something about the way Miebi was looking at it, lightly running a finger over it. Obiefuna worried he would cut himself and draw blood.

"Patricia had a point," Obiefuna voiced on impulse.

Miebi exhaled, shook his head. "Edward is getting married," he said. His voice sounded muffled and he cleared his airway before continuing, turning to look fully at Obiefuna. "This wasn't entirely about Tunde."

MIEBI HAD BEEN INVITED to a party in town. He asked Obiefuna along. The party was not what Obiefuna expected. Held at a small compound, the event took place without tents or dancing, and with only the sound of low music from a stereo; casually dressed people of varying races sipped from tall glasses and spoke in measured tones. The compound was in a government-reserved area, and the attendees had about them an air of well-being. It took Obiefuna a moment to notice that something about the environment felt out of place, and then suddenly everything became clear—the cluster of men holding hands with other men, the women seated on the thighs of other women, the unusual dress sense. He looked at Miebi, who had been looking at him, expecting a reaction.

"Is this—"

"A gay-friendly gathering, yes," Miebi said with laughter in his eyes.

"I see," Obiefuna said. He had heard about this kind of party, mostly from the mainstream blogs he had read about the raids, where policemen stormed the venues and carted away attendees. And, although he could feel the power the attendees exuded in the relaxed manner with which they interacted with one another, he could not stop picturing a raid, his hands clamped with handcuffs, his face splattered on a news site.

"I needed to show you this," Miebi said, holding his hand. "The country might be trying to tell you otherwise, but we exist, Obi. In mass numbers."

A man was walking towards them, his face lighting up from behind his glasses at the sight of Miebi. "You were the last person I expected to see here," he said, attempting to hug Miebi but he was met with a handshake instead. "How have you been?"

"I didn't think you'd be here," Miebi said.

"Well, we do what we have to do," the man said. His eyes darted to Obiefuna. "And this is?"

"Obiefuna," Miebi said, simply.

"Very nice," the man said. His eyes settled on Obiefuna, only momentarily interested before he forgot about him altogether. Miebi and the man fell into conversation, the man animated, Miebi looking bored. Excluded, Obiefuna extricated himself to properly observe the party. In the distance, he could see bodies rocking to the sound of slow music, laughter ringing out. From time to time, he looked at Miebi and the stranger, discomfited at the man's insistent and unnecessary need to touch Miebi's arm as he spoke. Finally, with a pause in the conversation, Miebi excused himself and guided Obiefuna away.

"You deserve an award in patience," Obiefuna said.

Miebi said, "You don't know that man, do you?"

"Should I?"

Miebi chuckled and slid his arm into Obiefuna's, as if they were a couple headed down the aisle. "Well, only if you're remotely interested in politics. That's Diri. He's a lawmaker. Pretty influential."

ON THE DRIVE BACK HOME, pleasantly drunk from only a few glasses, Obiefuna said, "Only one senator voted against the bill."

Miebi said, without looking at him, "It wasn't Diri, if that's what you're asking."

"It's just hard to believe there's someone like us in that house," Obiefuna said.

"Of course there is," Miebi said. "There are people like us everywhere, darling."

"Are you all right?" Obiefuna asked.

Miebi slowed the car's pace. He was driving without his glasses and seemed to be second-guessing every turn he made. "What do you mean?"

"You haven't been yourself all night," Obiefuna said. "Didn't you want to come?"

Miebi was quiet. He leaned slightly sideways, as if to whisper in Obiefuna's ear, and then he retreated, seeming to change his mind. "I just have this funny headache," he said. "It hurts my eyes."

TWENTY-SEVEN

One Saturday, Obiefuna woke up craving oranges. It was mid-June, and the soil was still damp from the first rains. While Miebi remained in bed, Obiefuna rode his bicycle to the fruit vendor down the street and bought some oranges, adding cucumbers and watermelons for Miebi. When he returned, Miebi was awake, sitting upright in bed. He was flipping through a magazine without reading it. He received a watermelon slice from Obiefuna's hand, took a bite and set it aside on the bedside table, returning to the magazine. Obiefuna went to the kitchen for a tray and a penknife, and set them on the table beside the watermelon. He took up a piece with the knife and circled the bed to sit on the other side. He watched Miebi turn another page of the magazine.

"What's wrong?" Obiefuna asked.

Miebi looked up from the magazine. His eyes rested on Obiefuna's face. "You look beautiful this morning."

Obiefuna laughed. "I look beautiful every day."

"Hmm," Miebi said. His smile was distracted. "Hard to argue with that."

"Babe, what's wrong?"

Miebi took a breath before passing his phone across to Obiefuna. He kept his eyes on Miebi's face, trying to gauge his expression, as he accepted the phone from Miebi's hands. The screen was opened to a WhatsApp message, a girl's picture filling the screen. Obiefuna studied her face, a pretty, smiling face, her braided hair gathered in a bun. The contact read "Mum." She needed Miebi to at least meet the girl in person, give her a chance. It was the last thing she was asking of him. If he cared any bit for her, for their family, he would grant her this one favour. It was a full one hour before Miebi responded, with a single word that spelled the end: "Okay." Obiefuna held the phone in both hands. He felt like a splendid performer before Miebi's appraising eyes. He wanted to smash the phone against the wall. His appetite for oranges was gone.

"You seemed different," Obiefuna said. He wasn't making complete sense, and yet he hated the bitterness in his tone, the tears clogging his voice. He rose from the bed and walked into the living room, shutting the door behind him. Sitting on the sofa, he tried to still the furious beating of his heart. His head throbbed painfully. Above him, the air conditioner was on full blast, and he was soon cold to the bone, but he remained still. After a few minutes came Miebi's soft knocks on the door, his voice, "Babe, please just open. I haven't said yes or anything. Please."

But he would, Obiefuna realized. He was aware that the estrangement from his parents was getting to Miebi. The possibility of their forgiveness and acceptance was something he had always held on to, regardless of how much he tried to mask it. He remembered Chinedum in his finely tailored suit, smiling in that photograph behind Edward. He remembered the wife, how happy she had looked next to Edward, how blithely unaware. By the time he rose from the sofa, it was evening. He found Miebi in the dining room, a dinner table set for two.

"I made spaghetti," Miebi said.

Obiefuna rounded the table and sat next to him. Platters of chicken sat next to each plate of spaghetti. The oranges were arranged in a small circle next to the watermelons that had by now been expertly chopped into cubes. He took one and slid it into his mouth, trying not to look up, aware that Miebi's eyes were on him.

"When's the wedding?"

"Babe, please. We don't have to go through this now."

Don't call me that, Obiefuna wanted to say. You no longer have the right. "You're getting married," he said instead, with a throaty laugh. He hated the surliness creeping into his voice. "We're going to have to talk about it at some point."

Miebi sighed. "I don't know when it will happen. If it will happen," he said, and then added, "My parents might decide that."

Obiefuna half nodded. In other circumstances, he might have been amused by the formal proceedings. He reached for another bite of watermelon, enjoying the bland taste of the cubes, melting without effort on his tongue, giving off no distinct, lingering flavour. He wanted to stuff all the watermelons into his mouth at once.

"You're leaving, aren't you?" Miebi said.

Obiefuna paused in the middle of picking up another watermelon cube and looked up at him. It was odd, how the implication for their relationship had not fully registered with him. The prospect of a decision seemed to elude him. What he felt now, he realized, more than betrayal, more than hurt, was despair: for Chinedum, for Miebi, for all people of their kind all over the country, building relationships, investing so much of themselves over time. How do you begin something beautiful with the certainty of its end? You gave yourself over to love and lived the rest of your life knowing you never stood a chance; all it took was a girl somewhere and family pressure to end it. He wanted to laugh. And then he realized that what he really wanted to do was cry.

Miebi reached out across the table for his palm, missing it by an inch. "Please, Obi, don't leave. We could always work things out."

There it was again, the beautiful glint of hope in his eyes. In a way, it reminded Obiefuna of why he loved him, why, no matter what happened, he would always think of him with fondness. As Miebi moved his hands towards him, enclosing his palm, Obiefuna thought again of how large and soft they were, how perpetually warm. Briefly, he allowed himself a fleeting vision of their relationship through Miebi's pleading eyes. They could stay together; they could stick it out and have each other's backs. He could be the perfect friend or distant cousin who occasionally visited at weekends, especially on the weekends when the wife was away. And he knew even then that he could never abide that life indefinitely, that he wanted no part of it.

Obiefuna lay flat on his back on Patricia's woolly rug, his hands folded behind his head to serve as support. He watched the ceiling fan, the swirl of its metal blades as it sent down cool air.

"This road is twisted," she said. "Something about it—like it catches up with you eventually." She paused. "But, then again, Miebi was never Edward. Even I couldn't have seen this coming."

Obiefuna rose and walked to the balcony. He had to admit that there was something comforting about the view from up there, the expansive glimpse of the outside world, the promise of a merciful descent from above if he were simply to let himself go.

"Ever thought of leaving?" Patricia said.

Obiefuna sighed. "It'll never be the same with anyone else." He was struck, now that it was voiced, by the truth of it, by the crushing defencelessness he felt, the urge to cry and cry.

Patricia walked up to him and placed a hand on his shoulder from behind. "I don't mean Miebi." She paused, took a breath. "I meant home. The country."

Obiefuna turned around to look at her.

"I spoke with Mathew. Remember the organization that helped Tunde? He's willing to help facilitate an asylum application for you if you need it."

"Asylum," Obiefuna repeated. The word tasted bitter in his mouth, unreal to his ears. "My life isn't in danger."

Patricia nodded. "I just thought you should know there was the option."

"I can't," Obiefuna said. He thought of Tunde, smuggled out of the country under the cover of night, disorientated for weeks on end, leaving behind all he had, all he knew. "Everything I have is here," he said. "What would Miebi say?"

"Actually," she said, "it was his idea." She stepped forward to hug Obiefuna. "He wants nothing but for you to be free, darling."

In mid-August, lying astride Miebi on the cool tiles in the living room, Obiefuna turned twenty-three. Miebi rolled over on his stomach, right as the clock struck midnight, to whisper,

"Happy birthday!" in Obiefuna's ears, and that single gesture, the ease of it, made him want to cry.

"My father hated watching me dance," Obiefuna said instead. He voiced it without rancour, as if merely presenting a simple, objective fact. "He slapped me so hard one time, I almost lost hearing in that ear."

Even with eyes closed, he could sense Miebi prop himself up on his elbow; and when he opened his eyes, he beheld Miebi's eyes on him, their tender expression piercing Obiefuna, reviving him. Miebi hauled himself off the floor and held out a hand to help Obiefuna up. He went to the stereo, filling the room with Onyeka Onwenu's "You and I." At first he danced alone, in the middle of the living room, waltzing from one end to the other. Obiefuna watched him, alert to Onyeka Onwenu's melody as she seamlessly alternated between English and Igbo, celebrating the enduring wonder of easy, lasting companionship, admonishing them to feel less sad and seek solace in the knowledge that God was taking notes. The beauty of the moment brought sharp, stabbing tears to Obiefuna's eyes. After a while Miebi held out a hand to him and Obiefuna hesitated only slightly before he took it. Their first movements were bumpy, lacking harmony, Obiefuna occasionally stepping on Miebi's toes, so that they stumbled a few times, fell over themselves, giggling all the time. But soon they gained rhythm, and Obiefuna found himself twirling, spurred by Miebi's firm grip, assured of a safe landing on Miebi's chest when, finally, he wore himself out. He stood motionless at the centre of the living room, enclosed in Miebi's embrace, encased in soft light and the fading melody of the track as it came to a slow end; and then there was silence, and in it he found a sweet and sad contentment.

TWENTY-EIGHT

Outside, the rain fell in slants, striking the windows like pellets. It had been a full week since he left Miebi's house. As he took the last of his things from the wardrobe, Miebi had called his name, and the devastation in his voice had been enough to induce Obiefuna's tears over and over on the ride back.

"It happens eventually, right?" he asked Patricia over the phone later. "I still don't understand why it's so shocking to me."

Patricia said, "You're not being unreasonable to expect 'forever' from the person you love. Don't let anyone make you think otherwise, even under the circumstances."

Now he slept alone in his childhood room, in the small bed he had shared with Ekene. The university lecturers were striking again, delaying his return for his final year, and he spent the time at home alternating between computer lessons at a cybercafé down the street and studying in advance of resumption. He had worried, at first, about the awkwardness of constantly sharing a space with his father, but, in the end, he needn't have, as his father, now in his mid-fifties and experiencing early signs of arthritis, kept out of Obiefuna's way, content to settle himself in the living room after work, watching television, empty cans of beer growing in a pile around his feet. Whenever their paths crossed, there was an expression on his father's face he could not pinpoint—something like confusion and relief at the same time.

"How are classes going?" he asked Obiefuna one day.

"We're on strike, Daddy," Obiefuna said. It was the third time he had told his father this.

"It's just one more year until you graduate, okwia?"

"Yes, sir."

"Hmm." His father nodded to himself. "How time flies. Very soon it will be Dr. Obiefuna!" he said, laughing. He reached out a hand to jab Obiefuna's shoulders playfully. "Or is it Dr. Aniefuna?"

Obiefuna said nothing. He stared instead at the empty cans on the floor. The doctor had warned of the consequences of such drinking, but his father seemed to have a death wish these days. He sailed through his days with a vacant, distracted air, as if nothing in the world could ruffle him. Obiefuna thought of Tunde's parents hanging up when the call for Tunde's ransom was made, and he wondered, occasionally, what his father's reaction would have been.

ONCE, his father asked him, "Who's he?"

"Who?"

"The boy who broke your heart."

Obiefuna drew back. It was an odd conversation to be having. How little they knew each other, how little they had in common.

He realized then that the terror his father inspired, ever present as it was, had been diluted somewhat with time and distance. In any other instance, he would have been armed with denials, the beating of his heart loud enough to be heard. But the days following his exit from Miebi's apartment had left him with a lethargic weariness. He contested nothing, accepted everything as it came.

Anozie smirked. He was drinking beer from a glass. His eyes were red, sleepy. "Your mother thought I was unfair to you," he said. "She believed I didn't love you as much as I should."

Obiefuna bowed his head. How odd it was, after so much time had passed, that the mere mention of her name still sent him into that dark, drowsy place, where he felt himself sapped of air? He wished his father would stop talking. He wished he had gone to his ex-roommates' instead.

"Everything I did, I did in your own interest," Anozie said. "It's not normal to live like this. There's even a law now against it. You could go to prison for doing this."

"I've been imprisoned all my life, Daddy."

"What would people say, Obiefuna?"

Obiefuna rose from the chair. It would be the first time he walked out on his father. He remembered a time when that would have been impossible, when Anozie would have promptly leaped up to grab him and slammed him against the door. But time had happened to Anozie, disabling his body, so that he could only react to Obiefuna's disrespect with a headshake. Obiefuna went downstairs and out into the open air. The neighbourhood was nothing like Miebi's, with identically built structures cluttered unprettily together, their ancient façades speaking of a faded lustre. It exuded an air of disorder, with commerce thriving in the mini-shops, slow-moving cars constantly navigating narrow lanes, the open sewers emitting horrible smells. And yet there was something to admire about this atmospheric life, the small children that darted about, keen in playful pursuit of one another, and the friendly, familiar faces that waved in recognition of Obiefuna as he walked past. A slow tune was playing in his head and soon enough he found himself humming along. Although the late-evening sun was receding in the sky, it felt too warm for a run, and he had no trainers on. But Obiefuna set off at a slow jog. He was aware, at first, of the odd glances he drew, of the children who stopped to stare, of the occasional blast of horn from an irritated driver, but soon he was conscious only of the soft thud of his heart in his chest. It was on this same street that he had suffered a cycle accident as a child. He remembered it now as happening on a school morning, he and Ekene already in their uniforms, waiting on the wooden slab just outside their yard for their mother. He still recalled, with startlingly vivid details, the sleepiness of the weather, as if the day was reluctant to begin. Their mother was taking longer to get ready and Ekene was being fussy. Without warning, he flung his lunch box out ahead of him, onto the street, and Obiefuna, without thinking, had stepped forward to pick it up. In that split second, he had been aware only of a blur of shiny metal sweeping him off the ground, his mother's panicked scream filling his ears and the crash of his body against the hard earth. It was a story his mother would recount over the course of the years, embellishing details with a tone that was intent on pointing out Obiefuna's heroism, the same light returning to her eyes. She had thought of him only as a thing of joy, choosing primarily to see him as goodness and nothing more. Her belief in him was simple, her love unquestioning. And this, he could see, after all these years, was his truest blessing. It was why, he had eventually come to realize, he loved Miebi. For Miebi felt, in addition to many things, familiar, instilling in him the same feeling he had felt with his mother—the relief of finally having arrived at a safe location.

Obiefuna thought, too, of his father. They had not always been friends, and Obiefuna's overwhelming memory of him was one of coldness. Still, there had been random, fleeting moments—on the long drive to the seminary, when his father had put a hand forward to touch Obiefuna's shoulder; at his mother's funeral, when his father had pulled Obiefuna up and held him—when he had felt nothing but love, even if reluctantly, even if tentatively. But he had never heard the man say the word, and he realized now, with his mind made up on calling Patricia later tonight, that nowhere else in the world would ever feel like home to him if he didn't go with the knowledge that the one parent he had left truly saw him.

From behind, the sudden blaring of a car horn brought Obiefuna to a halt. He leaned over his knees to catch his breath. When he straightened up, he saw that he had arrived at an intersection. Across the street from him was Ojukwu Field. Most of the fence was gone; Obiefuna could see from where he stood: a number of bare-chested boys playing around the field, footballs of different sizes swinging in the air. Obiefuna stood there watching. He wondered if there was a boy among them who felt out of place, who would rather be elsewhere doing something he truly loved. Other than the broken fence, the field remained the same, with the low grasses and makeshift posts—an unremarkable, unimpressive spectacle. And yet it had defined his childhood, had built and broken him. He remembered the taunting he had suffered there, the ringing laughter of the boys coming back to him now; he could still taste, after all these years, the saltiness of his own blood when Chikezie had struck him. He recalled the weight of the humiliation that day as he navigated his way home, just as he did now, picking up his run again. He did not stop until he approached the gate that led into his neighbourhood yard, at the open square where he and Ekene had, essentially, grown up. He remembered practising with Ekene, the ball refusing to bow to his will, and Ekene's voice: "Just dance, Obi." He remembered, finally, how the feeling of doing the one thing he truly liked, which required the least practised effort, had filled him with a delirious and liberating happiness.

Obiefuna paused in his walk and looked around the yard, to take it in one last time, and then he mounted the stairs that led to their home, where he knocked repeatedly on the door, until he heard the lock turn from inside and his father surfaced, stepped aside and let him in.

Acknowledgements

This book is the product of what is best described as a miraculous triangle, and I am deeply grateful to the two indispensable women who complete this triangle.

My agent, Emma Leong, for that early, steadfast belief, for that quiet zeal behind the scenes and for presenting only the best news in the best possible ways; and Isabel Wall at Viking, for being so heartwarmingly invested, for such extensive, generative edits and for that auspicious email on a random day that, quite literally, changed my life.

Equal gratitude to the whole Viking team, especially Donna Poppy for making me look good; to Olivia Mead, Amelia Evans, Alexia Thomaidis, Lou Nyuar and Olatoye Oladinni for holding the fort and spreading the word; to Richard Bravery and Tosin Kalejaye for rendering such visual beauty to my chaotic thoughts;

and to the good people at Janklow & Nesbit, especially Mairi Friesen-Escandell, Ellis Hazelgrove, Maimy Suleiman and Janet Covindassamy for all your hard work.

Thank you to David Ross at Viking Canada, Cara Reilly at Doubleday, Madlen Reimer at S. Fischer and Leonel Teti at Urano Group for taking on this book with so much love and enthusiasm.

This novel has benefited from the loving, critical insights, fact-checks and all-round generosity of friends who read through drafts with care and offered experience and perspectives—all shortcomings are, of course, mine only—and I am forever in their debt: Joshua Chizoma Emeka, David Emeka and Adachioma Ezeano; and those who quietly rooted for me from the sides: Franklin Okoro, Munachim Amah, Henry Ikenna Ugwu, Arinze Ifeakandu, Michael Powers, Roy Udeh-Ubaka, Olakunle Ologunro, Uzoma Ihejirika and Klara Kalu. Special thanks to Chimamanda Ngozi Adichie, so full of goodness and grace.

I owe so much to the nurturing creative-writing programme at Washington University. Sincerest gratitude to the faculty, especially Kathryn Davis and David Schuman, and to Natasha Muhametzyanova, Timi Alake, Gbenga Adeoba and Stephen Mortland.

Thank you to my family, my "people": Chimezie and Jacinta Ibeh, Chidera and Chinaza Ibeh, Ngozi Obinna and Obiageli Pamela Amadi, for loving, and for never doubting.

ABOUT THE AUTHOR

Chukwuebuka Ibeh is a writer from Port Harcourt, Nigeria, born in 2000. His writing has appeared in *McSweeney's*, *New England Review of Books,* and *Lolwe,* among others, and he is a staff writer at *Brittle Paper.* He was awarded a 2021 J.F. Powers Prize for Short Fiction, was a finalist for the Gerald Kraak Prize, and was profiled as one of the Most Promising New Voices of Nigerian Fiction by *Electric Literature.* He has studied creative writing under Chimamanda Ngozi Adichie, Dave Eggers, and Tash Aw and received his MFA from Washington University in St. Louis, Missouri.